INTULO

THE LOST WORLD

JE GURLEY

INTULO

ISBN: 978-1-925342-84-0

1

December 21, 2012   Van Gotts Ngomo Mine, South Africa –
Frederick Means studied the crumbling rock in his hand for a
moment through his magnifying lens, quietly muttering to himself.
He replaced the lens in his shirt pocket and tossed the rock to the
floor to join the many others that littered the mineshaft. *Too many*, he
thought. He examined the walls and pried loose a stone with his
fingers. It took little effort. The rock face was rotten, ready to
collapse.

A bead of sweat rolled into his eye. He took his handkerchief from
his back pocket and wiped the sheen of perspiration from his
forehead. A rivulet of sweat immediately ran from beneath his
hardhat to replace it. He removed his hardhat, swiped the
handkerchief across his thinning hair, and shoved it back down on his
head, sighing in frustration when another drop stung his eye. It was a
losing battle fighting sweat in the hot, humid tunnel deep beneath the
ground.

"Damn hot," he complained to his companion, Paul Mbussa, a
Zulu driller. The driller's ebony skin glistened with sweat, but his
broad smile revealed ivory teeth.

"43 degrees Centigrade, *baas*," he said.

Frederick flinched at Mbussa's use of the Afrikaans word for boss,
a term he despised as being too reminiscent of the old days of
apartheid. "Nothing ever bothers you, does it Paul?"

The driller dropped his smile and glanced uneasily at the tunnel
roof half a meter above his head. Tiny fractures were already visible
in the freshly drilled roof. "Thirty-nine-hundred meters of bad rock
like this does."

Frederick flinched, remembering why they were so deep in the
new *adit*, a short side tunnel drilled perpendicular to the main ore-

bearing rock. "Yes, it is much too friable. I can easily crumble it in my hand. I don't need a pick to scale loose rock from the walls. It sloughs away on its own. I see lots of kimberlite, some limestone, and greenstone, but hardly any harder dolomitic rock. I told Verkhoen it would be too dangerous to tunnel here, but he ignored me. Even if the gold vein continues this deep, I doubt it would be profitable to extract it."

Using his iPad, he snapped several photos of the rock face as proof with which he could confront Klaus Verkhoen. The often-captious Van Gotts Mining Corporation CEO resented any challenge to his authority, treating them as personal attacks. He had a long memory and no qualms about using his considerable power for petty and often brutal reprisals.

Mbussa hesitated, looked around to see no one was within earshot, and spoke quietly. "The younger Verkhoen is much like the father, Heinrich. He is ruthless and determined. More people will die here."

Frederick thought of the hundreds of miners, mostly poor blacks, who died each year from cave-ins, falls, lung disease, and machinery accidents, all for a shiny yellow substance for which men had fought and died for centuries. There had to be a point at which a human life was worth more than a few flakes of gold per ton of ore.

"Not if I have anything to do with it," he said. "I informed Verkhoen this morning that I would go directly to the Board if I must." A surge of determination swept over him, like a righteous cause. *He* could do something about it.

Mbussa frowned and shook his head slowly. "Verkhoen will not like that. He is a dangerous man. Not good to cross him, *baas*, or Duchamps."

Frederick thought of Henri Duchamps, Verkhoen's Chief of Security, a cold, calculating, vile man willing to do anything to further his career – Verkhoen's watchdog. Inside he cringed, but he laughed aloud to assure Mbussa he was not afraid. "All he can do is sack me. Eve has been begging me to quit and take a job back home in England." He shook his head at the idea. "No. Engineering some grubby coal mine in Wales does not interest me in the slightest. South Africa is where the real geology begins." He pointed to the walls of the shaft. "Why, some of this rock around us is as old as the Earth. The Kaapvaal Craton is a piece of the original continental crust 3.6 billion years old. There is some speculation the gold field itself was brought about by a meteorite impact."

Mbussa looked unconvinced. "Gold from the sky, *baas*?"

Frederick nodded. "Possibly."

"Our village *sangoma* says our god, *Unkulunkulu*, fell from the sky into a great swamp. I believe the gold is a lure to entice men into his underground lair where his demon, *Intulo*, devours their souls."

Frederick blustered. "Superstitious claptrap. You should know better than to listen to a witchdoctor, Paul. You are an educated man."

Mbussa looked chagrined. "Yes, I went to the white-taught schools, but inside I am still Zulu. The old legends are in my blood. Sometimes, when the earth moans and the rock speaks to me, I hear strange voices."

"It's just the rock strata groaning under pressure, especially this rock." As if punctuating his words, a chunk of rock fell from the roof and landed at their feet. "I think you had better gather the men. We should leave. The shaft will need additional shoring if Verkhoen insists on digging here."

He glanced at the stacks of fifty-meter-long nylon bags filled with viscous slurry of liquefied mine tailings lining both sides of the tunnel to support the roof. They were easier to use than hydraulic chocks and longer lasting than wooden pillars and beams; nevertheless, the bags were subject to the same laws of physics and gravity. Already, dewdrops of grey slurry coated the surface of several of the bags as the enormous pressure forced it through the tightly woven material.

He shook his head sadly and sighed. "I don't see how I can stop him."

Mbussa smiled and changed the subject. "Have you told your wife yet?"

Frederick replaced his iPad in its carrying case slung from his waist, reached into his pocket, and pulled out a small black box. Opening it, he produced a gold ring and showed it to Mbussa. "Not yet." Mbussa examined the ring, admiring its perfection. "Gold from this mine," Frederick said. "I had it made in Johannesburg. There's an inscription inside."

"What does it say?"

He dropped the ring back in the box, pocketed it, and smiled. "That's for her eyes only. It should make a nice Christmas gift."

Mbussa laughed. "She will love you forever."

Frederick hoped so. Eve Means was his wife, a biologist working for the South African Department of Education, a menial job for someone with her credentials. She hated South Africa with its politics and lingering racial prejudices. He had hoped she would come to love the country as much as he did, but to no avail. For him, a mining engineer with degrees in both geology and engineering, South Africa was paradise, albeit lately paradise at a price.

She was six years younger and much too beautiful for a man like him. When he had first met her vacationing in Brighton, he instantly fell in love. He courted her relentlessly like a teenage suitor, and in the end, she had accepted his proposal. She was his life.

The ground jerked sharply beneath his feet, and the walls shuddered and groaned. A loud wail repeated farther down the tunnel. Frederick knew the sound had not issued from a human throat.

"*Intulo!*" Mbussa cried out. His face was a mask of fear, as his eyes studied the tunnel.

The ground began to tremble more violently. The walls crackled as shards of rock became stony shotgun pellets peppering the frightened miners. Dust motes caught in the beams of the lights careened through the air like glowing charged particles shot from a cyclotron. The lights strung along the wall did an epileptic jig; then, flickered and failed. Frederick switched on his helmet lamp, as a blinding cloud of dust swept down the tunnel. Rocks cascaded from the roof, bouncing off his hardhat. Rock slurry sprayed from the crushed bags, drenching him in thick mud. He felt Mbussa's strong arms shielding him from falling rock as he and the burly driller crouched together. After a minute, the trembling stopped, but the choking dust remained.

"Cave-in," Frederick said, coughing savagely. "Probably from a small tremor. According to the seismograph, there have been clusters of small quakes over the past few days."

Mbussa looked at him in the lamp's diffuse glow, nostrils flaring as he sniffed the air. Slurry covered all but one of the reflector patches on his jumper. His helmet lamp played along the walls and down the narrow tunnel, now filled with rock and debris, blocking their escape. He shook his head. "I smell cordite. It was a blast."

Frederick looked at him in incredulous horror. "An explosion? Don't be ridiculous. Who would ...?" His legs weakened as realization hit him. "Verkhoen," he groaned as the answer became obvious to him. "He wants to silence me, keep me from going to the Board. He can pretend to dig us out, wait until we're dead, and start all over again. Bastard!" He worried about Eve. What hell would she go through, worrying about him?

One of the miners who had been farther down the tunnel ran up to them, his lamp bobbing in the dark like a cork on the water. His mud-covered face was a mask of fear.

"It was an explosion. The whole shaft has collapsed," he exclaimed before coughing violently from the rock dust. Frederick waited impatiently for him to stop. "The tunnel is filled for fifty meters or more with rock. They will never get through."

The man was near panic. Frederick knew he could not let the man's fear infect them all. It was up to him to quell his own fear and take charge.

"Quiet!" he shouted and waited for their muttering to die out. "Listen. They will dig us out, but we must conserve our air." The shaft was short and held little air in reserve. Rescue would come too late. He dredged his mind to recall blueprints of the area. "There is a second tunnel crossing directly beneath this one on 137 Level. The company sealed it because of water seepage. We must drill a small hole into the shaft to test the air for methane and carbon dioxide. If the air is good, it will help keep us breathing for several more days, more than sufficient time for a Proto-Team to reach us."

The rescue teams were trained and equipped to deal with emergencies, but Frederick knew it took time to organize a team and transport them through the kilometers of mineshafts. More time would be lost while they determined a course of action. Every cave-in was different. Proto-Teams had been lost by moving too quickly.

He didn't need to tell them that if the lower shaft was completely flooded, as it had been when the engineers had sealed it, they risked flooding their own shaft as well. They would drown as had the two miners caught in the flood two years earlier. Even considering the risks, it was their only chance for survival. A Proto-Team couldn't rescue them until they first removed the tons of debris sealing them in.

The portable generator powering the air compressor for the jackleg drills was distant enough from the collapse to avoid damage. Its small gasoline engine would foul their air quickly, but in addition to running the compressor, the light stand it powered would beat back the solid wall of darkness, providing a degree of comfort to the frightened miners.

Mbussa insisted on manning the drill himself. Frederick prayed he had picked the correct spot for Mbussa to drill. He had nothing to go by but his memory. Drilling a few centimeters either direction, they would miss it. The broad-shouldered driller handled the heavy pneumatic drill with ease, keeping the bit driving into the floor as it chewed through the rock. The other miners stood in a semicircle around Mbussa, watching the drill bit slowly disappear into the rock and the pool of slurry accumulating on the floor. Without the flow of cooler air from the ventilator fans, the tunnel was heating rapidly. The heat could kill them before the lack of air.

Frederick's heart skipped a beat, as the drill broke through the ceiling of the shaft below twenty minutes later. The ankle-deep slurry drained through the hole. He pulled out his portable sniffer to check the air quality. Every eye was glued to the three LED readouts on the device as they flickered; then, steadied on the percentages for oxygen, carbon dioxide, and methane. The air was stale but breathable – no methane.

"The air is good," he told them. The relief on their faces told him the effort was worth it.

The entire time they drilled, the tunnel had moaned and groaned, and rocks had continued to shower them periodically. The explosion had weakened the already delicate rock stratum. Frederick was greatly concerned the entire shaft might collapse at any moment.

Sensing Frederick's concern, Mbussa grabbed a pick. "The rock below us is less than a meter thick. I say we break through in case this ceiling lets go."

Frederick nodded and stood back, as Mbussa and another miner with bulging biceps the size of Frederick's thighs took turns pounding the rock floor with their heavy picks. When they tired, the other two miners took over. Less than an hour later, a large slab of rock broke away and fell into the shaft below. Frederick heard no splash, which was more good news.

Mbussa looked up and smiled. "We're through." He leaned over and shined his light in the hole. "Funny smell, but dry. I'll go down first." He sat on the edge of the hole and allowed two other miners to hold his arms and lower him through the hole. A few minutes later, he looked back up through the hole, shining his light upwards. "It's not flooded."

Frederick welcomed the good news. "Good. We'll …"

With a sound like a dying woman's scream, the entire wall beside the generator collapsed, crushing the generator and sending half-ton boulders bouncing across the floor. The lights went out, leaving them with only their battery-operated helmet lamps. The roof began to shake, ready to collapse at any moment.

"Down there," Frederick called out over the rumbling. "Quickly!"

Hands lowered him until his feet touched rock below. The others followed close behind him.

"Away from the hole," he yelled, as dirt and rocks rained down on them through the hole they had dug. He glanced up in time to see a section of the roof of the shaft above crumble. If they had remained where they were, it would have crushed all of them.

The rumbling subsided within seconds, but the dust was slow to settle. Frederick wiped his eyes, making things worse with his filthy hand. He would have killed for a drink of water, but their water cooler lay buried beneath tons of rock. The tunnel stretched into darkness in both directions. To his left, he knew the tunnel ended abruptly when the miners had struck an underground aquifer of hot water, flooding the shaft. To his right, the company had installed a waterproof steel door to seal off the flooded shaft from the rest of the mine. He hoped the door was unlocked.

He tried hard not to believe Verkhoen had ordered the explosion, sealing the new shaft and perhaps their fates as well. While the young CEO was ruthless, to wantonly kill five men simply to silence opposition was insane. Eve, a much shrewder judge of character than him, had warned him not to openly antagonize Verkhoen, but he had ignored her. He wished now he had heeded her advice. They had one chance. If Verkhoen did not guess they had entered the lower shaft, they could exit through the steel door and enter the main shaft system. Once out among the other miners, even Verkhoen would not dare attempt to harm him.

He quickly explained to them what he and Mbussa had discussed concerning the possibility of Verkhoen's complicity in the collapse. There were a few stunned faces, but most knew Duchamps well enough to believe him capable of such an act if ordered to do so.

"We'll continue down this tunnel to a point beyond the collapse and give them time to begin digging us out. Then we will leave through the old steel door. Once we reach the elevators, we'll be safe."

They walked a hundred meters down the tunnel. Along the way, Frederick noticed the complete absence of the water signs he expected to see in a once-flooded tunnel. Examining the floor of the tunnel more carefully, to his shock, he determined it had never been flooded. "More of Verkhoen's lies," he grumbled. "What really did happen here?"

They sat in total darkness for two hours to conserve their batteries and to allow the dust to settle. The air wasn't stale, but it carried an unidentifiable odor that made Frederick's stomach queasy. It reminded him of an abandoned animal den, but of no creature that he had ever encountered. He put it down to nerves. Strangely, the tunnel was not as hot as the one above. That concerned him, but only as an inexplicable datum. It presented no immediate danger. In fact, the cooler temperature could prolong their lives.

After a while, the unseen walls began to close in on him. As a mining engineer, he had thought himself immune to claustrophobia, but he had never been in the dark hemmed in by solid rock for hours on end. The darkness seemed to magnify his fears. Insane, horrific thoughts spawned by the blackness surrounding him found fertile soil at the edge of his conscience. He imagined he could feel the others' fear slowly seeping into his mind. Only by concentrating on Eve and the ring in his pocket did he manage to stave off the subtle onset of madness.

Finally, the muffled sounds of drilling reached them through the rock. The rescue attempt had begun. He switched on his iPad, using its flashlight function to scan the mud-caked faces around him. The stark contrast between their frightened faces and the smiles they offered him struck him as photo worthy. He snapped a photo for his album. Mbussa, exhausted by the digging, leaned back against the wall with his eyes closed.

His habit of jotting down notes and stray thoughts on the iPad's notebook was too ingrained to ignore. He wrote a brief summary of the cave-in, adding only the facts he could prove. Speculation and innuendo would only call his observations into question. His accusation against Verkhoen would be face-to-face. He added a quick note to Eve, just in case. He would erase it when he reached the surface. When he finished, he made sure the device backed up his data onto the memory stick and laid his iPad down beside him.

"What did you mean when you said *Intulo* earlier?" he asked Mbussa.

Mbussa at first looked embarrassed; then he smiled. "*Intulo* is a demon who lives in the earth. He heralds death."

Frederick nodded. "You believe in *Intulo*, and yet you make your living in a gold mine."

"I work below the earth because I must to feed my family. My belief in the ancient tales is much like some Christians' belief in God. I have doubts, but I believe just in case I am wrong."

"A very wise choice," Frederick conceded. He checked his watch. "I think it's been long enough." He stood and stretched his legs, stiff from sitting so long. "Grab the picks in case the steel door is sealed. Then …"

His voice trailed off as a strange sound drifted down the tunnel, louder and nearer than the rescue drills, a loud clicking, like the electric starter of a gas range. It came from the dead end of the shaft. He hoped the sound didn't presage another cave-in or a flood.

"What can that be?" he asked aloud.

"I'll check," Mbussa offered, as he stood and switched on his lamp.

Frederick followed Mbussa's progress down the dark tunnel until the darkness swallowed him. A few minutes later, Mbussa's blood-curdling scream echoed down the tunnel, ricocheting from the rock walls until it faded in the distance. The ghastly moan continued for only a few more seconds before ending abruptly.

"What the bloody hell?" Frederick exclaimed. His skin began to tingle, and his mouth went dry. He tried to swallow, but the lump in his throat was a fist crammed down it. Fear reached its icy hand into his chest, squeezing his pounding heart until his courage ran as cold as his blood. He wanted to run, but the eerie sound riveted him in place like spikes driven through his feet into the solid rock.

The clicking grew louder, as did the horrendous scratching of a thousand metal chisels on stone. Now, all the helmet lamps were on and pointed down the tunnel toward the sound. Beams of light danced along the walls, floor, and roof, searching for its source. Large, indistinguishable shapes moved in the shadows, making it difficult to judge their size. They moved rapidly and resolutely toward the fearful group of transfixed men.

One of the shadows separated from the wall and fell upon one of men. He screamed in agony, as sprays of blood splattered the stunned miners. The creature dragged him to the ground and savagely attacked him. Long, pointed sticks jabbed into the man's chest. Blood ran from his open mouth. *No*, Frederick realized. *Not sticks, legs*. It was a giant insect, an enormous black beetle twice the size of a miner's helmet.

More insects appeared, swarming as scores skittered from the darkness in an insect flood. The lights reflected dully from their shiny carapaces as if absorbed by the ebony chitinous material. Now, everyone was screaming; burly miners who considered themselves above fear blubbering like frightened children. Their cries roused Frederick from his own terror trance. He grabbed a pick, and with a mighty swing drove the tip into one of the creatures' back. It was like chipping stone. The pick's tip skidded across the rigid chitinous shell doing no damage. The insect tumbled away, but quickly regained its feet and attacked him. Stunned, he dropped the useless pick and raced down the tunnel toward the exit, praying the steel door at the end was not locked.

After fewer than a dozen steps, a searing pain brought him to the ground. Fire lanced through his leg, shooting up his back and stabbing his brain. He glanced in horror at his right leg dangling by a flap of skin. Two of the creatures had nearly amputated the leg with their razor-sharp mandibles. A spray of blood arced through the air, splashing the floor of the tunnel and drenching the creatures. They tugged the leg free and fought over their prize. The absurdity of two nightmarish creatures skirmishing over his unattached leg struck him as hilarious. He barked out a short, clipped laugh. The creatures, engrossed in their feast, ignored him. He dragged himself down the tunnel toward the steel door, leaving a bloody trail behind him.

He knew escape was useless. His life's blood was spilling from him at an alarming rate. The smell of blood and fear permeated the tunnel, driving the creatures insane. The hellish beetles were everywhere. His stump, rather than in excruciating agony, was numb. He realized his body was in shock and that unconsciousness was not far away. He wanted to document what was happening, a record of his death. He fumbled for his iPad and snapped two quick photos of the creatures, realizing too late that the flash attracted them. He rolled onto his stomach and tried to crawl away, but they surrounded him, relentlessly nipping and pinching at his extremities. As they scurried over him, their pointed legs were daggers stabbing into his flesh.

Eventually, their weight pressed his face into the ground. He didn't see the mandibles ripping into the soft flesh of his back, but he felt the intense pain as the creatures tore muscles and severed bone to reach his internal organs. Screaming obscenities, he slapped uselessly at the creatures with his left hand until one of the beetles snapped it off at the wrist.

As he stared dumfounded at the bloody stump, his helmet light went out, instantly plunging the tunnel into abysmal darkness. The darkness was a godsend. It saved him the horror of watching the creatures rip him apart. Strangely, he no longer felt pain, just an odd sense of separation, as if he was no longer in his body. He tried to laugh. He knew he must look a mess. What would Eve think? She had always said he looked so distinguished.

He pushed the box containing Eve's ring deeper into his pocket with his remaining hand to protect it. He wanted to look at it one last time, but it was too late. A chill came over him as he lay dying. He sensed something farther away, deeper down the tunnel from which the creatures had come. It was a malevolent presence, eager to feed. Even the ravenous insects feared it, pausing for a moment from their meal. They stopped their incessant clicking and turned toward the presence; then, life fled his body.

The sounds of drilling continued above as the insects feasted. Two-hundred-million years of evolution had made of them efficient predators and voracious scavengers, leaving nothing behind but dismembered skeletons. When they finished their meal, they lingered in the tunnel for a while, searching for a way out. Later, when hunger forced them, they returned through the crack in the wall to their lair.

2

June 10, 2016   Tosca, South Africa –

Alan Hoffman now knew what a side of barbecuing beef felt like. He was basting in his own juices as he squinted to take readings from the *Cerberus AT10* burrowing furiously into the hard granite of the hillside. Blasts of broiling air swept past him, so intense the ground shimmered. He stood just meters away from a whirlwind of super-heated gases reaching temperatures upwards of 1100^0C. One misstep and he would be toast.

Alan checked his figures – .12 meters per minute. That worked out to 7.2 meters per hour. *Not good enough.* He cursed and slammed his clipboard onto his thigh hard enough to bruise flesh. "Son of a bitch!"

"Alan, are you okay?"

Damn. He had forgotten his headset microphone was live. His father's voice was barely audible over the radio headset above the high-pitched screaming of the turbine. Even so, he noted the concern in his father's voice. He pushed the earplug firmly into his ear before answering.

"Yeah, Dad, sorry. I'm returning now. Shut it down."

He removed his L.A. Dodgers baseball cap and wiped his face with a towel before beginning the long walk back to the control room trailer they referred to as the Shack. Behind him, the deafening sound Doppler shifted from a shrill whine to a dull roar, as the Honeywell AGT1500 jet-turbine engine, stripped from a surplus M1 Abrams tank, and adapted for the *Cerberus*, gradually slowed. As the lasers shut down, the temperature plummeted from hot enough to melt stone to warm enough to scorch his skin. As he trudged to the control room, he avoided the inquisitive eyes of the workers operating the waste discharge lines. Even in their air-conditioned, heat-resistant suits, he was sure they were sweating as badly as he was.

It was difficult to wrap his mind around the fact that it was nearly the same temperature in the middle of South Africa's winter as it was in Carson City, Nevada, where it was the middle of summer. The reversed seasons south of the equator was disconcerting. *At least it's a dry heat in Nevada.* He shook his head at the old joke, but to some degree, it was true. Here, in spite of the fact he was in a desert, the humidity was killing him.

He had chosen Tosca as a test site because South Africa was where he hoped to sell the automated mining machines. The geology was similar to the *Witwatersrand,* the largest gold producing region in the world, and the Van Gotts Mining Corporation operated one of the largest mines in the *Witwatersrand.* Their tempting offer to test the *Cerberus* under actual working conditions could put Hoffman Industries back on its financial feet. Since Tosca was a privately owned town, it hadn't been difficult to negotiate a short-term lease deal, avoiding the tedious entrenched layers South African government bureaucracy. Located only a few kilometers from the border with Botswana, the Kalahari Desert locale was perfect for the test, sparsely populated with little agriculture. After weeks of failure, he was ready to pack it up and go home.

The others were waiting at the trailer for the good news. He hated to be the one to break their hearts. His father had leveraged everything he owned to finance the *Cerberus AT10* project. The crew had invested three years hard work in the project. If he couldn't make it perform up to the required specifications, he would lose everything his father had worked nearly sixty years to build.

Cerberus was his idea and his responsibility. An automated, laser-powered, boring machine capable of burning through solid rock at a speed of ten-meters-per hour would revolutionize gold and silver mining. A byproduct of the process was a reinforced tunnel liner spun from the molten rock. His machine could save hundreds of lives. Nearly four thousand miners had died in the last decade in South Africa alone. With his machine, mines could reach levels far below the depths men could now tolerate, opening up vast new mineral deposits. The reduction in the cost of mining would reinvigorate the declining mining industry.

But if he couldn't produce a speed of at least ten-meters-per hour, thirty-three feet, it wouldn't be cost effective, and more lives would be lost, as well as his father's company. His father had worked hard over the years building Hoffman Industries from a small, family-owned business supplying pumps and drill bits to Nevada miners into one of the largest mining supply companies in the world. He feared he could single-handedly tear it down within the next few weeks.

Opening the door of the trailer, Alan took a moment to savor the cool air washing over him. Trace Morgan, one of the young engineers, glanced up at him with a questioning look. Instead of the utilitarian jumpsuits everyone else wore, Trace wore his usual attire of a pair of ragged jeans and a heavy metal t-shirt. Today's selection bore the image of a skeletal clown holding a sniper rifle. Alan recognized it from one of Trace's CD covers as the band *Scelerata*. He shook his head in answer to Trace's unspoken question.

His father stood beside the monitor console wearing his ubiquitous green coveralls with its multitude of pockets, tapping his large, black frame glasses against the console's side, running his hand through his disheveled, thinning gray hair. Alan suspected his hair would look like his father's soon. He was ready to pull it out by the roots in his frustration.

"Well, how did we do this time?" his father asked.

Though he tried to hide it, Alan suspected his father knew the results weren't good. He couldn't meet his father's sympathetic green eyes. Instead, he stared at his dusty boots as he replied, "Just over seven meters, twenty-three lousy feet." He slammed his clipboard down on one of the desks, startling William Bakerman, one of the engineers. Bill sensed Alan's foul mood and ignored the interruption. "I can't seem to increase the power output without building up too much heat in the GPS unit. When it heats up, we lose positioning integrity."

The elder Hoffman nodded. "That is a concern."

Alan winced at his father's polite assessment of the situation. Without the Global Positioning System working accurately, the *Cerberus* could be off by meters after a day's tunneling, making it useless as a precision mining tool.

"I've tried more insulation, but it doesn't seem to help." He threw down his clipboard on the console in disgust. It skidded across the surface and fell off the other side. He let it lie. "I don't know what else to do, Dad."

His father walked over and patted him on the back as he had often done when Alan was facing a childhood disappointment. "There, there, son. We'll get it worked out soon."

Alan flinched and pulled away, feeling sorry for himself and undeserving of his father's benevolent understanding. "I'm letting the family down. This whole thing sucks. I wish I had never started it." He turned and stormed out of the room, feeling foolish for his unprofessional behavior and doubly foolish for talking his father into what was proving to be a hopeless venture.

Outside, he almost ran into Vince McGill leaning against a wall of the trailer smoking a cigarette. "Still overheating the GPS, huh?" Vince asked casually. He pulled a second cigarette from the pack and offered it to Alan.

Alan nodded and automatically accepted the cigarette Vince handed him. Although he had stopped smoking three years earlier, the urge had been a rampaging water buffalo dancing on his spine all week. He needed something to take his mind off the fiasco the *Cerberus* Project had become. He pulled the battered Zippo lighter he kept as a reminder not to smoke from his pocket and lit up, relishing the cigarette's strong taste as he pulled the smoke deep into his lungs. He held it there for several seconds, allowing the nicotine to absorb into his lungs and into his bloodstream to relax him. He slowly exhaled a large blue cloud of smoke. The breeze whipped it around his face.

"Too bad we can't pack it in dry ice or something," Vince suggested while exhaling his own cloud of smoke. "Maybe hit it with the liquid nitrogen."

Alan shook his head. "That wouldn't work. The liquid nitrogen would freeze the delicate components, and the dry ice wouldn't last thirty minutes in that kind of heat." He took another deep drag off the cigarette before tossing it to the ground in disgust and grinding it into the dirt with his boot heel. He had enough problems without becoming hooked on cigarettes again. It had been difficult enough giving them up the first few times.

"Too bad the new insulation didn't work."

Alan had been optimistic for the new multi-layered foil thermal insulation developed by NASA for rocket engines, but it, too, had fallen short of their needs. "Yes, it sucked just like this whole project is beginning to suck."

"Don't worry, Alan," Vince said, grinning from ear to ear. "They don't call you 'the best geo-engineer in the field' for nothing."

Alan laughed. The praise had come from a magazine article in *Popular Science* two years earlier when the *Cerberus* Project was just beginning to attract attention in the mining industry. He believed the young, blonde writer had been more infatuated with him than with the story.

"Maybe if I hadn't believed the hype myself, we wouldn't be in this mess. You and Trace both said I was moving too fast."

Vince plucked his cigarette from his mouth and laughed. It was a sarcastic laugh. "If Trace or I were in charge, we would still be tweaking the drawings. I'm good at following blueprints, but I don't have what it takes, up here." He pointed to his sandy-haired head.

Alan accepted Vince's self-deprecating statement as a gesture to bolster his sagging confidence. Vince was a mechanical genius who had been instrumental in many of the *Cerberus'* design changes. Alan brushed the annoying wind-blown sand from his face. The breeze was beginning to pick up, and the flat land around them did nothing to block its fury. Only the low hill caused by an anticline in the local rock stratum they were using as a test site broke the stark monotony of the landscape. Its remoteness was the reason they had chosen the area for their tests.

"This sucks," Vince yelled at the landscape, as he lit up another cigarette. "There was none of this dust for Doctor Perry or David Innes."

Alan sighed and hung his head. "Not Abner Perry again."

"Well, aren't we just like David Innes and Doctor Abner Perry in Edgar Rice Burroughs's *At the Earth's Core*? *Cerberus* is our *Iron Mole*."

Vince's infatuation with the Pellucidar novel series by Burroughs sometimes became tiresome, especially with his constantly drawing parallels between Burroughs's heroes and themselves.

"The Earth's not hollow, Vince," Alan reminded him. "It's hard as a rock. That's the problem."

"Yeah, just you wait. We'll find Pellucidar yet. But just the same, I want to get back to my room and take a hot shower." He lifted one

17

leg and wiggled his butt, frowning. "I'll probably have to vacuum this sand out of my ass crack."

Alan chuckled at Vince's lurid description and tried to dismiss the somewhat disgusting image it conjured as he considered their problem. He watched Vince take another deep puff of his cigarette and smiled. As solutions sometimes do, this one came to him full blown, floating like a 3-D diagram in his mind. Vince's off-hand witty comment had provided the catalyst. He swung around and confronted Vince.

"Vince, is it possible to run a secondary vacuum line into the GPS assembly and attach it to the main heat transfer vacuum pump without the heat back-flowing into the GPS unit?"

He watched as Vince ran the idea in his mind. His eyes lit up as he found a solution. "If we install an insulated, one-way vacuum switch, I don't see a problem. That new NASA foil should be able to handle that much heat." He furrowed his brow. "But what good would that do. Why do we need a vacuum? Dirt hasn't been a problem, has it?"

Alan smiled. "No, don't you see? We place the entire GPS assembly in an airtight compartment and…"

"Vacuum out all the air," Vince finished for him. "In a vacuum, the GPS shouldn't heat up as quickly."

"Right!" Alan knew Vince was a bright young engineer. He would be able to make the modifications in no time. "Come on. Let's get started on it. I don't want to tell the others until we test it."

Vince leaned into the rising wind, headed to the parts truck for the line and switch he would need. Alan rubbed his hands together in glee. Maybe they would be able to get the *Cerberus* up to specs after all. If the vacuum worked, they could run a full-speed test tomorrow.

In the distance, over the roar of the wind, he heard hammering coming from the *Cerberus* and smiled. Vince was wasting no time. He was young, fresh out of MIT, but he loved his work, thrived on the cutting edge of technology. Alan hoped everything went well with this next test. Vince deserved his reward for the time he had spent on the project. He had turned down dozens of more lucrative job offers to work with Alan, based solely on a single article Alan had written for *Mining Journal* magazine about the possibility of laser-powered tunneling machines.

Now, it was time to see if the years of work had been worth it.

3

June 30, 2016, 10:00 a.m.   *Ngomo* Mine   Klerksdorp, South Africa –

Three weeks after their first successful test, Alan Hoffman and his three top engineers were setting up the *Cerberus AT10* on 138 Level of Van Gotts *Ngomo* Mine twenty kilometers north of Klerksdorp. At a depth of nearly 3,900 meters, 138 Level was the deepest shaft in the world's deepest mine. In reality, 138 Level was presently only a three-meter-square vertical shaft one-hundred-ten meters below 137 Level. At that depth, the temperature was 60^0 Celsius, 140 Fahrenheit, making working conditions impossible. Only the massive air conditioning system the mine employed allowed men to work at such depths, and still the temperature was pushing 47^0C. *116 degrees Fahrenheit*, he thought, *that's about the temperature of a pleasant summer day in Vegas.*

Van Gotts' engineers had developed an ingenious method for cooling the deep mine shafts, a marvel of engineering equaling the mine itself. A large vacuum vat on the surface turned water to ice by helping the water quickly reach the triple point – liquid, gas, solid – by utilizing the principal that water in a vacuum simultaneously boils and freezes. A conveyor belt carried the ice three-hundred meters down into the mine to an abandoned tunnel used as a reservoir, where three-million liters of water was stored before pumping it through a forced air vat cooler. Massive fans blew the cool, moist air deep into the shafts, and additional fans sucked the hot air out. One such conduit opened just above the new excavation site, and freezing water dripped down Alan's back, as he peered into its depths of the pit at his feet.

"That's some hole," Vince noted, spitting into the opening and watching it disappear into blackness. His yellow hard hat slipped from his head, almost toppling into the hole. After a frantic juggling act to hold on to it, he jammed it back on top of his head.

"One-hundred-ten meters," Alan quoted from the figures Verkhoen's mine supervisor had provided. "That makes the new shaft we'll be boring just over four kilometers deep, officially the deepest manmade tunnel in the world." He grinned. "We'll be making history."

Vince whistled his appreciation. "Yeah, that means a pressure of over ninety-seven-hundred tons per square meter." He glanced up. "There's a trillion tons of rock hanging over our heads."

"Claustrophobic, Vince?" Trace asked, grinning ear to ear at his friend's discomfort.

"Not if the rock stays put," Vince replied with a forced laugh.

Getting the seven-meter-long *Cerberus* down into the mine had not been an easy task. Alan and his crew had worked feverishly for three days stripping the *Cerberus* down to its chassis and major components and transporting it to the deepest level using the two cages of the main elevator shaft. He had designed the machine with just such a reassembly in mind. Each section was just over two-meters long and weighed almost three tons. It had taken four elevator trips to bring all the components into position. Now, they faced the daunting task of reassembling it.

"Let's get started," Alan said.

With a hand signal to the crew chief, the crane operator gently lifted the first section of the eight-ton *Cerberus* and lowered it into the Stygian depths where, like its Greek namesake, it would rule the underground. Lights flashed on below them, revealing the true depth and size of the freshly excavated pit. Alan held his breath as the crane operator painstakingly eased the nose section lower a centimeter at a time until the machine rested safely on the bottom. Workers in the hole scurried to unhook the cables and send them back up for the next section.

"How do we get down?" Vince asked, eyeing the crane uneasily.

His answer came as the crew manhandled a large metal bucket measuring two-meters high by one-and-a-half meters in diameter into place at the edge of the pit. When the cables came up, they attached them to the bucket.

"That," Alan said.

"Great," Vince moaned surveying the swaying bucket, "a water bucket down a dry well."

"It's called a *kibble*," Alan corrected him.

"It's a big frickin' bucket," Vince insisted.

"You can wait until they install the ladder if you want."

Vince rolled his eyes at the thought of descending so many rungs. "No thanks, I'll travel by bucket, but I'll feel like a KFC drumstick. Would you like fries with that or mashed potatoes and gravy?"

The kibble's incessant rocking as it descended made Alan's stomach queasy. He fought down the nausea by concentrating on the *Cerberus* checklist. By the time they reached the massive machine, he had reassembled it in his mind. Two burly technicians manhandled the drilling section out of the way to make room for the rest of it, sliding it into a ten-meter-deep pocket previously dug in the side of the shaft to accommodate the *Cerberus*. As the kibble disappeared back up the hole, Trace and Vince quickly removed the bubble wrap protecting the flanges.

When the second section reached them, they moved it into place and slid five-centimeter bolts into the flanges. While Bill and Vince tightened the bolts with pneumatic torque wrenches, he and Trace removed a panel from the laser generator section and carefully checked the fiber optic cables and electrical connections. The job of assembly went quickly and efficiently, much to Alan's surprise and delight. Six hours later, the *Cerberus* was ready.

"Verkhoen's men can attach the gas exhaust lines and run the fiber optic cable to the surface," Alan said, laying down his wrench and rubbing his aching shoulder. "I'll buy the beer topside."

* * * *

Alan smiled into his headset camera for Trace, who had remained topside in the Shack monitoring the machine. In spite of the mine's cooling system, he was soaking wet with perspiration in the ninety-seven percent humidity. The heat from the racks of work lights on stands positioned around the perimeter of the hole didn't help matters.

"You shouldn't have drunk so much beer," Trace said. "You're sweating it all out."

"I only had two beers," Alan protested. "It's easy for you to preach from your air-conditioned perch in the Shack."

He had spent the last four hours double-checking the circuit boards and inspecting the rotating laser array to make sure every connection, every bolt was secure. He made one last check of the heavily insulated, six-inch-diameter poly-composite pipe that would carry the vaporized rock from the *Cerberus* to a discharge pipe on the surface. Because of the great distance involved, four heaters installed at intervals along its length reheated the gas to prevent it from cooling and clogging the discharge lines. Then, he connected the four-kilometer-long insulated fiber optic cable used to remotely operate the *Cerberus* and receive data from the onboard computer. Ideally, he could program the *Cerberus'* computer and dispense with the tether, but until they had a successful tunneling behind them, he was taking no chances. After a lengthy diagnostic check, he was finally satisfied everything was in good working order.

He turned to Vince, who was tightening a loose bolt on one of the treads. "Time to go." He spoke into his mic again. "Okay, Trace. Give us a couple of minutes to get clear; then start it up. Bring the power up slowly in increments of ten."

As he and Vince rode the kibble up out of the hole, the *Cerberus'* turbine slowly revved up until its shrill whine became deafening in the enclosed space. The temperature rose quickly as the *Cerberus'* three rotating lasers began to burn into the rock, turning part of it into a superheated gas quickly sucked back to the surface through the kilometers of exhaust pipe. The remainder of the rock became heavy, viscous, molten slurry, which *Cerberus'* rotating spinnerets, located in the middle of the vehicle, sprayed into a super-hard tunnel casing, quickly cooled by jets of liquid nitrogen, eliminating the need for gunite.

"We're at twenty percent," Trace announced over the headset. "Increasing to thirty."

So far so good, Alan thought.

"Forty percent, Alan." Trace's voice brimmed with tension as he called out the numbers.

Alan stepped out of the kibble. The roar intensified until the ground was shaking from the power of the rotating lasers disintegrating rock. "Let's go for it. One hundred percent," he yelled into his mic.

"One hundred percent capacity," Trace repeated.

Below, the rear end of the *Cerberus* slowly disappeared as it burned its way deeper into the solid rock. The temperature around them rose quickly as hot air billowed up from the pit. The discharge pipe sang a tenor note as hot gas jetted to the surface. Alan wiped his forehead and loosened his collar. Between the heat and humidity, it was like standing in a sauna.

"Okay. Everybody topside to the Shack. We've done all we can do here."

Because of the great depth of the mine, a single elevator shaft would have been ineffective. Two additional elevator shafts branched from the main shaft, descending to the lowest levels. Winding through the twisting, dipping tunnels of 137 Level, it took them nearly half an hour to reach the #2 elevator. The discharge pipe followed their route, singing its song of vaporized rock on its path up the shaft to the surface. They disembarked the #2 elevator and switched to the main elevator on 80 Level. Alan noticed Vince's lips moving during the ride to the surface.

"What are you doing?" he asked.

Vince, embarrassed, confessed, "I'm saying prayers to Vishnu, Allah, Buddha, Odin, and God. I believe in covering all the bases, just in case somebody's right."

Alan whispered a quick, silent prayer of his own for success. He wished his father were there to witness the event, but he had returned to Nevada to manage the company. He would have to be satisfied with monitoring the progress from the comfort of his office via a Skype broadcast.

* * * *

For the next twenty hours, Alan refused to leave the control trailer. He followed the steady progress on his laptop as the *Cerberus* bored through the dense igneous rock at over twelve-meters-per hour. He held his breath once when they stopped operations to allow two mining engineers wearing heat-resistant suits to test the tunnel casing the *Cerberus* deposited behind it like an earthworm. The tensile strength proved fifteen percent higher than they had expected, nearly twice that of gunite, the sprayed concrete normally used to reinforce tunnels. The quick-cooling nitrogen jets solidified the molten rock into a strong, crystalline lattice. There would be little chance of a cave-in, even in strata as brittle as the metamorphic sedimentary sand and gravel deposits through which they were digging.

The *Cerberus* bored a circular tunnel three meters in diameter, easily large enough for men to work comfortably in. Special protuberances beneath the *Cerberus* scored twin parallel grooves in the molten floor for the later addition of steel tracks for ore carts. It also left a meter-wide, twenty-centimeter-deep trough for water run-off. Alan foresaw a completely automated process. After reaching the vein, automated mining equipment could extract the ore, load it onto carts, and deliver it to the ore hopper, eliminating the need for miners and costly cooling equipment. With a few modifications, the *Cerberus* could melt the ore and pump the resulting slurry to the surface for collection. Such automated mines could follow the rich ore veins deeper underground or operate under the hostile conditions of the moon, Mars, or the asteroids.

From their starting point, the gold vein Verkhoen sought was twelve-hundred meters away, nearly one hundred hours boring time. After a full day following the *Cerberus'* progress, the tension began to wear at Alan's already exhausted body. His back ached from leaning forward in his seat, and his eyes burned from constantly staring at the monitor screens. His hands and fingers felt like slabs of raw meat after hours of grasping tools assembling the *Cerberus*.

He rose from the chair he had been sitting in for hours and stretched his long, cramped legs by pacing the narrow confines of the trailer. Glancing out the Shack's solitary window, he blinked back tears as the glaring lights atop the brickwork elevator tower struck his eyes. The bright floodlights lessened the gloom outside the Shack, but just the knowledge that it was night, a time normally reserved for sleeping, intensified his fatigue. The elevator tower, the entrance to the subterranean city below their feet, loomed like a stone sentinel over the collection of metal-sided and older wooden-plank buildings comprising the vast mine complex. In spite of the hour, men and vehicles streamed across the landscape like worker ants preparing the nest for winter. The twenty-four-hour activity of the mine provided a stark contrast to the endless inactivity within the timeless stasis-bubble confines of Shack.

He glanced around the control room, noting the condition of his companions. Vince sat bleary-eyed nodding at his desk, his body slowly slumping forward, and then waking with a jerk and shaking his head. His hand brushed a cup of cold coffee sitting by his laptop. Alan slid the cup a little farther away to prevent it spilling. Trace was alert. He had tapped into his store of youthful, nervous energy, bouncing the eraser end of a well-chewed Number 2 pencil on the desk to the rhythm of a thumping bass drum, a growling bass guitar, and screaming riffs of a shredding heavy metal guitar leaking from his earphones, while chewing gum and popping bubbles to stay focused.

William Bakerman, the oldest of the three engineers at forty-eight, lay face down at his console snoring, his long salt-and-pepper beard spread out on each side of his face. A small replica of the *Cerberus* dangled from his left earlobe fashioned, or so one of his recollections from his colorful past went, from a gold nugget he had discovered while panning in the Klondike. In spite of the air conditioner, his shaved head sprouted beads of perspiration.

"We'll work in shifts," Alan announced to the nearly comatose crew. "It's almost midnight. Each of you take a few hours off and get some rest."

"I'm okay, Alan," Vince protested. "I'll stay." Then he stifled a yawn with his hand.

"You look okay." Alan's sarcastic dig drew a forced, big-toothed smile from Vince. "Go get some real sleep. Be back here in six hours. You, too Trace. Trace, wake Bill." Trace kicked Bill's chair. He jerked awake and looked up, chagrined at being caught sleeping. "Bill, you go with the others. It might get hectic when we break through. Everyone needs to be their frosty best."

Alan watched them file out the door, leaving him alone in the trailer. He poured a cup of black coffee, leaned back, and watched the slowly moving graph representing the *Cerberus'* progress. "So far, so good," he said.

His baby was performing as well as he had hoped. He was a proud father. He hoped his father would be as pleased. He glanced up at the video camera near the ceiling in a corner of the room and smiled for Verkhoen. The Van Gotts' CEO had it installed the video feed to monitor their progress. Verkhoen should be delighted. He was getting his new tunnel free. His promise to purchase three of the machines would save Hoffman Industries, but Verkhoen's investment so far was nil, other than a small leasing fee.

Alan glanced out the window of the Shack and watched a crew of Verkhoen's men clad in heavy, heat-resistant suits maneuver the flexible metal discharge pipe to a new position. Their silver suits glowed in the floodlights. The superheated gas generated by the *Cerberus'* mining, filled with potentially dangerous particles of uranium and heavy metals, became a fine dust of minerals as it cooled near the end of the pipe. Large tanks had been set up near the trailer to collect the dust. The dust was still over 200^0 C when it exited the pipe. In spite of the suits' built-in air conditioners, he imagined the men were rather uncomfortable.

A tough way to make a living, he reflected.

By the time Vince returned five hours later, Alan had resorted to splashing his face with cold water from the small refrigerator and pressing a cloth filled with crushed ice to the back of his neck to stay awake. After five cups of coffee from his oversized Viva Las Vegas mug, he needed to pee so badly his bladder was about to explode. The one comfort the Shack didn't provide was a bathroom. He didn't want to walk the hundred meters to the crew's locker room, especially during the middle of a shift change.

Vince took one look at him and remarked, "You look like shit, boss. Go get some sleep."

Alan smiled and stifled a yawn. He raised his arm, sniffed his shirt, and grimaced. "I guess I could use a shower."

Vince pinched his nose. "That's what that God-awful smell is. I thought we had hit a sour gas pocket."

"All right, all right. I'll leave. Keep an eye on the GPS unit. It seems to be holding up, but watch the temperature. If it wavers, shut it down."

He stood and leaned over the desk to check a reading. Vince gave him a playful shove toward the door. "Go! Trace is on his way here. He and I can handle things for a while. Get some sleep. Take a shower. Eat some real food instead of this take-out crap." He picked up a Styrofoam container, sniffed the contents, and made a face. "I hate to think what kind of meat this *moo goo gai pan* is made from. It doesn't smell like chicken to me."

As exhausted as he was, Alan was reluctant to leave. The *Cerberus* was his baby, his brainchild. From concept to creation, the project has dominated his life for four long years. It had cost him most of his friends and his marriage. *No, not my marriage,* he corrected himself. *I did that on my own.*

He and Sharon had been married two years and two months before she finally informed him one night that she was tired of coming in second to the *Cerberus* Project. "That damned hairless mole," she called it. She had been calm and collected, presenting her case as would a defense lawyer. He had been too busy and too proud to fight her, and too naive to fathom the real reason behind her sudden departure. She left and he continued his work. He tried to fill the void she left in his life with endless hours on the job, hardly noticing how small that void had become. Finally, he realized the reason she had left him was that he had shown her no real love during their marriage.

Their rapid romance and courtship had been mostly at the behest of their two fathers, a merger of local dynasties, and they had merely gone along. In reality, they had nothing in common, and both were much better off out of the marriage. It had cost him half his savings, but he supposed that was a small price for freedom. Since then, he had gone on numerous dates and taken a few lovers, but no loves. *Cerberus* was his only love for now.

Cerberus was easy to love. It was a marvelous machine. The Honeywell AGT1500 jet turbine produced 11 kilowatts of power. A *Tesla* thorium generator pumped that up to 60 kilowatts. The U.S. Air Force had developed most of the technology, but he had added a few of his own concepts, such as a sixty-meter-long, Erbium-lined, double-clad optical fiber coiled to fit within the *Cerberus'* confined interior. The *Cerberus'* laser produced a short-pulsed, polarized beam of light capable of generating 3,000 BTUs/min. of heat. The short-duration, pulsed power reduced internal heat buildup, and the three rotating lasers, one for each of the *Cerberus'* namesake mythological guardian of the underworld's three heads, covered the optimal area for tunnel boring.

He and Vince had already drawn up plans for a much smaller version of the *Cerberus*, called the *Charon,* for possible NASA deep-space mining missions. Less than three meters in length, the *Charon* was nonetheless capable of boring a tunnel a meter in diameter through anything they would find on the moon or Mars. Equipped with a wide array of sensors, the *Charon* could analyze the composition of the rock to determine its commercial value. It could burrow beneath the lunar surface to excavate living quarters for future *lunanauts* to protect them from solar radiation.

If the Cerberus was successful.

Driving back to the hotel in Klerksdorp proved more difficult than he thought. Lack of sleep and the glare of the rising sun blinded him. He came within a meter of colliding with a ten-ton ore truck. Only the deafening blast of the truck's air horn jolted him back to reality in time to swerve into a ditch. The eight-meter-high truck looked like a railroad locomotive as it raced by his window. Luckily, he hadn't been driving his usual breakneck speed. Neither the automobile nor he suffered any damage, and after a few minutes to calm his jangling nerves, he made it to the hotel in one piece.

When he reached the quiet comfort of his room, he tossed his keys on the nightstand and headed for the bathroom. While relieving himself, he eyed the shower wistfully but considered it too much trouble. Instead, he fell onto the bed fully clothed. He was asleep within seconds.

4

July 4, 2016, 7:00 p.m.   *Ngomo* Mine, Klerksdorp, South Africa
—

The *Cerberus* was less than ten meters from its intended goal.
Trace, looking as if he hadn't slept for the entire four days of
tunneling, sat with his feet propped up on one of the desks. His
uncombed blond hair stuck out at all angles. His bloodshot blue eyes
peered out from within bands of dark circles at his laptop screen.
Today, his ubiquitous t-shirt displayed an image of the band *Korn.*
Alan believed Trace's entire wardrobe consisted of dozens of heavy-
metal band t-shirts and faded denim jeans. Numerous coffee stains
and blotches of spilled food spotted the image of the metal skull from
the band's *DJ Death* tour. In spite of Trace's haggard appearance,
Alan didn't have the heart to exclude him from the grand finale. Of
them all, he most deserved to be there for the end.

Alan glanced at the date on the right-hand bottom of his screen,
the Fourth of July, Independence Day. For most Americans, it was a
day of celebration, fireworks, picnics, and family outings. Alan
hoped the date was auspicious for him as well. If they succeeded, it
would mean financial independence for Hoffman Industries. Here, in
a foreign land, it was simply another date on the calendar. They had
no time for celebration.

Nor did they have time for housekeeping. The Shack resembled a
college dorm room after a four-day keg party. Styrofoam coffee cups,
empty plastic water bottles, and crushed soda cans lay scattered about
the trailer like losing betting slips littering the grandstands after a
horse race. Take-out food containers spilled over the rim of overfilled
garbage cans and onto the floor. Strewn across the desks were half-
eaten sandwiches and used condiment packets. A dust of finely

trodden potato chips sprinkled the carpet.

Alan glanced at the camera suspended from the ceiling in the corner of the room, wondering if Verkhoen was watching from his office in Pretoria. He was certain the prim and proper CEO would disapprove of their cluttered workplace, but he didn't care. The Shack was a small piece of America, an embassy on foreign soil. Outside the Shack, they were visitors. Inside it, they were home.

His mind focused on seeing *Cerberus* through the job. He caught a glimpse of himself in one of the monitor screens and noticed he could do with a shave. He rubbed his hand over the three-day stubble and quickly dismissed the idea. *Later.*

"Eleven-hundred-ninety-eight meters. Two meters to go," Trace called out, as all eyes in the room focused on the monitor screens. "One-point-five meters."

To Alan, Trace sounded like a NASA astronaut calling out a docking procedure. He had one eye on the GPS reading and the other on the monitor. So far, they were right on the nose of their projected position.

"Touchdown," Trace announced, raising his arms in the air like a referee making a call.

Alan's shouted 'Yahoo!' startled everyone. "We did it."

The uneasy tingling sensation living in the in the pit of his stomach the past week slowly faded. Oddly, he felt no adrenaline rush. He simply felt relief. He had lived on caffeine and nervous tension for so long that success was anticlimactic.

He leaned back in his chair and laced his fingers across the top of his head. "Okay, shut her down."

He watched the bars on the power graph drop to zero, as Vince began shutting down the turbine and laser array. For the first time in a long time, he felt contentment.

His respite was short-lived. A red light on one of the monitors began blinking rapidly. Simultaneously, an alarm sounded. He shot forward in his seat.

"What the hell is that?" he shouted. The *Cerberus'* outboard camera showed a dust storm raging around the machine.

Vince slapped his computer keyboard with the palm of his hand, silencing both the alarm and the blinking light. "I don't know," he replied, as his fingers danced across the keyboard. "It looks as if the

Cerberus surged forward five meters past the designated stopping point, just before I cut power."

Alan shook his head, quickly running numbers through his head. "That can't be right. It would take twenty minutes to bore that far. Check your readings again."

Vince double-checked his screen, frowned, and scratched his head. "They're correct."

Alan watched the monitor screen for several minutes. Slowly, the dust dissipated, and the readings returned to normal. Everything checked out. He shrugged his shoulders at the short-lived enigma.

"I don't know. The GPS might be off a little." He hoped not. Such an error would cripple the *Cerberus'* effectiveness. He chose to go with the next best reason. "We might have hit a layer of softer rock. There's no indication of moisture. It doesn't seem to be a seep; still, we might want to wait a while before we send anyone down there."

If the *Cerberus* had bored into an underground aquifer, it could flood the new tunnel; however, that was Verkhoen's concern, not his. He looked at Vince, Bill, and Trace and grinned. "We did it, guys."

"Your father will be proud," Vince replied.

"Yes, he will be." *His father.* He had forgotten. He sat down in front of his laptop and brought up his father's image on the screen. His father, probably everyone at Hoffman Industries, had been watching the *Cerberus'* progress on Skype. "We did it, Dad. The *Cerberus* did it."

The noise level of the celebratory din at Hoffman Industries drowned out his father's words, but from the gleam in his eyes, Alan guessed his father was proud of him. That was enough for him. His father continued speaking and gesturing at the crowd of people gathered in the company warehouse. It looked as if every employee was on hand for the party. The phone rang. He turned down the volume on his laptop and answered. Verkhoen was on the other end.

"Congratulations, Mr. Hoffman," he said in his clipped Boer voice. "Your machine worked as well as you claimed. How long before I can send down a crew?"

Alan checked the readouts again. The temperature was stabilizing quickly,   and there was no sign of seepage. Whatever they had hit didn't seem dangerous, but he didn't want to take any chances.

"I would wait about eight or nine hours," he replied. "The tunnel is still hot. I'll send down a man in a heat suit in a couple of hours to check out the *Cerberus* and take a few core samples."

"Good. One of our security personnel will accompany him. He can assist your man if needed."

Alan knew Verkhoen wasn't sending a security man down just to lend a helping hand. If there was a rich vein of gold down there, he intended to see no one helped themselves to a nugget or two. Alan laughed at the absurdity. Gold nuggets were the last thing on his people's minds right now. They had spent three years working with him developing the *Cerberus*. They wouldn't leave its side until convinced everything was working perfectly; besides, the gold in this case was invisible, a few ounces per ton. Someone could walk out with a truckload of ore and not have enough for gold fillings.

"Thank you, but that isn't really necessary. My people are used to mines."

"Nevertheless, I insist," Verkhoen replied.

Alan gave up arguing. Verkhoen was in charge. "All right. I'll pick one of my engineers to go. I'll join him after a few hours sleep."

Trace raised his hand and waved it frantically above his head. "I'll go."

As badly as Alan wanted to go himself, he knew it would look too much like vanity if he insisted on going first. Alan looked at Trace and shook his head. "You're dead on your feet. You're going back to the hotel for some sleep. Maybe you could change shirts, too."

Trace pulled the front of his t-shirt out to look at it and grinned. "It's just food," he said.

"I'll go, boss," Vince said.

At twenty-six years old, Vince was the youngest of the three engineers, with all the inexhaustible exuberance of youth and the skill of an engineering wizard. He had designed most of the *Cerberus'* remote systems and the laser alignment guide. Without his help, *Cerberus* would be just another idea on the drawing board like its little brother, *Charon*. Of them all, he most deserved the chance to be the first person on scene.

"Okay, Vince, but stay away from Pellucidarian women if you find any."

Vince laughed. "All of them except Dian the Beautiful. If I see Doctor Perry, I'll tell him you said hello."

Vince's infatuation with Edgar Rice Burroughs's legendary land at the center of the earth had been a standing joke since he had joined the firm. He had tried many times, unsuccessfully, to convince Alan of the possibility of giant cavern systems deep in the earth, sealed away for eons, perhaps holding treasures of proto-bacteria or lichens loaded with the next cure for cancer or AIDS.

Alan didn't claim to be an expert, and his biology was limited to required college courses, but he tried to stay informed by reading the latest scientific journals. While he considered the likelihood of sealed, deep-cave systems a remote likelihood, recent deep-rock discoveries of various extremophiles hinted at the possibility. He felt it unlikely that anything larger than bacteria could survive the rigors of the depths or the inevitable decline of a species through DNA decay. Without fresh input of from different strains of DNA, mutations would eventually eliminate a species due to climatic or environmental pressures.

While Vince waited for the security guard to arrive, Alan decided a shower and a few hours of sleep on fresh, clean sheets would go a long way in restoring his health and personal hygiene.

"See you guys later," he said. He checked his watch – eight p.m. "Bill, you keep an eye on Vince. When Trace gets back, it's your turn for a few hours off. In eight hours, we'll all go down and check things out."

Bill nodded, broke a rare smile, and continued monitoring the readings from the *Cerberus* as the machine cooled down after its four-day ordeal. His taciturn manner belied his keen wit and proclivity to wax eloquently on any subject ordinary or arcane after a few beers. Some mistook his laid-back manner for laziness, but after twenty-five years as an engineer, his efficiency and knowledge of his profession made the job look easy. A smile was about as celebratory as he got.

Before Alan could leave, Trace stopped him. "There was something odd about those last few meters of rock."

Trace's solemnity alarmed him. "What was that?"

"The stratum was more like kimberlite than the igneous or dolomitic rock we expected. The *Cerberus* practically ripped through it like butter."

"Kimberlite? But that's found in diamond formations. The nearest diamond mine is a hundred kilometers from here."

"Nevertheless," Trace insisted.

Trace was seldom wrong, but Alan dismissed the information as interesting but requiring no immediate action. He had no problem with exceeding expectations. "Okay, tell Vince to be careful. Have him take some samples for analysis." He grinned. "We just dig 'em. After that, it's Verkhoen's problem."

He received a few hearty pats on the back as he left the tiny control trailer. The sounds of jubilation followed him across the parking lot to his car. Even some of the workers, having learned of the breakthrough, shouted their congratulations. His success elated him, but something nagged at him, something he couldn't put a finger on. Maybe it was just the usual post-partum depression of seeing his baby delivered, but he knew he had missed something important. He shook his head to clear it. He was too exhausted to think clearly. He needed a few hours of uninterrupted sleep to regain his momentum. He would take a fresh look at the data later.

The night was cloudy and cool with no moon. Ominous dark clouds scuttled across the sky hinting at rain. He smiled. Where he would be in a few hours, four-thousand meters underground, weather wouldn't be a problem. He drove past the yawning, three-hundred-meter-deep open pit, abandoned when the sloping gold vein dove deep into the earth and became too difficult to mine by conventional methods. Now, it saw new life as an armada of heavy haulers raced up and down the roadway winding along the pit's steep sides hauling ore.

In another first for gold mining, Van Gotts Corporation had bored a one-and-a-half-kilometer-long shaft from 70 Level to the pit and installed a heavy-duty belt conveyor to move the ore from the depths of the mine to the pit. There, bucket loaders filled large ore haulers for transport to the crushers. Ore mined from 65 Level or higher dropped through a converted airshaft to the skip lift room on 65 Level, which delivered the ore directly to the surface conveyors. Electric locos pulling ore carts hauled ore mined from the lower levels to the belt conveyor. The ingenious split-delivery system had saved millions of dollars and freed the elevators for three work shifts.

Back in his room at the *Protea Hotel*, one of two hotels in Klerksdorp, Alan checked to see what time it was in Nevada – one p.m. – and made a phone call to his father. They hadn't had much chance to talk during the celebrating, and he wanted a few words in privacy, away from the crowd. His father answered on the second ring.

"Hello, Dad."

"Alan," his father barked into the receiver. The background noise of the continuing festivities drowned him out. "Let me go someplace a little quieter," he yelled. "They're breaking out the champagne here." Less than a minute later, with the din of the celebration at a tolerable level, he said, "Nice job, son. You did it."

Alan's heart swelled with pride at his father's praise. He was thirty-two years old; nevertheless, it felt good to have his father acknowledge his accomplishments. They had been rare lately. "No, *we* did it, Dad."

"It was difficult to keep people's minds on the job this past week," his father continued. "Everyone made excuses to drop by my office to watch the progress on my computer."

"I hope you and mother got some sleep."

His father laughed. It sounded good to hear mirth from his father where there had been only unspoken anxiety for so long. "Oh, a few hours here and there. Your mother was worse. She insisted on checking in every few hours. I've never seen her so concerned. What about you?"

"I've been living on coffee and adrenaline. I'm going to get a few hours sleep, and then join Vince down in the mine to check on the *Cerberus*."

"You be careful. Verkhoen has a reputation for cutting corners. Watch yourself."

His father's voice took on a darker tone that puzzled Alan. While his father was usually a good judge of character, Verkhoen seemed a nice enough person to Alan, cold and calculating, but reputable. He wished he had FaceTimed his father to see the expression on his face.

"I will," he promised. He wanted to query his father more thoroughly about Verkhoen, but decided it could wait as he stifled a yawn so wide it made his jaw ache. "I've got to get some sleep now. Talk to you later."

"Goodnight, son."

He hung up the telephone, still baffled by his father's veiled warning. *Nothing I can do about it now*, he thought as he undressed. In the shower, he let the jet of hot water hammer his back and neck, massaging away the tensions of the past few weeks, turning the water off only when it began to turn tepid.

Next, in spite of the late hour, he dialed room service and ordered a meal of steak and fried potatoes, called *kruisskyf* and vinegary 'slap' chips in *Afrikaans*, and a bottle of *Jakkals Fontein Shiraz*. He had grown to enjoy the local South African red wines from the country's *Svartland* coastal region. Van Gotts Corporation had paid for the rooms, which included an open room service and bar tab. He intended to test the limits of their generosity.

While sipping his second glass of wine after the satisfying dinner, wearing only his underwear, Alan sat on the balcony staring out into the night. Lightning flashed in the distance, illuminating the underside of the heavy clouds. A russet *hoopoe* slept safely nestled in the branches of a thorny acacia tree just outside his window, its long, insect-digging bill tucked under its wing. Alan's troubled thoughts returned to Trace's comments about the kimberlite.

The *Ngomo* Mine had been in operation for over five decades. Verkhoen should have been fully aware of any anomalies in the geology of the area. The *Witwatersrand* was gold country, the sediment bed of an ancient lake tilted on its side and folded by geologic pressure, subsequently brought to the surface by a meteorite impact. There shouldn't be any kimberlite in the area.

The diamonds associated with most gold mines were of poor quality, their greenish-to-black tints caused by eons of radiation exposure from natural uranium in the rock. The real diamond-producing mines were farther south and west near the city of Kimberly associated with ancient volcanic pipes. Before he allowed any more tunneling, he would have to check out the formations to see what they were getting into. He yawned again, rose from his chair, and returned to his room.

Now for some sleep.

* * * *

His cell phone woke him with a start. Was it his wake-up call? It felt like he had just dozed off. *No, the hotel desk would use the room phone.* He picked up his watch to check the time, startled to see he had been asleep for less than four hours. He fumbled for his cell phone, managing to turn it on after the third try.

"Boss, we've got problems." The sharp concern in Trace's tense voice yanked him from his drowsiness.

"Wha ... what's wrong?" he managed to croak, tossing off the covers and sitting on the edge of the bed.

"Vince is missing. So is the security guy."

Missing? His stomach churned, and he knew it wasn't from his last repast. "I'll be right there."

4

July 4, 2016, 10:00 p.m.   *Ngomo* Mine, 138 Level –

At first, Vince resented his companion, the security guard, Ntulli Masowe. Having an armed guard around seemed like overkill on the mine's part. The last thing he was interested in was gold. While Masowe stood around arms folded and acting officious, he checked out the *Cerberus'* systems by attaching a USB cable from the external port to his laptop. Except for a little more knocking around than they had expected, everything looked fine. The *Cerberus* was a success, and he felt a surge of excitement at his part in its development. He was also a bit sad. Now that the *Cerberus AT10* was a viable product, he could no longer ignore the many offers of work he received each month.

He craved excitement, surfing the cutting edge of technology. It was like a drug to him. He needed a new challenge that could keep his mind occupied. The camaraderie at Hoffman Industries had been like a second home, and while he liked Alan as a friend, Alan would be tied up for the next few years fine-tuning the *Cerberus* for mass production, a job more suited to Trace or Bill than him. Both were equally capable of managing the *Charon's* progress. The details annoyed him. He preferred the overall big picture – the concept development.

"It is cooler than it should be," Masowe commented, one of the few full sentences he had spoken since they had arrived in the shaft. Vince had wondered if he spoke any English.

Vince sighed softly and glanced up from his readings. "Yeah, I noticed that," he answered in an offhand manner, annoyed by the interruption. He checked the temperature and whistled. "98 degrees." He noticed the lack of comprehension on the guard's face. "That's 36 degrees Centigrade. At this depth, it should be close to 60 degrees

Centigrade, even hotter with the heat radiating from the casing."

"Why is that?"

While he disliked interruptions, he appreciated the guard's attempt at conversation. The quiet of the tunnel, aside from the pinging of cooling rock, was disconcerting. A bit of conversation might keep the walls from closing in on him. He enjoyed machinery, even mining machinery, but he didn't like mines. One thing he had learned in a geology class he had taken one summer was that the earth moved, sometimes at the most inopportune times. The closest he wanted to come to being underground was reading one of Burroughs's novels, and yet, here he was, 4,000 kilometers underground.

He looked up at Masowe's strongly chiseled features visible through the clear Plexiglas of Masowe's oxygen mask. The security guard looked every centimeter the Zulu warrior he claimed to be. He also had an inquisitive mind, or he would have never reached the level of security officer at Van Gotts. There might no longer be legal apartheid in South Africa, but prejudice remained ingrained in many of its people. Ninety percent of the workforce was black, while only five percent of the managers were black. The ratio was slow to change.

"I'm not sure," he answered.

Masowe nodded his head, as if expecting just such an answer; then, he began removing his mask.

"Don't," Vince warned, but it was too late.

Masowe sniffed the air. "It is cool enough." He dropped the mask and attached a canister of oxygen to the ground, pulled off his heavy gloves, and slid the balaclava from his head, freeing his curly black locks. Vince noticed the grey around the edges, making the guard older than he had thought. Masowe unzipped the upper half of the heat resistant overalls he wore and tied the arms around his waist, leaving him in his short-sleeved undershirt. "Much better," he said, smiling.

Vince shrugged. The cumbersome gloves and confining mask made it difficult to work. He had been painstakingly typing on the laptop keyboard, slowing his work to a crawl. He didn't want to look like an American *skapie*, an Afrikaans word he had picked up since his arrival, a pussy. He followed Masowe's example and removed his mask; then, drew in a sample breath. The air was hot, but no hotter than a summer day in Nevada. He attributed the slightly bitter taste to rock dust particles floating in the air. Next, he removed his gloves, and balaclava, but only unzipped his overall to his waist.

Masowe pulled a long knife from his belt and pried a rock loose from the wall in front of the *Cerberus*. The rock was still warm to the touch. He turned it over in his hands a few times to cool it enough to examine.

"This is not gold gravel," he said, showing it to Vince.

Vince gave it a cursory glance, intent on continuing his inspection of the *Cerberus* now that the gloves no longer encumbered him. "No. It looks like kimberlite."

"I have seen much gold ore. I have also worked in a diamond mine. This is like the rock where diamonds are found."

Vince shrugged his shoulders. "I'm no geologist, but I think you're right."

"Something is wrong here," Masowe insisted, glancing around nervously.

"Well, the mine engineer will be down soon with Alan." He made a chalk mark on the rock face in front of the *Cerberus*. "Maybe he'll have an answer. Now, stand back while I fire up a laser to check the alignment."

The Zulu guard positioned himself behind the bulk of the *Cerberus* with Vince.

"Here goes," Vince said, as he touched the key on his laptop to fire up the jet turbine.

He was glad he had worn earplugs when the deafening turbine came on line, shaking the ground. He waited until the laser array spun up to speed before firing only one of the three lasers. A flash of bright light flared in the tunnel for five seconds, and a wave of heat blasted past them, followed by a loud hissing. Confused by the sound that should not be there, he killed the turbine and stepped from behind the *Cerberus*.

"I'll be damned," he said. Instead of the hole punched through the center of his chalk mark he expected to find, a small section of the rock face had slumped forward, and a rush of cool, moist air poured from an opening in the rock. He turned to the astonished Masowe. "We've hit a solution cavity, a void."

Masowe poked his head into the hole but jerked it back quickly as the heat of the rock hit him. "I see a great opening beyond." He began to kick at the rock with his heavy boot to enlarge the opening. The soft conglomerate broke apart with little effort. "I will look around. Perhaps this is *Uhlanga.*"

"Uh ... what?" Vince asked.

"*Uhlanga*, the place of God," Masowe replied reverently. "My father is a *sangoma*, a spiritual healer. He told me of such a place when I was young, the place of the spirits of our ancestors. *Unkulunkulu*, the Creator, fell from the sky into a great underground swamp. He took two reeds and made man and woman. "

"Have you ever heard of Pellucidar?"

Masowe stared at Vince. "Is this a country?"

Vince laughed. "Kind of. It's a land under the earth."

Masowe smiled. "Like *Uhlanga.*"

"Exactly." Vince pointed to Masowe's beaded necklace, just visible through his open collar. "Is that part of your magic?"

Masowe held out the colorful necklace for Vince to inspect. "It is an *ibheqe*, a lover's gift to her man." He smiled. "It is from my wife." He pulled a small bead-covered gourd from his pants pocket. "This is my *ishungu*. It contains *muti,* or medicine against misfortune."

"You take all of this seriously, don't you?"

"My people have believed in *Unkulunkulu* longer than your people have believed in your God Jesus. Our beliefs are diluted by your Christian myths now, but some remember the ancient ways."

"Do you?"

Masowe stared at Vince for a moment, as if sizing him up. "My father believed. I have seen ... things you would not understand." He scratched a design on the ground with the tip of his knife. To Vince, it looked like a mandala of some sort.

"What is this?"

"It is to ward off the *Intulo*, an evil being that lives in the earth."

"You won't find much living down here, I'm afraid," he told Masowe. "It looks pretty sterile. There may be some lichens or bacteria, but I don't suppose we'll find any jungles." *So much for childhood dreams*, he thought. "Still, I had better check the air quality for the presence of fire damp. We don't want a methane explosion." He held the probe of the air sensor just inside the hole. "The air pressure is slightly higher inside the cavity, but the air is mostly oxygen and carbon dioxide with traces of hydrogen sulfide, sulfur dioxide, and methane."

Masowe peered through the opening. "No. No swamp, but it is a very large cavity. The machine's lights do not penetrate its full depths." He turned to face Vince. "It is a strange place. I wish to explore it."

"Uh, that's not a good idea." He knew he should stay with the *Cerberus* and complete his tests, but Masowe's enthusiasm aroused his curiosity and sense of adventure; *besides,* he thought, *it's a cave. Maybe I'll find Pellucidar.* The chance to fulfill a childhood fantasy was too strong to ignore. He tossed a mental coin and it landed on heads. "Wait. I'll come with you. Let me contact Trace first."

He punched in Trace's number on his cell phone before remembering that he had no reception underground. He opened the outside panel in the *Cerberus* containing a telephone connecting to the Shack, but only heard static. "Damn phone. It must be a bug in the system. Oh, well, he can see us through the camera." He waved at the camera, smiled, and pointed at the hole for Trace or Bill's benefit, whoever was playing video chaperone.

Satisfied with his handiwork at enlarging the opening, Masowe disappeared into the hole he had made. Vince grabbed a flashlight and followed, his sense of adventure making his skin tingle. He emerged into a wide tunnel. The tunnel was about thirty meters wide and slightly less in height. It sloped at an angle of twelve degrees, running perpendicular to the gold-bearing vein. Verkhoen had informed them the new tunnel the *Cerberus* had dug would intersect the gold vein. The ground penetrating radar could not have missed such a large cavity; the change in density would have been obvious. Therefore, Verkhoen had known about the tunnel. Why was he keeping secrets?

It was impossible to see far because of the slope, even with the powerful flashlights they carried. The tunnel walls and ceiling were smooth, almost as regular as the fresh tunnel the *Cerberus* had bored, but the rock was more brittle. Large sections of the ceiling and walls had sloughed away to form long berms and piles of rock on the floor, around which they had to navigate as they explored the tunnel. Lacey stalactites, some as thin as pencils, others like folded velvet, ribbons dripped from the roof, their surfaces moist with mineral-laden water.

Accompanying stalagmites jutted from the tunnel floor, some needle sharp, others shaped like melted blobs.

"It looks like a lava tube," Vince said in wonder, examining the walls. "See how smooth it is, and the multiple ledges along the bottom indicate different levels of lava flow over time. I've never heard of a lava tube so far underground." He shined his light on one of the stalactites. "Surface water is filtering down through the differing strata."

Masowe played his flashlight up and down the tube. "It is very long," he said and began walking. Vince followed.

As they strode down the lava tube, each footstep reverberated loudly from the walls and echoed into the distance. Their lights picked out shiny striations in the walls that looked like metals. Vince scraped one with his knife.

"Copper, I think," he said to Masowe. "This other one looks like nickel. If there's more of this about, it could be worth a fortune in itself. It looks like pure metal."

He looked up and noticed Masowe was not paying attention to him. The guard focused his light farther down the tunnel. The light reflected on something brighter than the rich metal ore deposits. They advanced slowly, curious but cautious. As Vince rounded a small stalactite protruding from the ceiling, a cavesicle, he drew in his breath at the vista before him. Embedded in the wall were dozens of crystal nodules as large as his fist, glittering in the flashlight's beam. As he played the light about, he discovered hundreds more of varying sizes, shapes, and colors.

"Smoky quartz?" he asked, but he knew by the look of astonishment on Masowe's face that they were not.

"Diamonds," Masowe exclaimed, "thousands of carats of diamonds." He shined his light along the opposite wall, revealing even more diamonds. They had discovered a pocket of diamonds ten meters long on each side of the pipe.

Vince stooped to pick up a glittering stone as large as a walnut lying at his feet.

"Put it back," Masowe growled. His eyes narrowed as he stared at Vince. His hand gripped his knife tighter.

Vince looked at the towering Zulu him for a moment before dropping the diamond. He wasn't sure the security guard would resort to violence to protect the mine, but he wasn't taking any chances. "I was just looking."

Masowe's face softened to one of shame. He relaxed his stance and put away his knife. "I am sorry," he said. "I dealt with thieves when I worked in one of Van Gotts' diamond mines. They swallowed diamonds; stuffed them up their asses, in their ears, in the foreskin of their penises – any orifice they could find. It became a habit to be suspicious." He picked up a diamond about ten carats large and handed it to Vince. "Take it to your girlfriend. Van Gotts will not miss it in all this." He waved his hands about, indicating the riches around them.

Vince took the diamond and secreted it in the pocket of his laptop bag. "What about you? One of these would make you a rich man."

Masowe smiled. "I am a black man, a *kaffir*. They will search me inside and out when I leave the mines. If I managed to smuggle it from the mine, any dealer would believe it an illegal blood diamond and immediately report me to the authorities. I prefer to keep my job and feed my five children; besides, I am a Zulu warrior and I have given my word to Van Gotts Corporation and to my boss, Security Chief Duchamps. I will honor it." He looked around uneasily. "We should go back. I do not like this place. It smells *klankie*."

"Klankie?" Vince asked.

"Bad. The air smells bad," Masowe explained.

Vince sniffed the air. Now, he too caught a whiff of something strange, like rotten meat or dead vegetation. *No*, he realized, *it smells musty like the Egyptian mummy case at the Nevada State Museum in Carson City*. He checked the air with his portable gas analyzer. "No carbon monoxide, no radon; methane is below combustible levels ... wait, this can't be right. It shows the O_2 is much too high, three percent higher than normal. Okay, let's go. I need to double check these stats."

Masowe was reluctant to leave. He stared at the diamonds for several minutes before joining Vince. Once back at the *Cerberus*, Vince tried once more to report to the Shack. The phone still didn't work. He waved at the camera and smiled at whoever was manning the monitor. He wrote 'Taking a break' on his laptop screen and held it up to the camera. Then, he sat down and considered his good fortune. Between the diamond and his bonus for the job, he could just manage a down payment on that new Corvette he had been looking at, a chick magnet if there ever was one. A tour up and down the Pacific Coast, hitting all the beaches along the way, would make a nice vacation.

He checked his watch. The others weren't due to show up for another five hours. He had been running on little sleep for over a week. Now, he had time for a nap. He made himself comfortable just inside the lava tube where the air was cooler. Masowe sat cross-legged beside his flashlight, now set on end to become a lantern, softly singing in his native tongue and swaying his upper body while he tapped one foot against the ground. Vince, too, felt inebriated by the increased oxygen level. He felt his tension slide away, as Masowe sang quietly.

"What are you singing about?" he asked.

"I sing for the gods to protect me and to keep my aim true during the hunt."

"The hunt?"

"Yes, all life is a hunt, is it not? We seek that which we desire or need and use our skills to obtain it. Each man's skills are different, as are his desires, but all men hunt. My people hunt for food or for ways to prove their manhood. Your people hunt for fame, fortune, and the good life." He shrugged. "Both are the same. How we use our skill makes us what we are. If we use them wisely and correctly and with honor, we will obtain our goals. If we squander them or cheat others, the gods will keep our desires from us. I pray for wisdom and a true eye."

Vince hadn't expected such profound and perceptive wisdom from a security guard. "That's deep," he replied.

"Deep?" Masowe asked, not understanding. "Yes, we are."

Vince chuckled. "I meant, what you said was very wise."

Masowe nodded, but his gaze remained fixed on a point down the lava tube as he spoke. "There is something here. I can sense it." He grimaced. "It is evil."

Vince looked at Masowe and imagined him naked, wearing paint and ostrich feathers, sitting by the fire before a hunt, the years of civilization stripped away; or carrying a short *assagi* stabbing spear and stretched cowhide *isihlangu* battle shield, running across the veldt. Just such a Zulu warrior, Shaka Zulu, had almost defeated the

British army in the late 19th Century. He shook his head. Masowe was spooking him.

"Let's douse the lights and get some sleep. In a few hours, everyone will be down here, and it'll be a long, hectic day."

Masowe turned off the battery-powered lantern, plunging the entire shaft into pitch-black darkness. *No, not complete darkness,* Vince observed. Large areas of the wall were glowing softly. *Bioluminescent bacteria or lichen,* he thought. *Very interesting. I'll have to check it out, later.*

From the near darkness, Masowe said, "It is like the stars above my village at night when I sit outside my family's *kraal*. It is beautiful. You sleep. I will keep watch. The lion comes soon."

Lion, Vince thought. *It was hardly likely they'd find a lion down here.* He watched the patches of luminescence twinkle, as he slowly drifted off to sleep.

* * * *

Vince awoke with a large hand clamped over his mouth squeezing gently but firmly. "Do not speak," Masowe whispered in his ear. "*Intulo* comes." Then he disappeared.

He sat up slowly. He heard nothing, but by the dim bioluminescent light, he saw Masowe crouched beside a pile of rocks with his revolver drawn. He sensed no fear in the Zulu, only wariness, and perhaps a trace of excitement. He strained his ears to hear what Masowe heard, but they were not as acute as the Zulu security guard's.

A soft clink reached him as a chunk of brittle rock fell from the roof and shattered. He relaxed. *So that's what got Masowe so wired up, a piece of the lava tube breaking off.* He started to chide Masowe for his nervousness when the sound of running feet broke the silence, many feet. *What the hell could be down here?*

He crawled over to Masowe's side. The Zulu was staring down the tunnel with the intensity of a laser beam, his eyes unblinking. In the scant light, Vince could see nothing but layer upon layer of shadows, but he was certain the Zulu could see something more, something that frightened him.

"What are they?" he asked quietly.

"*Intulo* – Devils."

"Devils?"

"Yes. Their smell is unknown to me, but I sense their evil, their hunger."

Without taking his eyes off the tunnel, Masowe reached into his belt, pulled out his long, bone-handled knife, and handed it to Vince. *No, not bone*, Vince realized as he grasped the smooth handle, *polished ivory*. The knife was heavy in his hand but perfectly balanced.

"Use it well. I count six of them."

"Six what? Are they rats?"

He had seen rats in the mineshafts, some as large as cat. The miners used them as canaries, noting their ability to detect minute shifts in the rock preceding cave-ins and following them from the tunnels. As he said it, he knew rats wouldn't be so deep underground. Masowe was beginning to frighten him. Masowe said nothing. He simply stared down the lava pipe.

Vince realized that they were off camera. No one in the Shack could see them. "I'm going to try to call in," he said.

Masowe placed his hand on his shoulder to stop him. "If you raise your voice, they will attack," he warned. "They are scouting us now."

"What about the lights?"

"We will be blinded for a few seconds as the lights come on. That would leave us vulnerable. I do not know if the light will blind them or not. It is best not to find out."

They sat for several minutes, as the slight scuffle in the rocks grew louder and bolder. And closer. Occasionally, Vince heard a scraping sound like metal on stone; then, a cacophony of loud hisses filled the air, coming from several different points of the tunnel. To him, it sounded like hunters calling out to one another, signaling that they were in position.

"They come," Masowe announced.

Masowe's calm voice didn't lessen Vince's apprehension. Vince stared into the darkness, but in the dim light saw only shadows dancing in and out of even deeper shadows along the wall. Masowe fired his pistol twice, startling Vince, and one of the shadows fell. The report of the gun almost deafened him. The blinding muzzle flash lit up the tunnel for a few seconds, but revealed nothing. The sounds died away down the tunnel slowly. The flash reminded Vince of something he needed to tell the Zulu, but he couldn't remember what, something about the gun. Masowe began crawling over the rocks. Vince pulled at him.

"Where are you going?" he demanded.

"I killed one," Masowe said, smiling with pride. "I must examine it." "Don't be a fool. We don't know what these things are."

Masowe ignored him, pulled away, and scrambled over the pile of boulders. "All the more reason to examine it," he called back. "I have only four more bullets."

"Then let's get the hell out of here," he yelled into the shadows, but there was no answer from the security guard turned hunter. He peered into the darkness, and thought he could see Masowe's outline as he swept from one pile of rock to another in careful movements like the stealthy hunter he was. More shadows were moving around him.

"Masowe," he yelled. "There are more of them." He knew Masowe probably saw them before he did, but he couldn't keep silent. A deep, guttural scream erupted from the darkness, a shriek that chilled his blood. He had never heard such a horrific cry except on television. It went on and on, the horrible sound reverberating down the lava tube until drowned out by two quick shots from the pistol. Immediately, a blast of fire erupted from beyond the rock berm, sweeping back toward the *Cerberus*. Vince fell flat on his face and hugged the ground with his hands over the back of his head, as the flames swept over him.

The gunfire had ignited a pocket of methane. That was what he was trying to remember. Increased oxygen levels and high temperatures lowered the LEL, the Lower Explosive Level of methane. Even a small concentration of methane became combustible under those conditions. He should have remembered earlier, but the extra oxygen in the air had made him euphoric and giddy.

More chirps and whistles and the sound of scuffling erupted beyond the rocks. *The hell with this*, he thought. *I need to see what's out there.* He scrambled back to the *Cerberus* to switch on the lights. Bright light immediately flooded the tunnel, and just as Masowe had predicted, the brightness momentarily blinded him. At a sound just behind him, he turned.

"Masowe?" he asked. Instead of the security guard, he caught a quick glimpse of something razor sharp slashing down at his head. He held up his hands in a reflex action and felt searing pain explode as the object broke his radius, ripped deep into his flesh, and knocked the knife from his grip. He turned to the phone on the side of the *Cerberus*, but before he could lift it from its cradle, claws ripped into his right shoulder and spun him around. In intense agony, he fought the urge to pass out to get a glimpse of his unknown assailant. His fear of the unknown paled to the horror of the known.

His last vision was of two large, multi-faceted red eyes set on each side of an enormous maw and a pair of mandibles red with blood. *His blood*, he thought numbly. His last thought was, *"What next, a Mahar?"*

As its companions dragged Vince's corpse away to feed, two of the creatures slipped through the narrow opening between the *Cerberus* and the tunnel wall and scurried down the tunnel, seeking escape from the dark, hidden world that had been their home for millions of years. They became a part of the shadows as they sought the source of the tantalizing odors coming from the warren of tunnels, a smell and taste with which they were now familiar – human flesh.

5

July 5, 2016, 1:00 a.m.   *Ngomo* Mine, 66 Level –

Judith Ainsley checked the wiring inside the electrical panel in Shaft B106West on 66 Level. The high humidity played hell with the connections, creating dangerous short-circuits that plagued the lights, plunging the shaft into darkness with alarming frequency. Though the shaft was no longer in operation, the inspector had written the lights up on his last report, and as an electrician, one of the few female technicians in the mine, it was her job to fix it. She would rather be home in bed. She was nearing the end of a long double shift and eager to go topside.

"Hand me that brush," she said to her assistant, Dylan Pitt. He was a young man ten years her junior, but she often caught his gaze straying to her ass. She didn't mind. Her husband was a slob, and a tumble with the strapping eighteen year old might be fun. So far, he hadn't made any advances, and she was reluctant to. The company frowned on dalliances between employees.

Pitt handed her a wire brush. She double-checked the wires with her current meter to make sure the power was off before scrubbing the rust from the connecting strip. The shadows cast by her helmet light made the job difficult. Finally, satisfied it was as clean as she could get it, she attached the wire for the lights and tightened the connection; then, she sprayed waterproof coating over the strip to seal it.

"That should do it," she said and threw the switch. The lights flickered for a moment before settling down to a steady glow.

"You do good work, Judy," Pitt said.

"I'm the best," she retorted. "I've been doing it for fifteen years."

"Good, I want to learn from the best."

"Just stick with me and … What was that?" Something had caught her attention.

Pitt glanced behind them. "What?"

She shook her head. "I don't know. I thought I saw something."

"Rats," he said.

"It was bigger than a rat." She couldn't think of anything else in the mines. An animal could have ventured down the skip elevator two levels above them, but most didn't like the heat or the noise. She laughed. "Only we humans are stupid enough to come down here. It must have been a shadow."

"Or a mine ghost," Pitt said, smiling

She handed Pitt her tools. He returned them to her tool bag, carefully wiping each one and storing it in its proper place. She smiled at his thoroughness. She had been caught in the dark too many times to fumble around for the proper tool when she needed it. Though he had been her assistant for only three months, he was a fast learner. He picked up her bag and slung it over his shoulder.

"Come on," she said. "Let's get out of here. I could use a bit of sunshine and some lunch."

"It's after midnight," he reminded her.

"Then a midnight snack will have to do."

As they approached one of the ventilator shafts, she noticed the screen bent outward from the half-meter-diameter opening. She stopped and knelt in front of it, enjoying the cooler air blowing from it. "I didn't notice this on the way down. Oh well, I had better fix it while I'm here. No reason to write it up and send a maintenance person back down."

"I'll do it," Pitt volunteered.

"My, aren't you eager. Okay. Have at it."

She stood back to watch as Pitt pulled a hammer, a battery-powered drill, and a handful of screws from the tool bag. He knelt in front of the opening and drilled new holes in the wooden frame. Just as he began pushing the wire screen back into place, something almost as dark as the shadows within the opening reached out, grabbed his head, and yanked him inside. His scream was short-lived, but the sound of his body banging against the sides of the shaft as it fell the hundred meters to the ventilator fan below sickened her. She had seen what the fan's meter-long blades could do to flesh, after once removing a mutilated bat from a stalled fan in the upper levels. She had barely recognized the mangled mess.

The horror of the manner of her assistant's death paled in comparison to the reason for it. He hadn't fallen. Something had pulled him inside. There was no ladder, so it couldn't be human.

She picked up the hammer and raised it in the air; then, she inched closer to the opening. She was so intent on discovering what was within the opening that she forgot about the shadow she thought she had seen earlier. A scuttling sound above her head distracted her. She glanced up at the row of bleeder pipes running along the wall near the roof. Sitting atop one of the pipes was a creature from one of her worst nightmares. The meter-and-a half-long, eight-legged cross between a scorpion and an ant lion stared down at her with two pairs of multi-faceted insect eyes. The monster was as black as a funeral dress and had vicious claws as long as her arm.

"What the fuck?" she whispered.

She swung the hammer at the creature's head. It was like hitting a stone wall as the hammer bounced off the creature's hard carapace. It clacked its mouthparts together rapidly. As she prepared for a second swing, its companion from the airshaft clamped down on her leg with its claws. The pain was excruciating, a raging inferno that swept up her leg and into her chest. She dropped the hammer and glanced down. White bone was visible through the deep gash in her leg. As she bent over to staunch the bleeding with her hand, the creature on the pipe slashed at her head, slicing away her right ear and cheek, exposing her jawbone.

Her panic turned to terror. She began screaming, swinging her arms wildly to fight off the creatures from hell. She fell to the floor. She picked up the drill and drove its ten-centimeter bit into the nearest creature, feeling a rush of satisfaction when the bit pierced the hard carapace and struck softer flesh beneath. Yellow ichor oozed through the small wound. The creature emitted a keening sound and tried to crawl back into the airshaft. She clung to the drill until it pinned her hand against the frame before letting go.

The second giant insect fell on her from its perch. She had no time to defend herself. It sank its stinger into her chest. Instantly, she felt the venom spreading through her lungs. Each breath became a battle she knew she could not win. The claws closed around her neck with more pressure than she would have thought possible, choking her. Her vision swam. Gradually, the pain receded. Where once she felt fire, a numbing cold crept through her body.

Is this what it feels like to die? she thought.

She heard disgusting wet crunching sounds and suspected it was the creature devouring her, but she no longer cared. She was drifting away like a feather on a breeze, no longer attached to her useless body.

This isn't so bad. I thought it would be much worse.

Then, pain exploded in her entire being, and she knew what death really felt like.

6

July 5, 2016 1:00 a.m.   *Ngomo* Mine, Klerksdorp, South Africa –
When Alan rushed into the Shack, he found Bill pale and trembling, quite a change from his usual imperturbable demeanor. "I called Van Gotts' security," Bill said. "They should be here any minute."

"What happened?" Alan was breathless after his sprint from the parking lot to the trailer.

Bill tried to remain calm and professional as he delivered his report, but Alan detected the underlying current of uneasiness in his voice. "Vince failed to report in on schedule. The phone was out, but I could see him on the camera holding up his laptop with the message 'Taking a break'. I assumed we lost the audio connection. It's been a little quirky all day. He doused the lights and everything went dark. I didn't think anything of it. We were going down to join him in few hours. Later, I noticed that the lights were back on. I began to pan the camera and found this."

Alan watched the monitor. The *Cerberus'* lights were on, bathing the end of the tunnel in bright light, but there was no sign of Vince or the guard; then, he noticed the irregular opening in the rock face. "What's that?"

"It looks like Vince busted through a void."

Alan's apprehension backed down a notch. Vince's curiosity had gotten the better of him, and he had entered the opening. It even explained the sudden surge of speed at the end of the *Cerberus'* run. "He's probably looking for Pellucidar, and the guard went with him," Alan said. "It was a dumb move but typically Vince."

Bill shook his head. "Not the opening. This."

Alan peered more intently at the screen but couldn't see what Bill meant until he zoomed in on an object lying on the ground and slid a control to sharpen the image. It was a long knife, its white handle smeared with blood. Alan's heart began pounding, and he had difficulty swallowing.

"I'm going down there," he told Bill.

Bill frowned. "Why don't you wait on security? We don't know what happened."

He realized Bill was right and cursed under his breath. He shouldn't go alone. Walking into an unknown situation could be dangerous. He wasn't even sure he could find the way back down. "Okay, but when the security team arrives, I'm going down there."

Bill nodded, still staring at the bloody knife. "Do you think the guard went crazy or something?"

Alan said nothing. An intense sense of dread gripped his intestines, twisting them like into balloon animal shapes, but speculation served no purpose. *No reason to conjure the Devil.* He stared at the bloody knife as if willing it to tell him what had happened.

Without knocking, four security people burst into the room, all armed with pistols in holsters on their hips. He wondered if he should ask for a weapon as well, and then decided he was being silly. Four armed security men should provide ample protection against anything or anyone they would encounter in the mine.

One of the two Caucasians, his crisp, blue uniform bearing a captain's insignia, stepped forward, his gaze directed toward the knife on the screen. "My name is Henri Duchamps," he said without looking at Alan.

Alan barely noted Duchamps' deeply tanned face and muscular arms, but he did take notice of the man's piercing eyes, which were a shade of flinty brown almost as dark as the rock on the monitor screen and just as cold and unsettling. He had seen such eyes once in an old newsreel clip of Heinrich Himmler, Adolf Hitler's right-hand man and architect of the Holocaust. They were the cold, calculating eyes of a predator. A scar running from the left corner of his mouth to just below his left ear bisected Duchamps' cheek, diminishing the effect of his twin, gold-incisored smile.

Alan suspected the security chief was not a man to underestimate. Despite his unimposing 5'9" frame, his arms bulged with muscle, and he walked with the cocky, self-assured confidence of a man used to getting his way.

"We've come to investigate the disappearance of one of our security men," he announced.

"My man is missing, too, Captain," Alan replied brusquely, irritated by Duchamps' gruff manner.

"They cannot leave the mine unobserved," Duchamps continued, ignoring Alan's outburst. "There are cameras on each level and on each of the elevators."

Alan pointed to the knife on the screen. "I don't think they left."

One of the black guards spoke up. "That is Ntulli Masowe's knife. He would never leave it. It was a coming-of-age gift from his father. It is a *sangoma's* knife, very sacred."

Just then, Trace threw open the door and raced in, colliding with the second white guard standing in the doorway. The guard growled under his breath, shoved Trace aside, and then stepped between him and Duchamps. Duchamps glared at the disheveled, young, blond engineer for a moment before dismissing him. He turned to the black guard who had spoken.

"You're certain of this?"

The guard nodded. "*Yebo.* It is his knife. I have seen it many times."

Duchamps faced Alan. Assuming what Alan considered a well-practiced pompous pose with his thumbs thrust into his belt on each side of his waist and his arms cocked outward at a sharp angle, he proclaimed, "We will investigate. You will wait here, *ja*?"

"Hell no," Alan replied. "I'm going with you. Vince is my friend and my employee, not to mention the fact that I have a fifteen-million-dollar piece of equipment sitting down there."

"I'm going too," Trace declared from the doorway. He tried to force his way past the guard blocking his path. The guard glowered at him and refused to move. Trace stared at him, clenching his fists, daring the guard to stop him. Alan, fearing the guard might try, spoke up quickly to prevent a confrontation. They didn't need a brawl distracting from the missing Vince.

"He comes with me."

The guard's fingers caressed the butt of the revolver in his holster.

"Bekker," Duchamps snapped.

Bekker grumbled under his breath and moved his hand away. Duchamps promptly ignored the guard and turned to Alan.

"If you insist," he said, "but I am in charge. Do not get in my way."

Alan resented the security chief's deprecatory tone, but swallowed his pride. After all, it was Duchamps' backyard, and he needed him for the search. He wouldn't piss on another man's grass. He grabbed a remote headset from the desk and followed the security team out the door. He glanced back at Bill, looking downcast at not being included in the search. He held himself responsible for Vince's disappearance. It had happened on his watch. Alan knew he needed to ease the engineer's guilt.

"Stay here," he told him. "Keep an eye on the monitors, and keep us posted if you see anything."

Immediately, the tension left Bill's body, and his clenched jaw relaxed at Alan's vote of confidence. He swiveled his chair around to face the video monitor screen and said, "Be careful down there."

"We'll find him," he said to assure Bill, but mostly it was to assure himself.

It took the group an agonizing fifteen minutes to don jumpsuits, helmets, and all the extraneous gear Duchamps insisted they wear – kneepads, shin pads, earplugs, safety glasses, and a self-rescuer pack containing a mask and oxygen supply for emergencies. He made them empty their pockets of anything combustible. When Duchamps wasn't looking, Alan palmed his precious Zippo. Besides reminding him not to smoke, it served as his good luck charm. Though not overly superstitious, he thought he might need the luck.

The elevator ride to reach 30 Level took less than four minutes, but seemed like an eternity to Alan in his impatience to reach Vince. They switched to the #3 elevator to reach the lowest level. From there, it took another thirty minutes to wind through the lower tunnels using the electric locos, called *cocopan* by the Zulu workers, transferring to electric golf carts for the smaller tunnels, and finally walking to the new *Cerberus* shaft.

Before, Alan had been too intent upon his job to notice the myriad of smells wafting through the mine: the sharp bite of chemical residue from blasting; the pungent trace of overheated lubricating oil and hydraulic fluid; the flinty taste of blasted rock that coated the tongue with each breath; and the overpowering stench of hundreds of unwashed bodies. Now, even the acrid reek of mineral-laden water seeping from the rock like the Earth's tears at the violation of her sanctity fought for recognition in the sea of aromas assaulting his nostrils.

"Anything, Bill?" he asked into his headset mic.

"Nothing. No sign of anyone," Bill answered. The link was tenuous, fading in and out because of the density of the rock. "I hacked into the security cameras to review the last few hours. Neither Vince nor the security guard exited the tunnel."

Alan was beginning to have a bad feeling. He knew Vince might be prone to wander off in search of Pellucidar or something equally intriguing, and the unexpected opening in the rock face would have been too tempting to ignore. However, the guard was experienced. He would not simply abandon his post. *And that damn, bloody knife; what did it mean?*

A crane operator met them at the hole and lowered them in the kibble. Entering the newly bored tunnel, Alan half-heartedly observed the walls as they followed the *Cerberus'* path. The tunnel ran as straight as an arrow into the darkness. The new shoring material was stronger than gunite and required no work crew to apply it. The AT10 did it for them.

At last, they came to the idle drilling rig. The last few meters of earth were of a different composition from the rest of the tunnel. He picked up a handful of the still-warm rock. It was much softer and crumbled easily with very little pressure. That explained the burst of speed during the last few seconds of drilling. It had cut through the softer rock like a warm knife through brie. The lights of the *Cerberus* outlined the opening in the rock face.

"It looks like they broke through into a second chamber or shaft," he said.

Duchamps shook his head. "No shaft down this deep." He leaned into the opening and shined his light about. "It's a bloody cavern," he exclaimed.

Alan's gaze followed Duchamps' light. "It's a volcanic lava tube," he said, amazed by the discovery. He entered the opening and played his light around the tube, noting the veins of metal ore. "Vince was right." He confronted Duchamps, who had come up behind him, shining his light in the security chief's eyes. "Verkhoen must have had some idea this was here. This isn't gold-bearing stratum."

Duchamps stared at Alan, blinking in the bright light. "If he did, he didn't feel I needed to know. My concern is my man and, of course, your engineer."

Alan backed down and lowered the flashlight. He could confront Verkhoen later. Right now, he needed the surly South African. "You're right, of course."

They searched the immediate area inside the lava tube and found nothing but the battery lantern and Vince's laptop. Alan picked up the laptop, powered it up, and checked the *Cerberus* readings.

"The readings look normal. The air is a little stale in here, and the oxygen content is slightly above normal, but there's no methane." He addressed Duchamps. "There's no indication of a volcano above ground, no *tuffing* from an eruption, or a circular depression. The geological survey maps don't indicate its presence. This is an ancient volcano, buried by geologic upheavals. How did Verkhoen know about it?"

Duchamps stared him in the eye and said, "I have no idea."

Despite Duchamps' repeated insistence that he knew nothing of his boss' plans and his unblinking delivery, Alan didn't believe him. He doubted anything happened in Van Gotts' mines of which Duchamps was unaware. If anything, it was a matter of culpability. Duchamps might not know Verkhoen's exact end game, but he certainly knew something was afoot.

"If you say so," Alan said. He placed Vince's computer in his backpack.

They split up into two teams. Duchamps sent two of his men upslope. Alan asked Trace to accompany them with a stern warning to avoid a fight with the quarrelsome white guard. He watched them walk away, the reflective patches on their jumpsuits glowing like LED lights, until they disappeared into the darkness.

He and Duchamps continued downslope with the other two guards, scouring the ground for signs of either missing man. When they reached the diamond pocket, Duchamps' eyes grew wide, and a big smile creased his lips. At that moment, Alan believed he might be wrong about the security chief. He was sure now that he had not known about the diamonds.

"Perhaps this explains our missing men," Duchamps said, nodding his head at the wall of diamonds.

Alan didn't believe that possibility. He didn't like hearing his friend accused of theft. "Vince wouldn't steal diamonds. He's more interested in the *Cerberus*. Maybe your guard was tempted and did away with Vince. After all, your guard had a knife and a gun. Vince was unarmed."

"So you say," Duchamps replied.

He was tired of Duchamp's surliness. He strode over to Duchamps and stood in front of him nose-to-nose. Unlike Trace, he despised fighting, but sometimes you had to drive home a point, with your fists in necessary. Neither of them flinched, but neither did they back down. In that moment just before confrontation became conflict, the other guard intervened, his eyes flicking back and forth between them.

"No one left by the new tunnel," he said. "I found tracks all over, but no human tracks go back into the new tunnel past the machine."

Alan backed away from Duchamps. "How do you know?" he asked the guard.

"Because he is the best tracker in the company," Duchamps replied icily. "If he says no one left that way, then no one did."

"Where are they?"

"That's the big money question, isn't it? We will continue our search." Duchamps radioed the other group with his walkie-talkie. "Go back to the machine and watch the tunnel. We will follow the tracks farther downslope."

"Wait for me," Trace yelled into the guard's walkie-talkie.

A few minutes later, Alan heard him trotting down the tunnel, his hardhat lantern bobbing, as he weaved around piles of rock and boulders. His loud steps reverberated and echoed until he sounded like a mob racing toward them. Duchamps cast a reproachful glare at him for the noise he made. Trace whistled appreciatively when he saw the cache of diamonds. Alan warned him to silence with a quick gesture. They didn't need to arouse Duchamps' suspicions, or he might send them back to the surface.

They continued downslope, passing several more diamond deposits before the tracker stopped, knelt, and searched the ground, running his hand over the rock. After a few minutes, he whispered in

Duchamps' ear. Duchamps turned and began striding purposefully back to the *Cerberus*.

"Where the hell are you going?" Alan yelled after him.

"Claude says there are no footprints beyond this point, only marks of a kind he has not seen before. We go back to search the area around the *Cerberus*."

Something didn't sound right to Alan. What was Duchamps hiding? He ran up behind Duchamps, grabbed his shoulder, and spun him around to face him. "What did Claude find?"

Duchamps shrugged off Alan's hand. "Blood."

"Human blood?"

"I don't know. It looked as if a struggle took place. The ground is disturbed." He continued walking, leaving Alan standing there with many questions and few answers. He didn't know whether to be relieved or more concerned for Vince's safety.

At the *Cerberus*, Duchamps and Claude performed a more careful search of the area, while Alan turned to Vince's laptop for answers. Trace paced nearby, clearly disturbed by Vince's disappearance. After ten nervous minutes, he walked over to Alan.

"Do you think Scarface is lying?" he asked.

Alan tried to suppress a grin at Trace's apt nickname for Duchamps. "I'll give him the benefit of the doubt for now."

"You're too trusting," Trace replied and stalked off.

Alan wondered if Trace was right. Should he be more forthright with the security chief? He didn't want to risk alienating Duchamps based solely on a gut feeling. Thirty minutes later, Duchamps returned. Alan had found nothing on Vince's computer in his brief scan to indicate what had happened to him. He hoped Duchamps could provide some answers.

"We found more blood on the rocks nearby," Duchamps informed him. "Masowe had a revolver. We have not located it or a body. I will not wander around down here aimlessly while someone has a weapon." Before Alan could protest the veiled accusation against Vince, Duchamps raised his hand to stop him. "Masowe was a big man. I do not believe your man could have taken his weapon from him, nor do I think Masowe would kill for no reason."

He paused, staring around the lava tube. "Someone else might have entered the lava tube, seen the diamonds, and killed them both.

He might still be here. I will leave two men to guard your machine and to report to me if either missing man shows up. We will return later with enough men to search the area more thoroughly."

He picked up the knife with his handkerchief and dropped it into a Ziploc bag. "We will see whose blood is on this."

Alan waited for more. When he saw that Duchamps was through speaking, he said, "You're not telling me everything, Duchamps. Your tracker looked frightened. Why?"

Duchamps stared at him for a moment, as if choosing his words carefully before replying. "He says he found tracks of a creature he has never seen before, a devil, an *Intulo*." He rushed on to add, "These Zulu are a superstitious lot and can't be believed, but something strange happened down here." He stopped talking and scrubbed his foot on the ground.

"What else?" Alan asked, seeing his hesitation.

"Can't you smell it?"

Alan sniffed the air. "Smell what? I don't smell anything."

"Death," Duchamps replied. "The air smells of death."

He spoke quietly with the two guards he was leaving behind and began to walk back down the tunnel Cerberus had carved. Alan looked at Trace, shook his head, and followed close behind. Along the way, he had the feeling something or someone was watching them. He kept glancing over his shoulder as they made their way back to the surface, but saw no one.

7

July 5, 2016, 4:00 a.m.   Protea Hotel, Klerksdorp, South Africa –
Alan spoke with his father over the phone while Duchamps
gathered more men for the search. His father was heartbroken at
Vince's disappearance.

"Do all you can to find him, Alan. Perhaps the poor boy fell down
a fissure and needs medical assistance. He's one of ours, and we need
to do everything in our power to find him."

Alan agreed with his father, but deep down in his heart he felt
Vince was probably dead, maybe at the hands of the security guard,
Masowe, in spite of Duchamps' denial.

Vince had been missing for over six hours; still, there was no
reason to upset his father, at least not yet. "I promise you, if Vince is
there, we'll find him."

"Do you need more men or resources?"

"No, Duchamps is calling in his off-duty officers. He has enough
security personnel available. I'll call when we have something more
tangible. Try not to worry," he added, knowing it was useless advice.
He knew his father too well. He treated everyone at Hoffman
Industries like members of the family. That was why the company
had managed to stay on top for so many years.

* * * *

When Alan returned to the control room two hours later, both
Trace and Bill sat around the monitors in stony silence. Their dour
expressions revealed their belief that Vince was dead. Alan refused to
give in to the morose cloud that had descended over them.

"Trace, I want you and Bill to stay here and watch over things.
When we get to the *Cerberus*, I'll attach a remote hook-up to the
USB port so you can follow us with this." He pointed to a small

camera mounted on a gyrostabilizer attached to the side of the hardhat Duchamps had insisted he wear. Surprisingly, Duchamps had given him the camera as a sort of conciliatory gesture.

"It has infrared and telephoto capabilities, so you can use it to pinpoint things for us in the dark. Duchamps claims it has a range of about five kilometers down in the mine. I have my doubts about that, but we shouldn't go that far." He looked at his two friends, obviously numb at the disappearance of Vince. "I'll find him, I promise."

Trace gave him a thumbs-up signal. Bill attempted a smile, but it fell flat.

He looked out the window and saw Duchamps leading a large group of people to the Shack. "Okay, I think the rest are ready to go. See you later."

Outside the trailer, he was surprised to see seven heavily armed security guards. All wore revolvers on their hips and three of them carried automatic rifles. He recognized it as the 5.56 caliber Denel R4, the mainstay of the South African Defense Force. Only the SADF had the authority to carry such weapons, but he imagined Verkhoen had enough political pull to bypass the regulations. It seemed like overkill on Duchamps' part, but Alan didn't argue the point.

Accompanying Duchamps was a woman about twenty-nine-years old.

"Hoffman, this is Evelyn Means, one of our field biologists. She is coming with us."

It was difficult to tell under the concealing hardhat, but Alan thought she had long, auburn hair, now pushed up beneath the helmet. She was about Duchamps' height, so she had to look up at Alan's 6'2" frame.

"Hello, Mr. Hoffman. I am so pleased to be joining you."

British, he thought. He recognized her clipped accent as from southwest England. One of the women he had dallied with for a short time had come from Somerset. Alan looked into her hazel eyes, which sparkled like a schoolgirl's on prom night. He imagined she would look every bit the prom queen in the right dress. Her green jumpsuit was baggy on her, but he saw the faint outline of a shapely hip and two firm breasts. While pleased by her presence, her function on the team puzzled him.

"Call me Alan, Miss Means," he said politely.

"Doctor Means, please." He flinched at her rebuke, but just as he was about to arrive at the opinion that she was another stuffy professional, she smiled, held out her hand, and said, "You may call me Eve. I like that better."

Her hand was delicate – slim, soft, and neatly manicured – the exact opposite of his rough, calloused mitts. The strength of her grip took him by surprise.

He turned to Duchamps. "To what do we owe the pleasure of Doctor Means' company?"

Duchamps held out the knife they had found, Masowe's knife. "The blood on the knife did not belong to your engineer."

A surge of relief coursed through him; then, the implications of Duchamps's words hit home. "What are you getting at? Are you saying Vince killed your guard?" His voice rose at Duchamps' accusation. He knew Vince better than that.

Eve broke into their conversation. "Alan, the blood on the knife wasn't human."

It took a few seconds for the implications to sink in. He stared at her to ascertain if she was joking, but her mien was one of deadly seriousness. He shook his head several times in confusion. "Not human? What do you mean?"

"The blood on the knife seems to be from a member of the arthropod family, but unlike any I've ever seen. I couldn't match it at all. I found similar blood on the electrician's drill bit. I sent samples to various laboratories for analysis. Captain Duchamps asked me to come along as an observer. I must say I am intrigued."

From the sour look on Duchamps's face, Alan imagined the order came from higher up the command chain, perhaps from Verkhoen himself. It was obvious he considered the woman an encumbrance to his mission.

Alan shook his head. "You're telling me that Masowe or Vince cut a bug with the knife and some electrician drilled into one. What's that have to do with Vince's disappearance?" He waved his hands in the air and shouted, "People are missing, and you want to go on a bug hunt. Lady, we don't have time."

"I don't know if it has anything to do with the disappearances," Eve replied in a soft voice, disarming his hostility. "The fact that one man has died and three have vanished may have nothing to do with this mystery, but it certainly calls for an investigation."

What she said finally broke through his wall of righteous rage. "Did you say one dead and *three* missing?"

Caught up in her excitement, she ignored his question. "Look, Mr. Hoffman, if there are arthropods down that deep, what else might there be? Cave spiders and scorpions inhabit the deepest cavern systems we have explored, often completely blind or even lacking eyes, adapted to their world of total darkness. If this lava tube or cavern system, whatever it is, has no opening to the surface, we could be looking at an entire ecoculture reaching as far back as the late Paleozoic Era."

Alan turned to Duchamps. "What does she mean by one dead and three missing?"

"An electrician assistant is dead," he said. "We found his body mangled by a ventilator fan at the bottom of an airshaft. He could have fallen, but ..."

"But what?"

"The electrician is missing. We found her bloodstained tool bag near the airshaft opening. The blood is hers."

"You think her disappearance and that of Vince and your guard is related."

Duchamps shrugged. "It is possible they were killed by the same person, but it does not explain the strange tracks."

Duchamps seemed to dismiss the missing electrician as a possible suspect. If he had a reason, he wasn't revealing it. Alan turned to Eve. "Would any of these insects be large enough to take down two men, one armed with a pistol?" Before she could reply, he raised his hands in mock defeat. "Okay, Doctor Means, Eve, I see your point, but remember, this is a search and rescue mission, not a bug hunt."

"I say what the mission is, Mr. Hoffman," Duchamps chimed in. "However, at this point I agree with you. One of my men is missing, too, remember."

Alan nodded. "Then we both have a reason to be anxious. Let's go."

* * * *

They made the long trip down into the mine in silence, each lost in his or her private musings. Alan knew he should apologize to Eve for the bad start he had made, but didn't quite know how to begin. He had never been very good with women, as his ex-wife would quickly attest. First, he had seen her only as a good-looking woman instead of the professional she was. Second, he had questioned her motives for coming along. Worst of all, he had questioned her expertise in her field while having nothing with which to refute her. She probably thought him another crude, rude American.

He was relieved when she made the first move. "Mr. Hoffman, Alan, I am sorry I did not make a good first impression. While it's true I came because of the intriguing blood on the knife, I do feel sorry for your friend's disappearance. I am here to help search for him. In my field, I've been in many caves and mines, and I am knowledgeable about what we might possibly find. I have made an extensive study of the local *Microchiroptera* that inhabit the upper levels of the mine, especially the sheath-tailed, tombs, and leaf-nose species. In addition, I've identified fifteen species of *Orthoptera*, two of which are indigenous to this mine. "

"Bats and crickets," Alan said, recognizing the sub-order for bats and the order for crickets. "I don't think either one is responsible for the disappearance of three people. Nor do I believe insects are the culprit, but I'm afraid my quick temper got the best of me. Vince is my friend, and I'm concerned about him. I spoke hastily, and I regret my harsh words. Why don't we start over?"

Eve smiled. "I agree."

"We're here," Duchamps announced, as the #3 elevator jolted to a sudden stop.

Duchamps' men walked two abreast. *Like soldiers*, Alan thought. He lagged behind with Eve, hoping for an opportunity to speak with her, but the tunnels near the elevators were noisy with ventilator fans, electric locos moving ore and men, rattling water pipes, and bleeder pipes controlling airflow from the tunnels. At first, the shafts were wide and well-lit, like underground thoroughfares, with offices, locker rooms, and mechanical rooms. The further they ventured into the network of shafts and tunnels, the passageways became dark, narrow, and twisting warrens. Side tunnels branched out at irregular intervals, each filled with the sound of drilling.

Eve seemed quite at home in the maze of winding tunnels and managed better than he did. His height made banging his head almost a certainty. He was thankful for the hard hat. To his inexperienced eye, it seemed they were taking a different route than earlier. Some sections seemed unfamiliar and weren't wide enough for the *Cerberus*.

"This isn't the way we came before," he said.

"This is a shortcut," she answered.

"You've been down here before?" he asked.

She looked startled by his question. She nodded and walked away, pretending to examine the wall.

What had he said? Duchamps, overhearing the exchange, dropped back to walk beside him.

"Doctor Means lost her husband down here four years ago in a tunnel collapse. He was a mining engineer. The company tried to rescue them, but it became impossible because of the loose rock. The company sealed the shaft. None of the bodies were recovered. She was down here the entire time the rescue effort was underway, even sleeping here. She refused to leave. She explored the tunnels for another way in. It hit her very hard, I think."

"Then I've put my foot in my mouth," Alan said.

"Perhaps, but she must learn to get on with her life. She is much too beautiful to grieve forever, is she not?"

"It's difficult to tell in that baggy jumpsuit, but yes, she is a very attractive woman."

Duchamps winked and walked on ahead of the group. When they reached the open pit, Alan saw that a work crew had installed a metal ladder with a safety cage. It made the descent a little safer but just as daunting.

"Kibble or ladder?" Duchamps asked.

"Kibble," Alan replied looking down into the hole. "It's quicker."

As soon as the kibble deposited them on the floor of the pit, Eve began to carefully examining the walls of the tunnel the *Cerberus* had dug, even taking out a geologist's hammer to chip at it.

"Your machine did this?" she asked in awe.

"The *Cerberus AT10*," he said with pride. "It will revolutionize mining. I'm sorry we didn't have it four years ago."

She blushed. "I see Henri told you about Frederick. Yes, your machine would have made a difference." She peered at him and added, "It will make you a lot of money, I suppose."

"It will save a lot of lives, I hope," he countered, slightly offended by her characterization of him as just another callous, money-grubbing American. "That's why I designed it."

She glanced away as if suddenly realizing what she had implied. "Then it will be worth it."

The two other guards met them at the *Cerberus*. There was a lot of grumbling and a loud exchange as Duchamps talked to them. Alan made himself useful setting up the remote feed from his helmet camera to the *Cerberus*. He turned his head, stopping to watch Eve bend over to retrieve something from her pack.

"Receiving great," Trace said. "Looks like we're missing out on something up here."

Alan realized he was staring at Eve's ass and panned the camera around the tube. "Switch to Infrared."

"Switching to IR. My God!"

The excitement in Trace's voice startled him. "What is it?"

"The entire pipe is glowing with some kind of low-level light. It's in the walls. It's beautiful." Trace sounded awed by the spectacle.

"Cave bioluminescence," Eve explained.

Had she overheard the entire conversation?

"What?" he replied, trying to hide his ignorance.

"Bacteria, some lichens, even some insects produce a cold light by utilizing a chemical called *luceferin*. They use it to attract mates or prey."

"Some come on. Doesn't work as well as a dinner with wine, though?" Alan replied and was pleased to see her smile at his lame attempt at humor.

Duchamps walked over. "Can your machine be positioned to point its cameras upslope?"

"Certainly. Why?" Alan asked.

"We will go downslope to examine the disturbed area Claude found, but I don't want anything to come up behind us."

Eve stopped examining the *Cerberus* and asked, "What are you afraid of?"

"The two men I left here say they've been hearing strange noises, whistles and clicks, things like that. One even claims he heard a voice."

"Someone is still alive," Alan exclaimed. He felt a renewed hope it was Vince.

"Perhaps, but my tracker says he smells many different odors, an evil smell, he calls it. I'm leaving the two men here, but I'm afraid they'll bolt at the first sign of trouble. The camera would keep our backs safe."

The security chief's voice had remained flat, but Alan detected a hint of fear in it. If Duchamps was concerned, he wanted to know of what. "That sounds a little paranoid, Duchamps. What kind of trouble are you expecting?"

Alan studied Duchamps carefully. The security chief added nothing more, but his apparent unease convinced Alan to comply with Duchamps' request.

"I'll have Trace move the *Cerberus*. You copy, Trace?" he said into his mic.

"Copy, Alan. Moving it now."

The *Cerberus* used a jet turbine to provide power while in operation but could travel a short distance on battery power alone. Alan smiled, as both Eve and Duchamps jumped, startled by the silence of *Cerberus* as it lumbered to the end of the tunnel. Trace swiveled the lights and the camera, pointing them both upslope.

"In position," Trace called out.

"Happy?" Alan asked Duchamps.

"Very. Let's get going." He looked around his small group and frowned. "Where is Doctor Means?"

Alan had been watching the *Cerberus* and had lost sight of her. "Eve!" he called out.

Faintly, they heard, "Over here."

They found her about twenty meters away by a large pile of rocks, vigorously shaking a test tube. Alan's gaze fell to her breasts bouncing beneath her jumper as she moved. He turned away before she caught him staring.

Duchamps chided her. "Doctor Means, you must stay with the group at all times. Do not go wandering off."

"Sorry," she replied, still engrossed in her test tube.

Her keen interest in her test tube aroused Duchamps' curiosity. "What are you doing?"

"I found blood here and here." She pointed to two small splotches of blood on a rock. Duchamps walked over to examine them.

"This one is human blood. See how it forms strings of proteins in the solution." She picked up a second test tube. "This one is the same blood as on the knife, at least the same species."

"The knife was found beside the *Cerberus*," Alan countered.

"All I know is that I have found human blood, either your friend's or the guard's, and I have found more of the same type of blood this is on the knife."

Duchamps called for Claude, the tracker, and asked him examine the area carefully. After a few minutes, Claude pointed to a chip in the rock. "Gunfire," he said.

What could be down here dangerous enough that two men with a large knife and a pistol couldn't defend against? Where were the bodies? The bloodstains didn't bode well for Vince's safety. Alan was getting a bad feeling about the whole situation.

INTULO

8

July 5, 2016, 8:00 a.m.   *Ngomo* Mine, 138 Level –

Pieter Bekker detested his boss, Henri Duchamps. To him, the arrogant chief of security was a half-breed Afrikaner, more French than Boer, while his family had been among the first *voortrekkers* to enter the Transvaal in the 1830s. He resented the offhand manner in which Duchamps had ordered him to remain near the American mining machine with John Khosa, his companion, and for rebuking him in front of the blond American surfer boy. Most of all, he didn't like the smell of the strange cavern the machine had discovered.

"What do you think happened to Masowe?" he asked Khosa, who stood staring upslope into the darkness of the lava tube.

"I do not know, but I fear he is dead."

"You think the American killed him?" Personally, he doubted anyone could kill Masowe. The big Zulu was one of the toughest bastards he had ever met.

Khosa shook his head. "No. Something else killed them both, as well as the electrician. Can you not feel it?"

"Feel what?" He looked in the direction Khosa stared. "I don't feel anything but the bloody heat and the imprint of Duchamps' boot on my ass."

Khosa arched an eyebrow. "You make your loathing of him known. That is why he does not like you." He smiled. "That is why he put you with me. Your loathing of me is well known."

"Nothing personal, Khosa. I just don't swallow that lost tribe of Israel bullshit. You Lemba may eat Kosher and have the tips of your penises snipped, but that doesn't make you Jews."

Khosa glared at Bekker. "I am Mwenye. Lemba is the Afrikaans name for my people."

"Whatever," Bekker said. He got tired of hearing how white men had taken away the blacks' history, changing names and territorial boundaries. As far as he was concerned, Africa would still be a bunch of ignorant savages fighting each other over land they couldn't farm if not for the whites. To some, that made him a *gomgat*, a redneck, but he saw it as the truth.

"My people brought the Ark of Covenant, the *ngoma lungunda*, with us on our holy journey from Jerusalem to Africa. We worship, *Nwali*, your Christian God."

"I don't worship no God," Bekker snapped at Khosa. The volume of the echo of his voice startled him. Quieter, he added, "If there is a God, he's not down here."

"You are Boer. Your people worshipped God, even though they went to war with the British to keep slaves."

"We fought the British for the right to be left alone," Bekker countered. "We left Cape Colony to settle new, open lands in the Transvaal. We tamed this country."

"You stole it from the Zulu and the Bantu."

"Savages," Bekker growled. "They ran around half naked and fought each other over cattle."

He stalked away from Khosa past the boring machine, careful not to stray beyond the range of its lights. Khosa's remarks had only intensified his unease. He patted the R4 rifle cradled in his arms. He was an excellent shot and didn't fear anything he could see, but like Khosa, he felt that something in the darkness watching them, something inimical and hungry.

"How long have they been gone?"

Khosa checked his watch. "Thirty minutes. Do you miss Duchamps?"

Bekker exploded. He marched up to Khosa and shoved his face up to his. "To hell with Duchamps and to hell with you!"

Khosa sneered. "Do not try to intimidate me, Bekker. I can smell your fear. If you do not wish to be here, you may go join the others."

He pointed downslope into the darkness. Bekker's gaze followed Khosa's pointing finger. He flinched at the thought of walking into the darkness alone. He licked his lips.

"No, I'll remain here. We must guard the machine."

Another half hour passed; then Khosa looked downslope and

asked, "Did you hear that?"

Bekker was still irritated at Khosa for calling him out as a coward. He heard nothing and suspected Khosa was trying to goad him into another argument. "Hear what?" he snapped.

"It sounded like gunfire."

Bekker listened more closely. After a minute, he heard a muffled sound that could have been gunfire. It could just as easily have been falling rock. Pieces of the roof had been dropping since they had arrived. He considered himself lucky one hadn't landed on his head and crushed his skull, hardhat notwithstanding.

"It's nothing," he replied.

"It was gunfire," Khosa insisted. "I am certain."

"Then let's go check it out, anything to shut you up."

"No, we have our own problem," Khosa answered.

"What do you mean?"

"Can you not feel it?" He touched the Star of David suspended from a chain around his neck. "It is something evil whispering from the darkness." He turned to stare at Bekker.

Bekker noticed the look of terror in Khosa's eyes and felt some of the man's panic. He raised his rifle and stared into the shadows, waiting for whatever was out there. There was no sound, no breeze, but the air around them grew colder. He stiffened when something brushed the edges of his mind. It felt like a soft whisper, but he knew it came from nothing human. He sensed hunger and longing. He sensed evil, the complete absence of kinship with any living creature. It was a strange feeling. Even the most dangerous predator interacted with its own kind, felt some affinity with them. This ... thing radiated a deep loathing and contempt of everything lesser than itself.

He glanced at Khosa, who had his eyes closed, mumbling the words of the *hashkiveinu*, the Hebrew prayer of protection from dark things, while clasping his Star of David to his chest.

"Open your eyes," Bekker snapped at him. "Pull out your pistol."

Khosa stared at Bekker, his eyes displaying his resignation. "It will do no good."

"Damn you, *kaffir*," Bekker shot at him.

Khosa ignored the racial slur. His eyes remained fixed on the shadows. Bekker expected some animal to charge out of the darkness. The rest of it, the strange feeling, was just Khosa messing with his head. He prepared himself, rifle to his shoulder set on full auto. Instead of an animal, the shadows of the tunnel grew darker, thicker, becoming a living, inky, undulating blackness that surged down the lava tube, flowing toward him like liquid tar. Just as the writhing shadow reached his feet, it broke apart, becoming dozens of giant black insects.

"*Shongololo*," Khosa said.

The creatures looked ancient, like distant primitive cousins of millipedes with which he was familiar, except these were twice as long as he was, and he could feel their ravenous hunger.

The shadowy creatures billowed upward, enveloping both him and Khosa. Bekker did not have time to scream as the creatures ripped into his flesh.

9

July 5, 2016, 7:00 a.m.   *Ngomo* Mine, 138 Level –

Duchamps waved his hand in the air, and his men formed a line across the width of the tube. They moved out with the tracker Claude in the lead. Alan and Eve marched at the rear. Occasionally, she took photos with her cell phone. She surprised him by snapping a photo of him.

"What was that for?" he asked.

"For me," she replied, smiling.

A few minutes later, Claude called them to a halt. He bent over and picked up a broken beaded necklace.

"What is that?" Alan asked.

"It is an *ibheqe,* a lover's charm. It must be Masowe's. He would never leave it."

Eve moved closer to Alan and whispered, "I'm frightened."

As much as he wanted to reassure her, he couldn't. His state of uneasiness increased, just as when he knew a support beam was going to give way in an old mine, a kind of sixth sense he had developed over the years that had saved his life more than once. Goosebumps sprouted on his arms. "So am I," he confessed to her.

They passed the diamonds with only a brief glance by Duchamps; however, Eve became excited, oohing and aahing as she spotted each large deposit. She snapped several photos before Duchamps warned her to stop. Alan supposed it was in a woman's nature to appreciate a jewel's beauty more than its worth. Duchamps merely saw dollar signs, something someone might steal, and he was doing his job to protect it. Alan's mind was busy trying to devise a way to tunnel through such pockets without damaging them. Perhaps a sensor that lowered the laser temperature at the first sign of diamonds would work, and then extract them by hand.

His mental calculations so intrigued him, that he failed to hear Duchamps' call to halt. He bumped into Eve.

"Sorry," he said. He looked around. "What's up?"

"The tracker found something up ahead," she replied.

He remembered the camera on his hardhat. "Trace, can you pan ahead and see what they found?"

"Affirmative."

He heard the whine of the camera as it moved on his hardhat. After a few seconds, Trace said, "It looks like a side tunnel of some kind. I can't tell from here if it's another lava tube, merely a pocket, or a deep fault." Trace paused. "Wait a minute. Infrared indicates it's cooler than the tube, but there's a lot of that bioluminescent stuff."

"We'll check it out," he told Trace. He walked over to Duchamps. "Trace says it's cooler in the cleft. Can we rest out of this heat?" The lava tube was cooler than the mine, but the high humidity drained him. His energy level was bottoming out. The others appeared to be handling the humidity with no problem, but he was a Nevada boy used to a drier climate. He needed a break.

Duchamps nodded. "Claude says the opening is clear."

The group entered the vertical crevasse and dropped their heavy packs, relishing the cooler air. Alan noticed it was fifteen degrees cooler than in the lava tube, about 80 degrees Fahrenheit.

"Everyone please extinguish your flashlights," Eve asked.

Duchamps looked at her for a moment before nodding to the others to comply. As soon as the lights went out, the entire grotto lit up like the inside of a Christmas tree. The grotto was a narrow chasm in the side of the lava tube, as high as it was deep. It had formed from a fractured fault line sometime after the lava tube became inactive. White, blue, and yellow lines radiated throughout the walls and roof of the crevice, often merging to form large splotches of color. As his eyes adjusted to the lower light level, Alan found he could see everything and everyone perfectly well. He could even read the names on the uniforms by the glowing cave light.

"We could save our batteries if we use only the cave light when we can," he suggested to Duchamps. "That would allow us to search longer."

Amazingly, Duchamps agreed with him. "It is a good idea, but keep your flashlight nearby at all times," he cautioned.

The light spectacle around them delighted Eve. She moved around the crevice, using her cell phone as a video camera, oblivious of the leering stares of some of the guards as they drank water from canteens they passed among themselves. Alan couldn't understand their jokes, but he was sure they were much like the jokes of men in any country and at Eve's expense. He chewed on a protein bar to raise his sugar level, but he couldn't get the image of Vince lying dead somewhere out of his mind. He had promised his father to find him.

"Alan?"

Alan keyed his mic to answer Bill. "What is it, Bill?"

"I've been replaying the *Cerberus* video. Most of it is dark after Vince shut down the lights, except for the glow of a lantern. They turn it off after a while."

"So?"

"Just a few seconds before Vince turns the *Cerberus'* lights back on, there's a quick, bright flash. It overpowers the camera's sensors, but I ran a spectrum analysis on it. I could be wrong. I mean, it's a video not a direct observation, but ..."

Alan rolled his eyes and sighed, wondering where Bill was going with his report. His need to be precise was great for engineering but could be a pain in the ass in a discussion.

"Get on with it, Bill," he urged.

"It looks like a methane explosion." The words burst from him so quickly Alan thought he had misheard. The sniffer indicated no high concentrations of methane.

"A methane explosion?"

"I'm ninety percent sure."

In Bill's mind, ninety percent was a certainty. Alan considered the possibilities. There was very little methane present now, but the air from the mines and the air in the lava tube had mixed for several hours. With the slightly higher oxygen content, even low levels of methane could have combusted. There was only on problem with that scenario.

"But we found no bodies. The heat from a methane explosion wouldn't be enough to totally cremate a human body."

Bill was apologetic. "I know. I just thought you might want a heads up."

"Thanks, Bill. The air checks out fine now, but I'll continue testing it just in case."

Sooner than Alan hoped, Duchamps ended the break by standing and picking up his pack.

"Leave nothing behind," Eve told everyone. "We don't want to contaminate the grotto any more than we have too."

This produced several chuckles from the men who had already left their own little spots of liquid contamination in the form of urine on the rocks.

Duchamps switched on his flashlight, erasing the iridescent graffiti of the lichen. He glanced at Eve, as she continued to photograph the crevice. "Doctor Means, we don't have all—"

Gunshots from down the tube erased his last words. Alan glanced around and quickly counted heads. Who was missing? *Claude, the tracker*. He must have gone ahead. More resembling a posse after an outlaw than a search and rescue team, the entire group grabbed their weapons and poured from the grotto. A high-pitched wail from the same direction as the gunshot elicited such visions of terror and pain it sent spasms surging through Alan's bowels. He managed to quell the disquieting rumblings before soiling his pants, but just barely.

They found Claude's weapon beside a pool of blood twenty meters downslope. Of the tracker, only a piece of cloth ripped from his shirt remained. The only sign of his attacker was a series of small droplets of blood leading from the pool of blood and across the rocks, but they disappeared as mysteriously as the tracker.

Eve began sobbing. One of the guards dropped to his knees and covered his face with his hands, mumbling something about *Intulo*. The other guards looked around nervously, searching for a target on which they could vent their fear and anger. Duchamps stood staring into the dark depths of the lava tube. After a few moments had passed, he pulled his pistol from his holster and told the guard, "Get up off your knees. We have company."

Alan couldn't see anything, but he trusted the security chief's judgment. "Trace, pan the tube again on Infrared," he said.

Again, he heard the camera whine.

"I see movement some sixty or sixty-five meters away," Trace reported. "Whatever they are, they're cooler than human bodies, barely warmer than the ambient temperature. They're merging and breaking apart, so it's difficult to get an accurate count, but they look to be two feet tall and about twice as long."

Alan relayed the information to Duchamps as Trace continued commenting in his ear. "They're headed your way," Trace yelled. "Watch out, they're moving fast."

The guards readied their weapons. Duchamps motioned his men to scatter among the rocks and hold their fire. "When they get close, switch on your flashlights. Maybe it will blind them."

"I doubt it," Eve warned. Rather than showing fear, she appeared anxious to see what life forms the tube had to offer. "Living in this weak light, it is likely they rely on a heightened sense of smell for hunting."

Duchamps paid her little heed, barking orders to his men.

"Here they come," Trace warned over Alan's earpiece.

"Now!" Duchamps shouted.

The lava tube lit up as all the flashlights came on at once. The shadows of the rocks made it difficult, but Alan could just make out the creatures coming at them. They appeared almost as dark as the shadows. Shots rang out all around him. The sharp report of pistols and the earsplitting blasts of single shots and short bursts from the R4 rifles filled the air with thunder and shrill screams. Duchamps jumped down from a pile of rocks and landed beside Alan, frightening him half to death.

"Here." He handed Alan his pistol; then leaped back over the rocks, firing his rifle as he went.

Alan stood and took careful aim at the nearest creature scrambling over the rocks, a nightmare with a segmented carapace and eight, multi-jointed legs. It was as large as a kitchen sink, a bastard cross between a giant black scorpion on steroids and a scarab beetle. Its nimble, long legs helped it leap over boulders, and the sharp claws on the forward pair of appendages made formidable weapons. A long tail tipped by a sharp barb dripping venom whipped the air around it. If that wasn't enough, the monster's wicked-looking mandible snapped open and shut with a loud click.

Alan emptied his pistol into the first creature. Just as he began to fear the bullets were having no effect, it fell dead at his feet, twitching and flopping on the ground with a thick liquid oozing from the bullet holes in its carapace. He stepped back to avoid its still-snapping mandibles and tripped over Eve, kneeling on the ground behind him calmly shooting more video. He collapsed on top of her as a second creature appeared above them on a boulder. He knew he could never reload his revolver in time. He pushed Eve farther beneath him to protect her.

The creature's head exploded into mush, as Duchamps fired at it pointblank with his rifle. He reached down, pulled Alan to his feet, and handed him a handful of cartridges.

"Reload," he said; then disappeared into the melee.

His trembling hands hampered him, but Alan managed to reload the gun. He searched for a target but noticed it had gone quiet. He searched for Duchamps and saw him standing with his back to the wall of the lava tube. Satisfied the fighting was over; Duchamps calmly replaced his pistol in its holster and began to check on his men.

"Call out," he yelled; then listened as they began to call out their names. Three men answered out of the six remaining.

Alan helped Eve to her feet.

"Thank you for protecting me," she said, "but you knocked my cell phone out of my hand. I missed most of the action."

"I'll write a paper for you describing every little detail, including the three dead men," he replied. His answer was brusque. He admired her coolness in the face of danger, but her one-track mind annoyed him.

She frowned at him, and then began to examine the fallen creature. He went to join Duchamps. He passed the mutilated remains of the three guards, now barely recognizable as human. The claws, stingers, and mandibles of the creatures were as deadly as swords and as sharp enough to slice through bone. A dozen of the creatures lay scattered around the area. Only the continuous fire of the rifles and pistols had prevented a slaughter.

"Well, we know now what happened to the others," Duchamps said. "They were killed and their bodies dragged off." He showed no remorse at the loss of his men. "We have to get out of here now, before they regroup. Doctor Means was correct. When we hit the lights, their eyes went golden, but they didn't even slow down. What the hell were those things?"

"They seem to be some type of *mandibulate*," Eve answered,

having completed her cursory examination of one of the dead creatures. Its yellow blood stained her hands. She wiped them on her jumpsuit.

"A what?" Duchamps asked.

"A *mandibulate* is an insect with mandibles, or moving mouth parts, thought extinct since the end of the Carboniferous Period over 300 million years ago. They were the ancestor to modern insects. It has a venomous sting like a scorpion, but the tail, the *telsun,* seems too short for a primary defense weapon, more an extension of the metasomal segment. However, the sting itself, the *aculeus,* is quite long and barbed."

"Those claws are pretty lethal," Alan noted, "as well as the mandibles."

"Yes, the *pedipalps* are quite enormous. They might also serve in a courtship ritual. The mandible, or more specifically the *chelicerae* as this creature is an arthropod, acts as a tool for grasping its prey as it devours it. Science had thought them solitary hunters, but these mandibulates hunt in swarms and are evidently quite adaptive. They show a remarkable degree of communicative ability."

"A smart, deadly bug?" Alan asked.

"Not smart, but organized. Perhaps some creatures sought shelter in deep caverns during the late Carboniferous Period and adapted to the environment. The gold lids are light filters. They can see in complete darkness or in full daylight, which is remarkable for creatures living in absolute darkness. Their sense of smell is extraordinary. These creatures' sinus cavities are twice that of known fossil remains. This is an entirely new species, a great find. We must bring one back for study."

"Before you fall in love with the *muggies*, Doctor Means," Duchamps called out, "we're getting the hell out of here before more of them come at us, and we don't have time to carry back souvenirs. We bring back our dead. I don't intend to leave my men behind as snacks for these bastards."

Alan's respect for Duchamps went up a notch. He seemed cold, but he cared for his men as much as Alan cared for his.

"I'll help carry a man," he volunteered.

"Thank you, Mister Hoffman," Duchamps replied, "but my men can handle it. You and I can best serve by keeping our weapons ready."

Duchamps handed him one of the R4 rifles and accepted back his pistol. The rifle was sticky from the previous owner's blood. Disgusted, Alan wiped the blood off on his pants leg.

Moving as fast as they could with each of the three remaining guards carrying the additional burden of a dead comrade across his shoulders, they rushed back to the *Cerberus* tunnel. The guards kept furtively glancing behind them. Feeding off their fear, Alan increased his pace.

When they arrived back at the *Cerberus*, Alan thought their troubles were over. To his dismay, Bill informed him that the two men that Duchamps had left to guard the tunnel were gone.

"Gone?" Alan asked. "You mean they ran away."

"No, something attacked them, something different from the bugs that attacked you. It was ... like a host of shadows, undefined, almost a liquid the way it moved, but ..." Bill hesitated.

"But what?" Alan urged.

"I don't know. There was something in the shadows, something deadly."

Alan swore. Bill was an engineer, detail oriented and not prone to exaggeration; and yet, he sounded mystified by what he had witnessed. "Christ! What have we stumbled into down here?" He turned to Duchamps. "Your two guards are gone."

Duchamps misunderstood and exploded. "Bloody bastard slacker!" he yelled. "Damn Bekker. I told him to keep watch. I will kill his sorry ass."

"You're too late," Alan said. "He's already dead. There are other creatures out there now, bigger than the insects that attacked us."

Duchamps' jaw dropped. His Adam's apple bobbed several times before responding, "Bloody hell. We're almost out of ammunition. If we try to run, those bugs could easily catch up with us in the mineshafts. Now you tell me there is a ... whatever took Bekker and Khosa running around. We can't allow them out of this lava tube. There are eight-hundred kilometers of tunnels in the mine. We would never get them all."

"We could block the tunnel with the *Cerberus*, I suppose," Alan suggested, "once we're gone. For now, we can certainly make use of the camera and lights. I'll have Trace turn the *Cerberus* downslope toward the scorpion creatures following us."

Eve paid no attention to their discussion. She knelt on the ground examining two small patches of whitish powder standing out in stark contrast against the darker rock. She picked up a piece of metal and held it out to Alan. He puzzled why her face had gone pale. He glanced at the metal, and then took it from her trembling hand to examine it more closely. He recognized it as the remains of a brass belt buckle.

"Can ... can this be your friend?" she asked, pointing to the powder. Her voice quavered in fear and with the realization that she was looking at the remains of a human being reduced to ash.

Alan's gut clenched with dread. He turned the buckle over in his hand and shook his head. Relief swept over him. "No. This is like the one the other guards are wearing."

"Now we know what happened to the two guards. A methane explosion?" she asked, her tone expressing her doubt.

"A methane explosion isn't hot enough to reduce bones to powder, much less melt brass. That takes a temperature of at least 900 degrees Celsius, over 1600 degrees Fahrenheit." He held the buckle to his nose and sniffed it. "This isn't melted. It's partially digested, as if it's been soaked in acid."

She nodded at the ashen remains of the two guards. "And this is not ash. It is pulverized bone." She shivered. "What kind of creature could do that?"

Before he could venture a guess, one of the guards yelled, "They're coming."

Too soon, Alan thought. *Too damned soon.*

"What do we do?" Duchamps asked.

That Duchamps had turned to him for advice spoke of the urgency of the situation. "Dig in. Have your men pile rocks together – over there." He pointed to an area near the wall beside a pile of fallen rocks. "I have a plan."

Duchamps stared at him, his face stern. "I certainly hope you know what you're doing."

Alan focused on the *Cerberus*. "Trace, move the *Cerberus* forty degrees downslope. Be quick about it."

The big machine groaned, as its treads spun it into position. Alan silently urged it to move faster. The guards, catching his panic, hurriedly piled boulders to form a low barricade against the lava tube wall a few meters distant from the pile of rocks, forming a low, three-side enclosure. Alan grabbed one of the guards to help him remove a section of the metal skirting protecting the *Cerberus'* tracks. The crimped upper edge of each three-meter-long pieces of metal slipped over a metal bar for easy assembly. *Thank you, Bill, for suggesting the timesaving design.* Carefully avoiding the moving treads, they unhooked the skirt and began dragging it toward the low wall. A second guard saw them struggling with the heavy metal skirt and rushed to help. He directed the guards to push one edge of the metal sheet up against the tube wall and lay it across the space between the pile of rocks and the wall they were building, creating a shallow bunker.

When they were finished, he yelled, "Everyone, crawl inside." Into his headset, he said, "Trace, fire up the turbine and the laser array."

They hesitated. He didn't have time to explain what he had in mind. He grabbed Eve's arm and shoved her toward the makeshift bunker. "Go," he said. She crawled inside without protest.

"Do it!" Duchamps shouted. His men complied.

Alan waited while they squeezed into the small space. The insect sounds grew louder than the rumbling of the *Cerberus'* treads. "Hurry," he urged, kneeling in front of the opening. Eve reached out and pulled him inside. He fell on top of her, scrambling out of Duchamps' way as the security chief crawled in behind him.

"Those things can dig us out, you know," Duchamps told him.

Alan nodded and began pushing rocks into the opening.

"What about the bodies?"

"There's no room for the dead," Alan said.

Now, it was Duchamps' turn to nod. "The living come first." He began adding rocks to Alan's pile.

"Trace," Alan called over the headset radio, "fire the lasers on full spread for fifteen seconds."

Duchamps looked at Alan as if he thought he was insane. "We're in the line of fire."

The laser array began to spin. "Help me seal the entrance," Alan said.

Duchamps worked frantically, shoving rocks into the gap between metal skirt and the floor of the lava tube.

"Everyone down," Alan warned, shouting over the whine of the turbine and spinning laser array.

Eve crawled over him and rested her head on his chest. He covered her with his arms and prayed his plan would work. The pulse laser could reach temperatures of 1000^0C in seconds. He hoped a short burst would be sufficient to kill the insects without frying him and his companions as well. The heat, when it finally washed over the lava tube, raised the temperature forty degrees Fahrenheit within seconds. The metal skirting above them quickly heated and buckled. Heat radiated down from it like the inside of an oven broiler. The air he sucked into his lungs instantly sucked the moisture from his throat, making swallowing difficult. His lips parched and the soft skin of his cheeks blistered. The acrid stench of singed hair and the burnt smell of scorched clothing mingled with the flinty odor of superheated rock. He cringed at the mad hissing of the creatures caught by the full blast of the laser. Popping sounds punctuated the hissing. *There's my Fourth of July firecrackers*, Alan thought.

After fifteen seconds, the laser array shut down. The turbine slowed; then stopped. Except for the pinging as the metal skirt cooled, a deep silence filled the lava tube. Deeming it safe to dig out, he pushed the rocks away with his hands, searing the tips of his fingers. The air was too hot to breath, but a blanket of heavier, moist, cooler air rushed down the tunnel to push it away. He faced the breeze for a moment before surveying the scene of carnage.

The laser had cremated dozens of insects, popping open their carapaces like popcorn. Their black bodies had turned a sickening cream color, like a broiled lobster changing color. The overwhelming stench of burned flesh filled the air. Steam and smoke rose from the nearly cremated remains of Duchamps' dead guards. Wisps of smoke curled up from their charred clothing. Alan felt a twinge of guilt at their grisly condition, but comforted himself knowing the dead felt no pain.

"Your plan worked," Duchamps said, as he crawled out and scanned the area for live bugs. "I admit I thought you were going to kill us all."

Alan smiled. "I hoped it would work. No one has ever been as close to that much unleashed power." He rubbed his arm where the heat had vaporized the hair as neatly as a razor. "I wasn't certain we could survive it."

Duchamps kicked one of the dead insects. It crumbled to powder. "That should keep them away for a while."

"I certainly hope so." He was more worried about the ebony shadow creatures Bill had reported, one that could turn human beings into piles of pulverized bone.

Duchamps' men followed Eve from the bunker. She stumbled toward Alan, eyes unfocused, still in shock from the intense heat. One of the guards nursed a badly blistered arm, but most of their wounds were minor. Alan brushed his scorched fingertips across his blistered lips, flinching from the sharp pain. His cheeks felt as if he had shaved with a hot poker. *But I'm alive,* he reminded himself, as he looked at the three corpses.

The additional security team Duchamps had requested arrived as they tended to their wounds. Alan would have traded the *Cerberus* for a tube of *Blistex* and a bottle of Aloe Vera lotion. Within fifteen minutes, the security team had placed the corpses and the more seriously wounded guard on stretchers and transported them from the lava tube. Alan watched them file out the opening, taking stock of their efforts to find Vince. So far, Duchamps had lost four security personnel to the creatures, and three were missing and presumed dead. Vince was gone. Alan no longer doubted he was dead. *How many more?*

Back in the tunnel the *Cerberus* had bored, he called Trace. "Trace, back the *Cerberus* into the tunnel."

Trace expertly maneuvered the vehicle until it stopped just inside tunnel. Alan and the two remaining guards removed two more skirts from the machine and placed them upright against the opening.

"Now, move it forward, slowly."

The machine inched into place, pushing the quarter-inch metal plates flush against the edges of the tunnel, effectively sealing it.

"That should keep the creatures out," he said to Eve, who had hovered around him since the attack.

"We have to come back down here to study those creatures," she told him. "They are a remarkable find."

In spite of her harrowing ordeal, Eve's shock had worn off quickly. Her adrenaline was pumping, and she was bursting with professional curiosity. Soot smeared her right cheek, and the heat had melted part of her nylon jumpsuit, blistered her arm, and singed the ends of her hair. She ignored these in her excitement over the creatures. Alan decided she needed a dose of reality.

"Eve, ten people are dead. These creatures are deadly. Unique or not, I'd blast the whole damned tunnel to seal it shut and call it a good day's work, but I'm sure Verkhoen will want his diamonds. Talk to him about coming back. I'm leaving. I've lost one good friend already. The *Cerberus* has proven itself. Now, I'm going home to help my father manufacture them."

He didn't tell her he was frightened down to his boots. The creatures acted with too much intelligence in the manner in which they stalked and attacked their prey. Sealed in the lava tube for 300 million years, evolution had ample time to play its tricks on them, a long time to hone their hunting skills.

Eve turned away from him, disillusioned. "I thought your scientific curiosity might have been aroused."

Her disappointment bothered him for reasons he couldn't quite explain, but he was out of his league and knew it. "Curiosity killed the cat. I'm an engineer, not a biologist. Certainly not a paleo-xenologist or whoever the hell studies these things. I develop, build, and sell mining equipment, not fight giant prehistoric insects. If you will excuse me, I have to go inform Vince's parents that I killed their only son."

He didn't turn around to witness her reaction to his statement. She was a good woman, but too caught up in the excitement of discovery. *If things had been different, maybe.* He mentally slapped himself in the face. *Enough of that.* Let Van Gotts handle everything. As soon as they could pull back the *Cerberus*, he and his crew were out of there.

* * * *

When he arrived at the Shack, Trace and Bill were relieved to see him.

"Great job, boss. You made it back alive," Trace called out after embracing Alan in a bear hug that nearly crushed his ribs. He held his arms out to his side to avoid hitting his blistered fingertips.

"You saved our skin with the *Cerberus*," Alan acknowledged. Without warning, his legs became wobbly and gave out beneath him.

He lurched backwards and collapsed in one of the rolling desk chairs. It skidded across the room, banging into the wall.

"Wow," he said, shaking his head to clear the cobwebs. "I guess it's all just hitting home."

He had never faced danger in such a personal manner. There had always been the possibility of cave-ins, industrial accidents, even his recent near miss with the ore truck, but nothing in which he felt lucky to be alive afterwards.

"It was your idea," Trace said, retrieving a bottle of cold water from the refrigerator and handing it to Alan. "I wasn't sure what you had in mind at first."

Alan twisted off the top, wincing at the pain in his fingertips, and downed most of it in one gulp. His felt a slight sting, as the bottle touched his blistered lips. His hand trembled when he raised it to take another sip, sloshing the water. He set it down before the others noticed. "Is the *Cerberus* still blocking the tunnel?"

Bill checked his monitor. "Nothing bigger than a rat can squeeze around it."

Alan's sharp laugh was bitter. "I'm not afraid of rats."

He stared at Bill for a moment. He had never seen the insouciant engineer look so dejected. Though often taciturn, he had never been withdrawn. Alan wondered if he still blamed himself for not keeping track of Vince.

"It's not your fault," he said. "No one could have predicted what happened."

Bill glanced at him, his eyes on the brink of tearing up; then turned his gaze back to the screen though there was nothing to look at.

"Hell, no, Bill," Trace added. "Once he saw that hole, Vince wasn't going to miss an opportunity to look for Pellucidar. It was … what do you call it? Synchronicity, that's it." He grew more somber. "What about Vince?"

Alan shook his head. "Not a sign of him."

"Could he still be alive, hiding from those bugs, maybe?"

Alan considered the question for a moment. It was a wonderful hope, one that he wanted to embrace, but after having seen the bugs in action, he knew the odds were against it. He shook his head and watched the faint glimmer of hope in Trace's eyes extinguish, as if he had snuffed it out like spitting on a candle wick. "I don't think so. Those things are everywhere."

Trace nodded and sat down in his chair. He sat in silence for a minute or two with his eyes closed, rubbing the bridge of his nose with his fingers. Finally, he said, "Your father wants you to call him as soon as you can."

Alan grabbed Trace's shoulder and squeezed it gently. "I will, after I take a shower. Try to get things organized here. We'll leave the *AT10* here as Van Gotts' first purchase." The bitter thought, *it's not the only thing we'll be leaving behind,* rolled through his mind. *I can't even bring back Vince's body for his parents to bury.* "If he balks, I'll give him a nice, fat, used-*Cerberus* discount to sweeten the deal. I want to be out of here by tomorrow morning. We're going home."

"None too soon for me," Trace whispered. He stood and began to yank files from the filing cabinet, tossing them in an untidy pile on the desk. He stopped and stood over the mess of graphs and printout strewn over the desktop, staring down at them. "I'll miss him."

Alan suspected Trace felt he was alive only because Vince had gone into the mine first. He was suffering from survivor's guilt, just as Bill suffered from false guilt. Alan felt a touch of it himself, but they had no time to dwell on it.

"We all will, Trace. Vince was our friend. Now, take the files and the laptops. Leave everything else for Verkhoen's engineers. If they have questions, they can call me long distance." He handed Trace Vince's laptop. "Put this one with the others."

Trace handles the laptop as if it were a holy relic. He stared at the black leather case with Vince's initials emblazoned in gold, rubbing his fingertips over the letters. "I'll handle it," he said.

"Bill," Alan said, "download all the video files from the *Cerberus* and the security cameras to Dad's computer back in Nevada."

He finished his water. His hand no longer shook. He didn't know if the water had replenished his dehydrated body, or if his decision to leave South Africa had hardened his resolve. Either way, he felt better. Sometimes one just has to accept failures and move on. *I'm getting good at that,* he thought bitterly. He tossed the empty water bottle at the garbage can and missed. He cursed and stormed out of the trailer.

10

July 5, 2016, 2:30 p.m.   Klerksdorp, South Africa –
Eve relaxed on her sofa in her home in Klerksdorp, a few kilometers from the mine. Freshly showered, she wore only her robe. She had disposed of the filthy, scorched jumpsuit she had worn into the mine. She knew she could never launder away the stench of death that permeated its fibers. In her hand, she held a glass containing a liberal splash of South African single-malt whisky over ice. She preferred *Glenfiddich Scotch*, but the Value Added Tax and import duty made it unaffordable on her salary. She needed the drink to settle her nerves.

Fear tempered her excitement over her discovery of the insects. Men had died, yet she knew she could not allow such an opportunity to slip through her fingers. Since her husband's death, she had been half-alive, simply going through the motions each day. She had remained in South Africa only because she hadn't the determination to leave. Now, she had stumbled upon the find of the decade, perhaps of the century.

The creatures in the lava tube system had been living for millions of years completely cut off from the outside world in a pristine environment, isolated from modern diseases and air pollution. Any other creatures in the tube could be equally unique. They provided a rare and unique study group. Who knew how they got there, or how they managed to survive for so long? She needed to learn upon what the creatures normally fed, what their environment was like, how long individuals lived. There was the potential for new drugs, new branches of biology, and maybe even new searches for similar creatures in cave systems throughout the world.

She would be right in the thick of it. She would see to it. Her paper on the creatures would make her famous. Their adventures today would provide material for a bestselling novel. The grisly deaths of so many, though she regretted the loss, would only enhance the mystique of the discovery. She felt the blood throbbing through her veins and delighted in it. She had been dead for so long. It felt good to be fully alive again.

When she had lost Frederick in the cave-in, she had been frantic, urging the company to do all it could, prowling around in the bowels of the earth searching for other ways in, fighting everyone who said they were dead and that it was time to give up. She knew Frederick would not give up. He would go on as long as he could draw a breath.

In the end, she had lost. They had sealed the shaft forever as being too dangerous for further digging. She knew it was to cover their mistakes. Her husband had warned that the stratum was too brittle to dig. He knew the roof would never hold.

If only they had Alan Hoffman's *Cerberus*.

Alan Hoffman. Just saying his name thrilled her. Something about him reminded her of her husband. They didn't look alike – Frederick was barely 5'8'' to Alan's 6'2", and her husband's thinning red hair couldn't compare to Alan's well-groomed, blond locks, but they both had that same look of determination that she cherished. Alan had saved them all with his quick thinking today. He had saved her. Perhaps when it was all over, she would ask him out for drinks and dinner in a show of gratitude. If that bold move didn't frighten him away, perhaps they could move on from there.

She was tired of being lonely. The excitement and the danger had not only awakened her from her long hibernation, it had reminded her just how alone she had been, deliberately cutting herself off from friends and family. Today had provided the catharsis she had needed to jumpstart her life. Pursuing Alan wasn't wrong. After all, she was a widow, and it had been four long years since she had a man in her life.

She knew Verkhoen wouldn't hesitate to eliminate the creatures to get to the diamonds. The World Wildlife Organization had the muscle to put pressure on Van Gotts. With the videos and her report, she could get enough backing from the scientific community to stop Verkhoen. The diamonds were not important; the creatures were.

Scientists would have to study them in their natural environment, install cameras in the lava tube to monitor them. They could even set up a website with a live video feed. The project could pay for itself through web hits at two Euros each. She would be on the cover of *Scientific American* and perhaps be asked to speak before the British Royal Anthropological Society. Her father would have been so proud. So would Frederick.

One suspicion she kept to herself. It was likely they had merely seen one small branch of an extensive network of lava tubes and caverns. She wondered what other wonders awaited discovery so deep beneath the earth.

She decided to enlist the aid of Doctor Simon Tells, a pre-eminent paleo-archaeologist from the University of Johannesburg she had met at seminars a few times over the years. With his credentials and contacts, word would quickly spread. Verkhoen could do nothing to stop them.

She checked her contact list in her cell phone, located Doctor Tells' number, and hit dial. He listened attentively, as she detailed the situation, but she could tell from his lack of questions that he thought her mad.

"Perhaps this would go better if you read the e-mail I just sent you. I've attached a video clip taken in the mine."

She waited for several minutes while Tells watched the video. When he came back on the phone, he was excited and full of questions.

"Did you manage to obtain a dead specimen?"

"I'm afraid not. We had to leave in a hurry."

"Were there other similar insects?"

"We didn't have time for a proper exploration. To do so, we will have to move quickly. Verkhoen will stop at nothing to recover the diamonds. We must present these creatures to the world before it is too late."

Tells paused, and said, "I'll be there in two hours."

When she ended the call, she felt she had gotten he jump on Verkhoen. She had no idea bugs in the lava tube weren't the only bugs she had to worry about.

11

July 5, 2016, 5:00 p.m.   Klaus Verkhoen's office, Ngomo Mine –
Duchamps' meeting with Verkhoen wasn't going as well as he had
expected. His first clue that Verkhoen had literally called him on the
carpet was Verkhoen's refusal to offer him a chair when the secretary
ushered him into the office. He stood across from Verkhoen's desk,
trying not to let his anger show, as Verkhoen berated him.

"You have been with this company for fifteen years, Captain
Duchamps, and have performed your job admirably until this point.
Now, through your gross incompetence, you have cost us the lives of
ten people and have jeopardized the find of the century."

Duchamps had expected Verkhoen to stand behind his actions, not
blame him for everything. How could he have anticipated giant bugs?
He protested.

"Surely you cannot hold me responsible for the deaths of those
men. We barely escaped with our lives. We went down there to
apprehend a suspect in a possible murder, not fight hordes of giant
insects."

Verkhoen waved his hand in the air. "Nevertheless, ten men are
dead, are they not?"

"Yes, but—"

"But nothing!" Verkhoen snapped. "I could forgive the loss of
lives, but you have allowed Doctor Means to broadcast a video of the
events. Now, the entire world knows about the diamonds, the
creatures, and the deaths. I will be lucky if the Board of Directors
allow me stay on as curator of their new wildlife museum."

Duchamps was well aware of Verkhoen's vicious temper. He had
witnessed others wither under Verkhoen's icy gaze, but he had never
been on the receiving end, especially not while being accused of

shirking his duty.

He offered what defense he could. "Doctor Means is an employee who signed the same nondisclosure contract we all signed. How was I to know she would contact her colleagues so quickly? I was in the process of setting up a tap on her phone per your instructions."

"Luckily, I was a step ahead of you and had her telephone bugged by a reliable outside agency. Doctor Means is an ambitious woman and still holds us responsible for her husband's death. She will use this opportunity to make a name for herself and to inflict as much damage to the company and to me personally as possible."

Verkhoen stood up and walked around his desk to confront Duchamps. Duchamps tried not to flinch, as Verkhoen circled him like a hyena probing for weakness. *A hyena wearing a 36,000 ZAR Desch suit and 12,000 ZAR Baldinini shoes.* "Your gross incompetence forced me to leave Pretoria and come here. Now, I will personally take charge. I must make a deal with Hoffman to procure the use of his laser to protect a team I will send to retrieve the diamonds. Humbling myself to that ... crass American irks me greatly. I will allow you lead this team, but let me assure you, if you fail in this task, I will see to it that you find no work in security anywhere in South Africa, ever again. You will not be able to guard a candy store in strip mall. Do I make myself clear?"

Duchamps swallowed hard. "You are being entirely unfair."

Verkhoen paced the length of the desk, returned to stand in from of Duchamps, and stared at him, saying nothing. Duchamps raged inside, but knew he had no choice but submit. Verkhoen still pulled all the strings.

"Yes, sir," he replied stiffly. "I understand."

Verkhoen turned his back on him and said, "We cannot waste time. Prepare to leave for the lava tube in six hours. You are dismissed."

Dismissed. Duchamps stared at Verkhoen's back, shaking with anger, fighting down the urge to plunge his knife deep between Verkhoen's shoulder blades. Then he would skin him like a gazelle and hang his carcass on an acacia tree for the vultures to eat. He had poured his life into the company, fourteen hours a day, and seven days a week. If Verkhoen thought he could get rid of him so easily, he had a surprise coming.

Since the moment he had first seen the diamonds, Duchamps had hardly thought of anything else. Not even the giant bugs held his attention as closely as the enormous, glittering raw stones. He had never carried out a single nugget from the mine in all his years as security chief. It would have been easy. He knew all the security procedures and all the myriad flaws and limitations of the mine's security systems. He had instituted most of the procedures himself. His integrity and his dedication to the company had forbidden such an abhorrent breach of trust.

Duchamps knew Verkhoen was capable of carrying out his threats. Indeed, he probably would do so as he had promised, despite the results of the coming expedition to retrieve the diamonds. Verkhoen was a spiteful, vindictive son of a bitch with a long memory. If fired, Duchamps would lose his company house, his pension, his bonuses, maybe even his stock options. He couldn't let that happen. He wouldn't allow it to happen.

He checked his watch. Verkhoen wanted him in the mine in six hours. That gave him just enough time to set in motion his own half-conceived plan. The idea had slowly formed in his head, the kind of thing a bank teller dreams of as he sits at his desk, ways to rob the vault and get away with it; impulses upon which a bank teller, or himself, would normally never act. They were fanciful daydreams to fill the long boring hours, dreams that would never have borne fruit but for Verkhoen's threats.

Duchamps knew he could count on three of his men, men who held their positions in spite of their dubious backgrounds simply because he had wanted them there. He would devise a way back into the lava tube and steal the diamonds, or at least as many as they could carry out. He would show Verkhoen just what he was made of. He would retire to a tropical island, perhaps Tahiti, a very rich man.

All he needed was a diversion, something to occupy everyone's mind while he made a clean getaway. He could be across the border of Namibia in an hour and aboard a jet for Tahiti in four. He smiled as he thought of what would serve nicely. The deaths of the electrician and her assistant had provided a clue. Everyone but him seemed to have forgotten that at least one of the creatures was loose in the mine already. All he needed do was to let more of crawly beasties out of the lava tube. With scores of those damn giant muggies running loose in the mines, eating drillers and causing a panic, he could walk out of the mine with a knapsack full of sparkling, white diamonds right under Verkhoen's nose. If a few miners died, so what? Hundreds died every year. If he were going to break a few dozen laws, a few more wouldn't bother him. He didn't intend to stick around afterwards to pay the consequences.

He would have no trouble convincing his three shady comrades to go along with his plan. A combination of their instinctive greed and threats of exposure would win them over.

Moving quickly, he retrieved several automatic weapons from the arms locker, as well as extra magazines of ammunition. He didn't intend to become insect meat. First, he had to move the *Cerberus* and free the creatures. He would have to convince one of Hoffman's men to do that for him. Hoffman and the young engineer were at the hotel, leaving only the old man with the salt-and-pepper beard on duty. If he couldn't bribe him, he would force him to cooperate.

* * * *

Bill Bakerman was listening to the recently repaired audio connection to the *Cerberus'* video camera. He couldn't see much, just the metal skirts sealing the opening, but he could hear the creatures' hisses and clicks. They were searching for a way out of the lava tube. When the door to the Shack opened, he turned around smiling, expecting to see Trace relieving him. Instead, it was Duchamps with three of his security men. Duchamps' dour expression troubled him.

"What can I do for you, Captain Duchamps?" he asked, bewildered by the security chief's presence and the automatic weapons they carried.

"You can move that great, metal beast out of the way for me, if you please," Duchamps replied.

Bill stared at him for a moment, uncomprehending, unconsciously stroking his beard. "Why do you want me to do that? The creatures could get out with no one on guard down there."

"Move the *Cerberus*," Duchamps repeated a little more firmly.

Duchamps' brusque manner made him uneasy. "I'll check with Alan." He reached for the phone. Duchamps slammed the butt of the rifle onto the back of his wrist. Excruciating pain radiated up his arm the carpus bones shattered. He jerked his throbbing hand back and cradled it against his chest. Duchamps shoved the barrel of the rifle in his face, letting the tip of the barrel brush his nose.

"If you pick up that phone, it will be the last thing you do. Move that machine out of the way. My men and I have business down there."

"At least let me wait until you're down there," he pleaded. "Otherwise, by the time you get there, those things could be everywhere."

Duchamps' cold, deadly smile startled him. The livid scar on the security chief's cheek danced as Duchamps replied, "Exactly. We want them out of the tube so they won't be a nuisance to us. Now, do it." To emphasize his point, he rapped Bill's forehead smartly with the barrel.

Bill swallowed hard. He had seen action as part of the 20th Engineer Battalion during the Gulf War. Attached to the Third Armored Cavalry in Kuwait, he had destroyed Iraqi bunkers and repaired destroyed bridges. That same rush of being under enemy fire returned. He knew without a doubt that Duchamps would pull the trigger.

"Okay! Okay! I'll do it."

Duchamps nodded. "Very good. Now, move it and do it quickly."

Bill was now in fear for his life. He had no choice but to cooperate and hope to delay Duchamps as long as possible until someone showed up. He bit back on the pain of his hand, which was making his head throb. Typing with only one hand was slow work as he moved through the various pop up screens detailing *Cerberus'* diverse systems. Duchamps grew more agitated and impatient, tapping his foot on the floor. Finally, Bill started the *Cerberus'* turbine. He didn't need the turbine's power to move the machine, but he hoped Duchamps didn't know that. Maneuvering the powerful machine using the joystick with his left hand was awkward. After several false starts, he began backing the laser driller away from the opening it had punched into the lava tube.

The steel plates barricading the opening fell backwards, covering the headlights, but not before he detected furtive movements all around the entrance, flickers on the edge of darkness. The bugs were breaking out, and he could do nothing about it.

"How do you operate the lasers?" Duchamps demanded.

He took a chance and pointed to Trace's laptop, which ran diagnostic programs on the *Cerberus'* systems. The pain hit his leg before he heard the report of the rifle. *The bastard shot me.* He looked down at his leg. The 5.56x45mm NATO round had blown an exit wound as large as a quarter in his calf. Blood flowed profusely down his leg, but it wasn't spurting. Through the haze of pain clouding his mind, he noted Duchamps had missed the artery. He hoped he had missed intentionally. That meant he might have a chance of surviving.

"I can read, asshole," Duchamps yelled. "That computer is running a diagnostic program. It shows 90% complete on the bottom of the screen. I ignored your clumsy attempt to delay me by cranking the turbine engine. I know the machine can move without it. Your second attempt at deception deserved a penalty. Now, show me the right one, or the next bullet goes in your head."

Over his pain, Bill pointed to his laptop with his good hand. "This one," he sobbed. "This one controls the lasers." He tried to hold back the tears, but the pain was too intense and his anger too deep. With his fingers, he pressed on the bullet hole just above his knee, trying to suppress the flow of blood running down his leg and soaking his pants.

Duchamps fired a short burst through both his and Trace's laptops before placing a bullet in the video camera in the corner of the room. Shards of plastic from his shattered laptop peppered Bill's face, adding to his misery.

"That should keep Verkhoen busy guessing," Duchamps said. He looked at Bill, frowned, and pursed his lips. "I am sorry for the pain I have caused you."

Bill sighed with relief. He might make it through alive after all. "Just leave," he said, angry with himself for cooperating, but most of his anger he directed at Duchamps. He noticed Duchamps' eyes narrowing.

"For your cooperation, I'll end your pain it now."

Before Bill could say or do anything, Duchamps placed the barrel of the rifle to his temple and pulled the trigger.

* * * *

Wiping the technician's blood from his face with a paper napkin beside the coffee pot, Duchamps turned to his men. "We go down, now. Stay together. If you see of the creatures, kill them only if they attack. The more creatures running loose in the mines, the better our escape. Come."

By the time they reached the lower level of the mine, the clicks and whistles of the creatures came from everywhere – mineshafts, elevator shafts, airshafts – with the screams of the miners mixed in. They had overrun the mine. How many of them were loose? Certainly, they numbered more than the few dozen he had expected. Nearly three hundred men worked the evening second shift in the mine, a lot of prey for the creatures.

He and his men encountered only a handful of the giant insects along the way. To his astonishment, only one was a scorpion. The others were a menagerie of nightmares, ranging from huge, ugly, hairy spiders the size of large dogs, a fearless black beetle bigger than a man's head, and cockroaches as large as his hand. After dispatching two of them with the automatic weapons, the others scurried away, as if sensing the weapons the men carried were dangerous.

Reaching the crane, all they found of its operator were a hardhat, scraps of clothing, and a blood pool on the floor of the crane's cabin. Bloody handprints smeared the windows. Duchamps ordered his men into the kibble, cranked the crane, and hopped aboard to join them, carrying the remote control for the crane. The remote only operated the winch, moving it up or down, but that was all he required. He shot one beetle that was climbing the ladder from the pit. It landed beneath the kibble, still wriggling. He smiled as the heavy bucket crushed it with a crunch and squishing sound.

They encountered nothing along the *Cerberus* tunnel, but he entered the lava tube cautiously. The lava tube was free of the creatures just as he had planned. They were busy feeding in the mines. His companion's eyes lit up when they saw the diamonds glittering in the walls. Now that he had delivered on his promise, they would follow him anywhere.

Duchamps was certain there were more diamonds elsewhere in the lava tube. He regretted he didn't have time for a proper search, but this wasn't the time to be greedy. Greed could prove fatal. He didn't want to become a victim of his own distraction. He would settle on a bulging knapsack full of the largest stones.

With hand-held picks and rifle butts, they pried the raw diamonds from the walls, some as large as golf balls. Most were pure white stones. The larger ones he left for Verkhoen. They would be more difficult to dispose of. They had nearly completed their work when the first of the enormous insects charged out of the darkness with no warning. They quickly mowed down the first four or five of the beetles with their R4 automatic weapons. The remainder pulled back and watched from the safety of the rocks. They were getting smarter.

He quickly discovered that giant beetles and scorpions weren't the lava tube's only denizens. Buzzing like a thousand electric shavers, a swarm of flies the size of sparrows descending on them; however, these flies had long beaks and sharp spines covering their bodies. Like giant mosquitoes, the flies dove at them, slipping between flailing arms to thrust their beaks into exposed flesh, sucking up as much blood as they could before a hand or fist connected with them. Even then, the sharp spines inflicted as much pain as their bite.

Duchamps had had enough. Hefting his knapsack, he yelled, "Come on. Let's get out of here."

Two of them dropped their picks and picked up their diamond-laden bags to follow him. One man, oblivious to the others fleeing, remained stubbornly at his task, attempting to free a particularly large stone from its stone cradle. Yanking it free, he held the diamond in his hand in triumph, smiling at his prize; then, realizing he was alone, picked up his knapsack and chased after them.

Duchamps turned at the sound of a bloodcurdling scream. The man had been too slow. He went down with three of the beetles swarming over him, driving mandibles into his back. Duchamps stopped to fire a short burst at them, but it didn't stop them from ripping the man to shreds. The others panicked. Duchamps saw his chance and rushed back to grab the man's bag of diamonds, which had spilled on the ground. It broke his heart to abandon the loose stones, but the beetles had noticed him. He snatched up the knapsack, shot one of the creatures, and ran.

"Keep together," he yelled at the others. "Keep your weapons ready."

A swarm of creatures pursued them – beetles, giant flies, cockroaches, and a second flying insect resembling an armored wasp. Their speed surprised him. The beetles and cockroaches scurried nimbly over the piles of loose rocks, while the flying insects darted around them, weaving through the stalactites like aerial combat fighters. He and his remaining men reached the tunnel safely ahead of their pursuers, but he knew the creatures would easily overtake them. He tapped one man on the shoulder.

"You, stay here and hold them while we get the kibble ready. Then, we'll cover you as you run to us."

The man nodded, dropped his pack, and knelt with his weapon pointed toward the creatures rapidly approaching.

"I'll carry this for you," Duchamps said, as he lifted the man's diamonds onto his shoulder, "so it won't slow you down."

The man stared at Duchamps for a moment but handed him his knapsack. Duchamps passed the partially filled bag to his companion and raced down the tunnel, as a rapid succession of shots rang out behind them. *The fool*, he thought. *He has his rifle set on full auto. He'll empty the magazine in seconds.*

"Do we stop for Bowers?" the other guard asked.

"You can if you wish to," Duchamps replied and continued running. The guard took only a second to make his choice and followed Duchamps as quickly as he could. Another half minute passed with rapid shooting; then, a loud scream reached them as the creatures overpowered Bowers.

"Thank you, Bowers," Duchamps whispered.

Laden with his two heavy packs, he fell behind his companion, who had learned from Bowers' example and did not intend to risk his life. When Duchamps reached the shaft, the guard had elected to climb the ladder rather than wait for him with the remote control. While he hauled himself up the ladder bearing his two cumbersome knapsacks of diamonds, Duchamp rode the kibble. Unlike the guard, whose two bags kept swinging wildly, throwing him off balance, he had anticipated the difficulty in climbing a one-hundred-ten-meter ladder burdened with a heavy load. As he passed the guard, Duchamps pointed below him. When the guard glanced back down the ladder, his face contorted with fear at the sight of several giant spiders in hot pursuit. He began clawing at the rungs at a frantic pace, but the spiders were faster. Still, he did not abandon his diamonds.

Reaching the top of the pit, Duchamps stopped the wench and leaped from the kibble. He stopped to wait on the guard, not because he felt any comradeship with him, but because the guard carried a fortune in diamonds in his two knapsacks. However, when he determined that the race between man and creature would be down to the wire, living became more important than wealth. He abandoned his co-conspirator and sprinted down a narrow side tunnel leading to elevator number three.

The guard climbed out of the pit half a minute later and bounded after him. Three spiders rushed out of the pit on his heels. Duchamps knew the guard would never make it. Each of the spiders' hops covered two meters. The guard saw the direction of Duchamp's gaze and turned to look over his shoulder. He didn't have time to fire his weapon. Two of the spiders bore him to the ground and made quick work of him, pumping him full of poison, and ripping their dagger-like fangs into his liquefying flesh. The latecomer spider joined in the bloody feast.

Duchamps stopped and watched with morbid fascination as the creatures fed. He waited until the spiders were engrossed with their meal, and then killed them with short controlled bursts from his rifle. He recovered the pair of knapsacks, dragged all four bags a short way down the tunnel, and loaded them onto the back on an electric maintenance cart. Keeping a close eye behind him in case the spiders decided on a new victim, he unplugged the cart from the charging station, hit the starter button, and headed for the elevator as fast as the cart would go.

The cart carried him two kilometers to Elevator #3, a secondary elevator shaft used mainly for moving freight. The elevator went only as high as 20 Level, but when the excitement died down, he could make his escape through the main elevator. Worst-case scenario, he would find an airshaft and climb out, hauling his load up the shaft one bag at a time. He knew the placement of every motion sensor and every camera. The sensors would be useless as evening fell and the bats emerged from the shaft for their nightly feeding. He could slip out the airshaft while the authorities were cleaning up the little bug infestation problem he had left them.

He chuckled at the audacity of his plan. The fool Verkhoen could have the mine. He would wind up rich, and Verkhoen would wind up with dozens of deaths to explain to the Board of Directors and the police. He would be lucky if he didn't wind up in prison with some big hairy bruiser drilling him like a boy toy just because he looked so damn pretty.

The #3 elevator was clear of creatures. He rode it to 30 Level and got off. A nearby drill bit room would provide him the perfect place to hide out until things quieted. The occasional scream still echoed up the shaft over the blare of the evacuation alarm. Duchamps smiled. His plan was working perfectly.

12

July 5, 2016, 8:20 p.m.   Protea Hotel, Klerksdorp, South Africa –
After leaving the Shack, Alan retreated to the solitude of his hotel
room. He turned off his cell phone and took the hotel phone off the
hook. He didn't want to see or speak to anyone. He was exhausted,
angry, and racked by guilt. He wanted to hold a private self-pity
party, and he didn't need witnesses. What should have been a
successful live trial of the *Cerberus AT10* had turned into a horror
story. Vince was dead, as well as seven security guards and two
electricians, killed by giant, prehistoric insects. He had been so eager
for a sale that he had allowed Verkhoen to use him. Events were
spiraling out of his control, and the only solution he could think of
was to run away, as he had his failed marriage. *Father will be proud
of me.*

He was disgusted with himself. He looked around for the wine
bottle from the night before, hoping there might be a few dregs left to
drown his sorrows, but the maid had taken it when she cleaned the
room. He could always order another bottle, but that wouldn't make
things any clearer.

A knock at the door drew a silent curse from him. "Go away," he
yelled.

After a second knock, a voice said, "It is Klaus Verkhoen, Mister
Hoffman. May I come in?"

"Perfect timing," Alan muttered, irritated at being disturbed.

He got up and opened the door. Verkhoen, dressed as if going to a
board meeting, stepped inside. Without waiting for an invitation, he
sat down in a wingback chair by the window and threw his leg over
the arm. Alan sat on the edge of the bed, placing as much distance
between as possible in the confines of the room. He frowned when

Verkhoen pulled a monogrammed, gold cigarette case from his breast pocket. He wondered what the M in the initials KMV stood for.

"Do you mind if I have a *skyf*?" he asked.

Alan had insisted on a non-smoking room. Going cold turkey was difficult enough without smelling someone else's old smoke in the pillows and the carpet. Verkhoen didn't wait for his answer. He fished out a cigarette and placed it between his lips. Lighting it with a gold cigarette lighter that matched his case, he inhaled, and then exhaled a cloud of smoke, which drifted tantalizingly near Alan. The aroma of burning tobacco corroded his willpower. He almost waved the smoke toward him to take in a lungful.

"Go ahead," he said. Verkhoen ignored him. "You didn't waste much time getting down here. I suppose Duchamps has kept you informed."

At the mention of Duchamps' name, he noticed a slight twitch in the corner of Verkhoen's mouth, but Verkhoen said nothing. Instead, he opened his cigarette case and offered Alan a cigarette. As much as he wanted one, he declined. If it had been anyone but Verkhoen offering, he might have accepted.

"Yes, Duchamps has contacted me about the incident," Verkhoen replied. "That is why I came down from Pretoria."

"Incident? You call enough corpses to start a baseball team an incident?"

"The deaths are regrettable, of course, but entirely beyond our control. In a way, it was like a freak of nature. Now, about your machine. The *Cerberus* performed beyond my expectations. I am well pleased."

Alan tried not to grin at Verkhoen's rapid switch of topics. The deaths did not interest him, only the success of the *Cerberus*. "Thank you."

Verkhoen waved his hand to dismiss Alan's gratitude. "It is a fact. I will submit an order for three of the machines to your headquarters, as I promised. They will substantially reduce mining costs. I believe the mine can once again become profitable. On my recommendation, other companies will follow suit. You will soon be a rich man."

"It won't make up for Vince's death."

Verkhoen crushed his cigarette into the top of the desk. Alan's gaze followed the wisp of smoke rising from the stub, wanting badly to pick the stub up and toke it back to life.

"Your engineer's death, as well as the deaths of my security personnel, was unforeseeable."

"Really? I think you knew what we would find."

Verkhoen glared at him but remained calm. His supercilious attitude rubbed Alan the wrong way. He wanted very badly to leap up and slap Verkhoen silly. The svelte, muscular Boer might beat him senseless, but it would feel good to get in a couple of good licks. Instead, Verkhoen said, "Is that an accusation of some kind?"

"You had to know about the void. You used my *Cerberus* because the rock was too soft for conventional mining. You tried that twice before and failed."

He waited for Verkhoen's reaction, but the CEO disappointed him.

"You've been listening to Doctor Means' distorted version of history. Do not let her beauty sway you. She is a vindictive woman." Before Alan could object, he continued, "As far as the lava tube, yes, I knew about it. We discovered it with a deep-penetrating ground scan. The chance it contained diamonds was too much to pass up. I need operating capital. If anyone learned of their existence, I could be in the courts for decades until ownership was established. I didn't have time."

"Did you know about the insects?"

Verkhoen sighed. "I swear I knew nothing about them. Who could have even conceived of such creatures?"

As much as he wanted Verkhoen to be guilty, he believed him. Whatever else the CEO had done, he hadn't known of the existence of the insects.

"We're leaving tomorrow morning. I'll leave the *Cerberus* here. You can have it as your first delivery. I'll knock off a couple of hundred thousand because the paint's scratched."

Verkhoen nodded. "That is satisfactory. I will pay full price. However, before you leave, I have a proposition for you."

"Not interested."

"Not even for, say, thirty million dollars."

Alan caught his breath. "Thirty ... million?" He stumbled over the word million.

"Yes. I must reach the diamonds before the authorities began an inquiry into the deaths. Even with my pull, I cannot avoid that. Doctor Means is going to make things difficult. From Duchamps' estimates, the diamonds he saw are worth over 1.75 billion ZAR. That is one-hundred-fifty-million U.S. Dollars. I will give you twenty percent of their value, in gold bullion if you wish. That comes to just under thirty million dollars at current exchange rates. I will make it an even thirty to make conversion easier."

"Just what do I have to do to earn this, er, bribe?"

"It is not a bribe. It is a fee. I must recover the diamonds. Those creatures infest the lava tube. I do not have enough manpower to do kill them with conventional weapons, and of course, explosives are out of the question. Your machine's laser has already proved its effectiveness at eliminating them. Use your remarkable machine to protect my men while they recover the diamonds, and I will pay you thirty million dollars. It is an aboveboard transaction, not a bribe."

Alan shoulders slumped and he hung his head. Verkhoen was untrustworthy, but how could he refuse an offer of thirty million dollars. Hoffman Industries badly needed money to begin production of the *Cerberus AT10*. For the first few years, capital would be tight. The diamonds were Verkhoen's, at least as far as he was concerned. He wouldn't ask his father's opinion. He was afraid his father would refuse on principle. They couldn't afford to be so cavalier; besides, Vince's parents needed some kind of compensation for his death.

Before he committed himself to a bargain that he was certain he would live to regret, he tried one last tactic, a graceful way out that didn't involve him turning down thirty million dollars.

"You have *Cerberus*. Why not use your engineers and save a butt load of cash?"

"It will take too long for them to become acquainted with its operation. I must act swiftly. I need you."

He wasn't sure if he felt relieved by Verkhoen's insistence on hiring him; or upset that the decision was back on his shoulders. He sighed. "Okay, I'll do it, but only me. I won't endanger any more of my men, and I won't hunt down the insects. I'll keep them out of your men's hair until they finish the job, but then we seal the lava tube for good."

Verkhoen smiled. "Agreed. I need you to be ready to go in five hours. Drop by my office shortly and I'll have a contract waiting."

Before Alan could protest the rushed timetable, Verkhoen rose from his seat. He didn't bother offering Alan his hand to seal the deal. A mere handshake wouldn't suffice. Verkhoen required an ironclad contract, perhaps signed in blood. Alan knew he had made a Faustian deal with the devil, and he needed something to wash the sour taste from his mouth. As soon as Verkhoen left, he picked up the phone.

"Room service? Send me up a bottle of *Jakkals Fontein Shiraz*. What? No, I don't need extra glasses. I'll drink it straight from the bottle." He slammed the phone down. "Damn Verkhoen, damn this place, and damn me for being such a goddamned greedy fool."

* * * *

He didn't finish the bottle of wine. He wanted to, but he needed to be sober. After two glasses, he shoved the cork back in the bottle, showered, and drove to the mine two hours before his scheduled meeting with Verkhoen. He wanted to inform Trace and Bill to hold off on packing the equipment. He couldn't wait to see their reaction. He wondered if they would think he was as crazy as he felt.

They hadn't brought enough fiber optic cable with them to move the *Cerberus* to the diamond site half a kilometer beyond the newly bored tunnel. He would have to accompany Verkhoen's men and control the *Cerberus* on site, using a laptop remote connection. The last thing he wanted to do was go back down in the mine, but he couldn't let Trace or Bill risk their lives. He was the one who had agreed to Verkhoen's offer. He already regretted his decision.

When he opened the door of the trailer and saw Bill slumped over in his chair, he thought the engineer had simply fallen asleep and opened his mouth to yell at him. He closed it again quickly when he saw the congealed blood pooled on the floor and the splatters on the wall. His heart skipped a beat; then, redoubled its effort by sledge hammering his ribcage. He went cold inside. Without checking for a pulse, he knew Bill was dead. Gunpowder residue surrounded the blood-crusted bullet hole in his right temple. Someone had shot the engineer at close range. The bullet had torn out the back of his skull, spraying the wall with bloody gore.

Bill's crushed and misshapen right hand and the bullet hole in his leg spoke of more than simple murder. Someone had tortured him before killing him. Both laptops were shattered with bullet holes exposing their damaged circuitry. Shards of glass littered the desktop and the floor. Alan's mind refused to make sense of what he saw. Why would anyone torture and kill Bill, and then destroy the laptops?

He checked the *Cerberus* video monitor. The screen was fuzzy; something partially blocked the camera, but he could see the tread skirt barricade had fallen from the opening. Someone had forced Bill to back the machine several meters into the tunnel, unsealing the lava tube entrance. Why would they do that? If the creatures got out . . . He let the thought die, as he saw that the insects were already out. A pair of scorpions scuttled past the *Cerberus*, giving it as wide a berth as the tunnel would allow, headed into the mine.

He picked up the phone. "Security, this is Alan Hoffman. The creatures are loose in the mine. You need to contact Duchamps ASAP and tell him what's going on." He looked at Bill's body, wanting to move it but knowing he shouldn't until the authorities arrived. "Please send someone over to the control trailer. One of my technicians has been murdered."

Rage filled him when the person on the phone said, "Captain Duchamps is not here. He and three officers entered the mine three hours ago. What was that about a murder?"

It all clicked into place. Duchamps! He was after the diamonds. He had forced Bill to move the *Cerberus*, and then killed him to prevent him from resealing the lava tube. The lousy bastard had deliberately let the flesh-eating bugs loose in the mines.

"Sound the alarm," he said. "The mines must be evacuated immediately."

Distantly, he heard the evacuation siren going off. If security acted quickly enough, they might confine the creatures to the lower levels and drive them back into the tube. When they did, he was going to seal the tunnel forever with explosives. He wasn't waiting for Verkhoen's permission. If Duchamps was still in the lava tube when he got there, he could damn well stay there.

Such deadly creatures had no place in the modern world. They had lived long past the time for their extinction. He knew from watching them in action that they were intelligent and cunning. They would quickly reach the top of the food chain. Humans could become the next animal to go extinct.

He realized the security guard on the other end of the line was still speaking. "I'm going to the lower level," Alan said, interrupting him. "Make sure those men you send over here are armed. I have to get the *Cerberus* operational from that end and reseal the tunnel. I'll need protection."

"This is Lieutenant Johansson, Mister Hoffman. I will send two men over. That is all I can spare. Please look for Captain Duchamps when you get there. I am worried about him."

Alan yelled, "Your murdering boss is to blame for this. He killed Bill Bakerman." He had no proof, but he knew he was right.

Johansson paused for a moment before continuing as if he hadn't heard or had chosen to ignore Alan's accusation. "See if you can locate Doctor Means' group while you're there."

Alan grimaced so hard he bit his lower lip. *Eve?* "What do you mean? Is Doctor Means in the mine?"

"Yes. She, Doctor Tells, and two others went down shortly after Captain Duchamps."

My God! Eve was down there with those creatures running around loose, although Duchamps might be just as dangerous as the giant insects. He had to rescue her before sealing the lava tube.

"Get those men to the lower level, damn it. I can't wait here for them."

He didn't bother hanging up the receiver. He tossed it on the desk and raced from the Shack. He drove to the explosives trailer he had passed every day on his trips to and from the mine. When he got there, a steel chain and padlock barred the door. *Of course*, he moaned. *Why would anything be easy?* Using a fourteen-inch pipe wrench he found in the back floorboard of the car, a '*bobbejaan spanner*' in Afrikaans, he hammered at the lock until it gave way. He ignored the hundreds of 50-pound bags of ANFO, premixed ammonium nitrate and fuel oil. They were useless to him, impossible to carry. He broke open a case of dynamite used as a primer for detonating the ANFO and grabbed half a dozen sticks. He added two pyrotechnic blasting caps, a coil of fast burning fuse, and shoved everything inside his shirt.

He drove like a maniac back to the elevator shaft, ignoring the blasting horns of ore haulers as he weaved among them. Sliding the car to a halt right in front of the elevator, he leaped inside and hit the down button, cursing it for being too slow as it descended into the mine. The cage had barely shuddered to a halt, when he shoved aside the sliding cage door and loped down the mineshafts toward the pit. He saw a flicker of movement ahead of him and leaped out of the way just as a giant beetle lunged at his legs from the shadows behind a support beam. As he flung himself against the wall, his feet kicked something, a rifle lying in a pool of blood. He grabbed it, prayed the safety was off, and fired two short bursts at the creature as it came at him again.

The beetle fell at his feet, thrashing its legs. He started to fire another burst into it to finish it off, but he didn't know how many bullets remained in the magazine. He might need them all. Slinging the R4 over his shoulder by the strap, he continued toward the pit. A scream erupted from somewhere ahead of him. He prayed it wasn't Eve.

Rounding a corner, he saw Eve and two others ahead of him. A pair of the scorpions had a third man pinned to the ground. The man's abdomen spurted blood as the creature stabbed him repeatedly with their sharp claws. As his movements stilled, the giant arthropods hungrily tore into the corpse with their mandibles, ripping strips of flesh from his corpse. Alan fired his rifle at them and was gratified to see one of the creatures shudder and die. The second, alerted by his shots, abandoned its meal and disappeared into the darkness.

"Alan," Eve yelled as she ran to him and fell into his arms. "Oh, my God! It was awful! Those things just grabbed Liles and ripped him to pieces."

"What are you doing here?" he demanded. Anger at her foolish expedition tempered his relief that she was still alive.

"I thought Verkhoen would try something shady, so I brought my colleagues down here with me to prevent him. When we arrived, we saw someone had moved the *Cerberus* away from the lava tube. When a horde of scorpions and beetles emerged, we ran. We thought we were safe; then, they attacked Doctor Liles."

One of the older men came over to him.

"You must be Alan Hoffman. Eve told us about you. I am Doctor Simon Tells and this is Doctor Jayden Sandersohn. That," he pointed to the corpse, "was Doctor David Liles, our bacteriologist." He shook his head. His too-large hardhat spun around. "You came at an opportune time, young man."

"Not soon enough for Doctor Liles, I'm afraid," he replied.

"Why did you move your machine?" Eve demanded. "Did you not know the creatures would escape?" She pounded her fists on his chest as she berated him. He grabbed her hands and pulled her to him.

"It wasn't me," he said. "It was Duchamps. He killed Bill Bakerman, one of my engineers after he forced him to move the *Cerberus*. He's after the diamonds."

She looked up, horrified. "But people could get killed."

"I think that was his plan. We'll be too busy hunting down and killing these creatures to worry about him."

"You can't kill them," Sandersohn said. "We must study them."

Alan glared at him. "You can study any loose bug parts you can find lying around, Doctor. I've seen these things in action. Any creature I see, I'm going to kill just as fast as I can. Now, I have to get you out of here and find a safe place to stash you. You can't go back up, and I have to reach the *Cerberus*." He turned to Eve. "You know these tunnels. Where's a good place to hide?"

She wrinkled her brow in thought before answering, "Each level has an emergency rescue shelter. There's one near here. It's airtight and has a week's supply of food, water, and oxygen for ten men. We could go there."

"Good. Lead the way."

As he followed Eve toward the shelter, he became concerned that they encountered no security guards. They should have already arrived. *Unless they're too busy elsewhere.* That unpleasant thought hurried his steps. He didn't know how much ammunition remained in the rifle, but he knew it wasn't enough to fight off a horde of giant carnivorous insects.

Relief flooded over him when he caught sight of the emergency shelter. With its wheel-operated airtight door and single observation window on the side, it resembled a six-meter-long, deep-sea decompression chamber. It sat snuggly in an alcove carved from the side of the mineshaft, protected from cave-ins by two steel beams supporting the rock ceiling above it. Four adjustable hydraulic chocks bore the weight of the beams. A steel rack beneath the window held four oxygen cylinders with flexible metal hoses attached to a regulator on the side of the shelter. For all that, it still managed to look claustrophobic. *Any port in a storm*, he decided.

He spun the wheel to open the door. A row of soft LED lights came on automatically, illuminating the functional but stark interior. Padded benches lined both walls of the rear of the shelter with blankets neatly stacked at one end of each bench. A storage cabinet stocked with bottles of water and packets of freeze-dried foods, similar to MREs took up most of the rear wall. A rack by the door held a dozen respirators, masks, and flashlights.

As Alan surveyed the shelter's contents, Eve said, "I hear something."

He stopped to listen, mystified by a fluttering sound growing louder. Something was coming their way. *Bats?* he asked himself, but dismissed the idea. It was too noisy for a bat. His sixth sense kicked into high gear. He stood aside and ushered the others inside, urging them to hurry. The two scientists politely waited for Eve, then followed her in. As he closed the door, from the corner of his eye he noticed two pairs of lacey wings rushing at him, attached to a meter-long dragonfly. He didn't have time to raise his rifle and fire, nor did he think he could hit it anyway. He swatted at the dragonfly with his hand but missed. It struck him in his chest, knocking him backwards into the shelter. He fell on his back, warding off the enormous dragonfly with his hands. He finally succeeded in gripping it around the thorax with both hands and tossing it away from him out the door. A giant spider leaped up from the ground and snatched it midair. It scurried away down the tunnel with its struggling prize.

As if he were a hurdle on a racecourse, Eve bounded over his prostrate body to pull the door shut. He crawled over to help. Claws reached around the edge of the door and raked his left wrist, leaving a long gash. He ignored the pain and helped her seal the door.

Something, or several somethings, began pounding on the door and trying to dig beneath the shelter, but the rock was too hard. He heard them scurrying back and forth, seeking a way in. By the vicious hisses and chirps, they were also busy fighting among themselves.

"Are you hurt?" Eve asked, her face flushed and breathing hard.

The wound burned, but didn't look too deep. Only a trickle of blood oozed from the cut. "Unless I catch some million-year-old flu bug, I'll be fine."

"Sit here," she said, guiding him to one of the benches.

She unzipped her jumpsuit to the waist, revealing a thin, white tank top that stopped just above her muscular midriff. Her breasts, barely concealed by the thin material, took his mind off his hand as she found a first-aid kit and began treating his wound. She was gentle but somewhat clumsy, her mind not focused on his wrist. The antiseptic she applied burned. When he groaned, she jumped and spilled most of it on the floor. He had to help her with the bandage when she wrapped his wrist so tightly it cut off the circulation. He noticed that she kept glancing out the window toward a deteriorated wooden door across from the shelter. She saw that he was watching her.

"Just beyond that door is where they sealed the shaft my husband is buried in," she said. Her eyes glistened with fresh tears.

Alan looked at the wooden door. "I don't guess there's a way out through there."

Eve shook her head. "No. When they saw it was going to take longer to dig through the rubble than they thought, they bored a shaft beyond the collapse from several levels above to supply air, but there is no other exit."

Alan sighed. "Then, I guess we sit tight until help comes."

"When might that be?" Doctor Tells sat on one of the benches wiping his glasses with his handkerchief.

"I'm not sure. I called the guards, and they're evacuating the mine, but they know we're down here. They'll get to us soon."

"Even through the insects?" Eve asked.

"They've got weapons."

Tells pointed his glasses at Alan. "My good man, these creatures have evolved for the last 250 million years beyond what they were at the end of the Paleozoic. Even then, they were the most vicious hunters of the eco system. They were the alpha predators – spiders the size of German Shepherd dogs, three-meter long centipedes, giant beetles and cockroaches, and flies as big as your fist. You simply do not understand of what these creatures are capable. They will not stop until they have eliminated what they perceive to be a threat to their colony."

"You make them sound intelligent."

"From the description Eve provided and the video she brought back, I believe they are, at least to a degree. They are at least as intelligent as dogs or cats, but much more deadly. I fear they will find a way out of the mines. Once on the surface in the open, they have all of Africa in which to breed. They could potentially wipe out most of the wildlife on the continent in a matter of years. We know so little about them, other than from a few scarce fossil remains."

"I'm more worried about us."

"If they breed as prolifically as do most insects, laying thousands of eggs, they could achieve a population so large as to pose a threat to mankind. Certainly here in Africa, where most people do not carry guns like you Americans."

"I thought you were eager to study them."

Till's face tightened. He drew himself up to his full height, which was slightly less than 5'7". "Study them, yes, but I do not want to be replaced by them."

Till's words sent a shiver down Alan's spine.

Sandersohn spoke up. "We have to get out of here and warn them. They'll try to herd the creatures like cattle back into the lava tube. They don't know how dangerous these things can be if cornered."

"Yes, I agree, but how?" Alan asked.

He peered out the window at a war scene fifty meters down the mineshaft. Groups of spiders and bands scorpions faced off like gangs in a turf war, hissing and chattering. Beetles raced in and out, attacking both sides indiscriminately. Hovering above the melee like a squadron of helicopters, the dragonflies swooped down and snatched bits of dead bug from the carnage.

"Not that way," he said. He nodded toward the wooden door in the tunnel wall. "That leaves this way."

"No, it's too dangerous," Eve cried.

"We can't stay here. The winners of the battle outside will eventually chew through the fiberglass walls of this shelter if they decide we might taste better than their fellow insects. We don't have much choice. Right now, they're ignoring us. That will soon change. We'll try the airshaft."

Eve slowly nodded her head, but she didn't look pleased with his decision. Alan picked up a pouch containing a respirator and dumped it out. When Eve saw him remove the dynamite from his shirt and place it in the bag, her eyes grew larger and her face paled.

"Dynamite? Are you crazy? You could bring the entire mine down on us."

"I may have to." He picked up his rifle and began unsealing the door. "I suggest you grab water, food, and extra flashlights." He opened the door a crack. No bugs were outside. The battle had moved farther down the tunnel. "I'll lead," he said.

He took a deep breath and stepped out of the shelter. He didn't know if he was making the right move, but he certainly didn't want to be around when the winners of the insect Battle Royale came to collect their purse.

Dry rot so badly damaged the door it looked ready to disintegrate at the first touch. However poor a barricade it was, he still preferred to keep it between him and the bugs. A rusty chain looped through a hole in the door attached to the staple part of a hasp secured to the equally rotten heavy-timber doorframe. He gripped the chain with both hands and tugged. The door squeaked. He paused, but the sound had gone unnoticed among the din of clicks, hisses, and clattering of the fight. The effort hurt his wrist, but he kept at it. He tugged harder, and the chain ripped the metal staple from the doorframe. The door, swollen in the wooden frame, resisted opening, but he persisted. With a final jerk, it finally gave. He pulled the door open, and a stack of lumber leaning precariously against the inside of the door collapsed with a loud crash. Instantly, the sounds of battle stopped and every compound eye in the mineshaft turned their direction.

"Run!" he yelled and pushed Eve inside the tunnel ahead of him. They had moved to the top of the insect menu.

13

July 5, 2016, 11:30 p.m. *Ngomo* Mine, 65 Level –
Five men worked with Pieter Wilhelmina in the new *adit,* a short side tunnel cut perpendicular to the ore face off Shaft C 211East. When the evacuation alarm sounded, he shut down the pneumatic drill he was operating and wiped his grimy, sweaty face on a rag as dirty as his face. With the thundering drill silent, the alarm clamored for his attention.

"Cave-in?" asked Lucas Bandile, Wilhelmina's Xhosa helper squatting next to the drill wrapping the water line attached to the drill to seal another leak.

The function of the fine mist of water spraying from the tip of the drill was to keep down the silica dust produced by drilling; great in theory, but it fell short in application. The ancient rubber hose leaked like a sieve. Most of the water ended up on the ground.

The dust caused *silicosis,* a deadly lung disease like Black Lung in coalmines. The company issued masks for protection, but they were uncomfortable and became coated in dust too quickly. Wilhelmina preferred to place his trust in God and in luck. Dust particles floating around Bandile's head sparkled in his headlamp beam, producing an aura. Shirtless in the heat, his jet-black torso glistened with beads of perspiration.

"I felt nothing," piped up tall, lanky Imbe Bhekithemba from the other side of the narrow shaft. The tall Zulu driller had to duck his head to avoid the low roof.

The other two men in the tunnel, both Zimbabwean immigrant laborers, glanced at one another nervously, but said nothing. They understood only one in five of the Bantu words spoken by Bandile and Bhekithemba and even fewer in Afrikaans. The mini-United Nations of workers Wilhelmina dealt with made the use of facial expressions and hand signals more important than language. When the others stopped working, the two Zimbabweans thought it was time to quit. They picked up their lunch pails, walked over to the half-loaded ore cart, and began pushing it back down the tunnel toward the main shaft. Wilhelmina stopped them with a shake of his head. They stopped and stood looking at each other in confusion.

"Well, whatever it is, we had best heed it." Wilhelmina took a big gulp from his water bottle. He was always surprised how thirsty a man could get when the air was almost damp enough to drink. The constant ninety-five-percent humidity and 48 degree Celsius temperature of the tunnel made working conditioners appalling, but it was a living. Too many men he knew had no jobs.

"Come," he said to the two Zimbabweans, crooking his arm and motioning them to follow, hoping they understood his meaning.

They heard the first screams as they entered the main tunnel. Bandile stopped and looked around, frightened. "What was that?"

Wilhelmina shrugged. "*Hamba,*" he said in Bantu, urging Bandile to go see.

"*Hhayibo,*" Bandile replied, shaking his head emphatically, and then repeated in English, "No way."

Wilhelmina smiled at Bandile's reluctance. Maybe he had trained the eager driller's helper right after all. "I'll look," he said.

He walked to the first bend of the tunnel, stopped, and stared dumbfounded at the spectacle in front of him. Dozens of the biggest spiders he had ever seen swarmed over two workers struggling on the ground. The nightmarish spiders were scaly and bristling with short, wiry hairs protruding from kitchen sink-sized round bodies, which attached to eight spindly, meter-long legs folded until they rose above the creatures' backs. The spiders repeatedly jabbed their fangs into the workers. As he watched in revulsion, the men's struggles slowly ceased. Then, the spiders began wrapping the men with silk extruded from twin spinnerets on their abdomen, rolling the bodies over with their legs as they spun silken threads.

As if giant spiders weren't enough, a dragonfly as long as his arm flew by on iridescent golden wings. One of the spiders leapt into the air, grabbed it, and dragged it to the ground. It immediately began enfolding it in the web with one of the men.

"What the fuck?" he mumbled, and then jumped in fright when

Bandile brushed up against his back. He glanced at Bandile, whose dark face was turning pale at the horrible sight. "We have to go."

"Go where? The elevator is that way." Bandile nodded past the creatures.

Wilhelmina tried to think. There had to be another way out. "The ventilator shaft," he remembered. "We can climb down to the next level."

Bandile stared at him. "Why not climb up and out?

"Because of the ventilator fan above us," he reminded him.

Bandile licked his lips nervously and nodded. "Okay."

The others were watching them from a safe distance. They had not seen the spiders, but they knew from the tenseness in Wilhelmina and Bandile's voices that something was wrong.

"We go," Wilhelmina said to them. Noting the fear in his face, they didn't question him, but followed mutely.

The ventilator shaft was a meter-and-a half-wide vertical opening drilled through the rock, connecting with a maze of similar airshafts regulating the temperature in the mine. A metal ladder inside the shaft provided an emergency exit. It was Wilhelmina's idea to reach the ore skip elevator three levels below them and ride it to the surface. The problem was that the shaft did not connect directly with the skip loading room. They would have to reach it in a roundabout manner.

He led the way down the airshaft, climbing hand over hand as quickly as he could. He wasn't quick enough. The first scream reached him from above just as he entered a second, horizontal airshaft.

He stuck his head out into the vertical shaft and shouted, "What's happening?"

Bhekithemba, sliding down the ladder using only hands and feet, almost landed on his head. He pushed past Wilhelmina with a look of abject horror on his gaunt face, slid into the horizontal airshaft, and scrambled down it on his hands and knees. Bandile stood on the ladder a few meters above the opening staring back up the shaft. Another scream followed the first. Bandile grimaced and began descending the ladder as fast as he could.

When he reached Wilhelmina, he said, "The two Zimbabweans did not make it. Spiders got them. We must hurry."

Wilhelmina was tempted to look back up the shaft to judge how much time they had but restrained himself. "Come on," he said and crawled after Bhekithemba.

They soon reached a shaft with a ninety-degree slope, a chute for delivering the ore to the skip elevator room over fifty meters below. Wilhelmina heard the grinding and squealing of the cable-driven skip elevator responsible for delivering the 3.3 tons of ore to the surface necessary to extract an ounce of glittering gold. In his ten years in the mine, he had yet to see a single gold nugget.

Without looking back to see if anyone was following, Bhekithemba entered the chute first, spreading his long arms and legs against the rock walls to slow his descent. Wilhelmina shoved Bandile in after him. Both men were younger and more athletic than he was. He didn't want to slow them down. He dropped his legs over the side and crossed himself. Reciting the names of the saints, he loosened his grip and dropped. He was soon glad for his heavy work gloves, as friction began to heat up his hands. He didn't bother slowing down. What was following them was far worse than minor friction burns on his hands and butt cheeks.

He slid out of the shaft and hit a pile of rock hard enough to jar his teeth. He rolled off the ore onto the raised steel-grate walkway and bounced into arms of Bandile. Bandile said something to him as he set him down, but he couldn't understand him over the noise of the skip elevator. He looked down into the grinding gears of the conveyor pulley on the opposite side of the walkway and was glad Bandile had been there.

He searched for Bhekithemba, but he was nowhere in sight. As he tried to catch his breath, he saw Bandile's eyes go wide with fright. He spun on his heel and saw one of the spiders drop to the pile of ore attached to a silk thread as thick as a clothesline. He grabbed a large chunk of ore from the floor and threw it at the spider with all his strength. Luck was with him. He missed the spider but hit a rock beneath it, dislodging it. He smiled as the spider tumbled into the opening. Yellow liquid squirted from its smashed body as the gears ground it into pulp.

As the pair raced for the skip elevator, a blood-curdling scream stopped them in their tracks. They entered the loading room cautiously. Spider webs festooned the entire room from roof to floor and draped over the front-end loader used to scoop up ore from the pile and deposit it in the line of moving buckets. Dangling from the webs were bundles Wilhelmina knew instinctively were humans, the loader crew. Spiders crawled over the web, some clinging to the bundles with their front legs with their mouths buried in the bundles. Wilhelmina felt sick to his stomach.

The scream had come from Bhekithemba. Half a dozen spiders had backed the big Zulu against one wall, and he was using a length of pipe to beat them back. One lay crushed beside him. Another oozed yellow ichor from its back and wobbled unsteadily as it moved, but there were too many of them. Bhekithemba saw Wilhelmina.

"Help me!" he screamed.

Wilhelmina looked around for a weapon to help him but saw nothing. More spiders were moving toward the Zulu from the sides like a pride of stalking lions, trying to surround him. He spied the open ore bucket ascending from below and wavered between rushing to safety and helping his co-worker. Bandile made his decision for him, grabbing him by the arm, and dragging him to the waiting skip elevator. He didn't resist. Spiders noticed them and began scuttling toward the elevator. Wilhelmina knew they weren't going to make it.

A sudden chill enveloped him, like an icy hand reaching inside his body and clutching his spine. Instantly, as one, the spiders turned to face the other direction. They became agitated, bouncing up and down on their legs, and then raced away down the tunnel. Whatever had frightened them was getting closer. He could feel it in his mind, growing like a dark cloud pregnant with lightning building to a summer thunderstorm. Most frightening of all, he knew the presence sensed him as well.

A creature entered the room, an ebony carpet sliding across the floor on hundreds of tiny legs. It paused for a moment, staring at the men with two large compound eyes almost as black as its body; then, began rising from the floor, heaving itself into a four-meter tower of dark terror scraping the ceiling. The dark orbs regarded the men leisurely, its hunger almost palpable in its intense insect gaze. Wilhelmina's bladder let go. He felt warm urine running down his leg, but he felt no shame. Men could not face such horrors. What did courage or strength matter to such a primordial creature? He felt a tickle in his mind and tried to fight it, but it was too strong. Had Bhekithemba across the room not chosen that moment to move, he knew he would have fallen into the dark abyss from which there could be no return.

The ebony creature swept across the floor and enveloped the Zulu in writhing bands of black. The tiny, needle-like legs punctured his flesh in a hundred places. His screams roused Wilhelmina from his trance. Bandile shoved him into the elevator bucket. He cast one last forlorn look at Bhekithemba, who had now stopped fighting and stood like a black statue, one eye visible through his shroud, watching him, accusing him of cowardice. The Zulu's blood ran down his body in crimson streams. Almost in a convulsion, the creature embracing him wrung his body dry of blood, its black carapace soaking it up like a sponge. Wilhelmina swallowed hard and made a move to help the Zulu. Bandile grabbed him and pulled him back.

"You will die," he warned.

As the bucket slowly groaned up the cables, Wilhelmina closed his eyes and fell to his knees sobbing, partially from abandoning Bhekithemba to his doom, but mostly out of joy that he had escaped Bhekithemba's grisly fate.

14

July 6, 2016, 2:05 a.m.   *Ngomo* Mine, 134 Level –

Alan frantically piled lumber, rocks, pieces of rusty machinery – anything he could find – against the flimsy wooden door. Eve helped him, handing him items she rushed around to pick up. He wondered if he looked as frightened as she did. Her eyes had the faraway look of someone not fully in the present, but to her credit, she didn't freeze or run. Her courage inspired him. His hands shook like a bartender with a cocktail shaker, and his feet did a two-step any square dance caller would be proud of as he fought the urge to run away, but he swallowed his fear and kept working.

Outside the rattling door, the horde of insects forgot their territorial disputes, and now concentrated their little bug minds on the removal of the only obstacle standing between them and food. They chewed, scratched, and propelled their bodies against the rotten wood. Powdered wood floated in the beam of Alan's light.

"Will it hold?" Sandersohn asked, as he watched the thin boards of the door bend inward.

"Not for long," Alan admitted.

"This was a stupid idea," he yelled at Alan. He held his clenched fists against the side of his head and closed his eyes, as if not seeing the door would make the threat go away.

"You could have stayed in the emergency shelter and taken your chances," Alan shot at him.

Sandersohn didn't hear him. He was repeatedly moaning, "We're going to die. We're going to die."

The frightened scientist's quick capitulation to death made Alan angry. "If you're so eager to die, stay here by the door and guard it while I get the hell out of here. Maybe you'll slow them down." His ire vented, he turned to Eve, "Where do we go from here?"

She took a moment to get her bearings. Alan suspected the tunnel was conjuring the ghost of her dead husband, but she would have to set that memory aside for the moment. He needed her in the here and now.

She nodded her head, as if convincing herself she was right. "The air shaft is about two hundred meters down the tunnel."

Alan led the way. As they hurried down the tunnel, the geologist side of his mind noted the brittle rock formations. The shaft would need massive supporting pillars and crossbeams to sustain a viable mining operation. No wonder Verkhoen had abandoned it. The *Cerberus* would be extremely effective in such soft rock formations, reinforcing the walls with the spun casing it produced.

They came to the cave-in. Snapped beams protruded from piles of rubble like broken bones. The path became a narrow, winding defile excavated through the rubble.

"This was the first collapse," Eve pointed out. "It took twenty hours to carefully dig through the rubble. The roof kept collapsing on the workers. The entire time, I half-expected to see Frederick's body beneath each stone they removed, but he and his crew were in an adit farther down and perpendicular to the main shaft."

Alan picked up a stone. It was brittle and friable, crumbling in his hand with only slight pressure. "This entire zone is unsafe. No amount of shoring could keep it stable in the event of even a moderate tremor."

Eve nodded. "That's what Verkhoen decided in the end. He simply abandoned the shaft and sealed it."

Alan located the airshaft by a slight breeze stirring the layer of dust on the floor. He swept the beam upwards. The tiny, round hole bored in the roof of the tunnel dashed his hopes of escape. The airshaft was less than two feet wide, barely sixty centimeters. Disappointed, he probed the shaft with the light; then turned to Eve.

"You and Doctor Sandersohn might be able to squeeze through. I'm afraid Doctor Tells is a bit too big in the belly, and I'm too broad shouldered to fit."

Tells smiled. "Don't apologize, young man. I freely admit I am fat. I have not regretted that fact overly much until now."

"It's three-hundred meters to the next level," Eve protested.

"There's no ladder. I could never make it."

Sandersohn eyed the narrow opening and became forlorn. He shook his head as well. "I am too claustrophobic for the climb. Only the thrill of discovering a new species brought me down the elevator. Even fear cannot force me up such a tiny hole. I'm afraid I would panic and kill myself or someone else."

Alan sighed. He tried to hide his disappointment. He might be able to shimmy up the hole if he pulled his arms in tight, but not while carrying the rifle and the dynamite, and he was reluctant to abandon either one. He couldn't desert the elderly Doctor Tells. Now, with the others refusing to try, it looked like a bust all around.

"What about the lower tunnel?"

"It's flooded," Eve reminded him.

"It was six years ago. Rock is permeable. It might have drained by now. Can we reach it from here?"

She shook her head. "No."

"Well, we can't go back." His head was pounding and his wrist throbbed. He leaned against the wall and closed his eyes to calm down.

"There's a place to rest a little farther down the tunnel," Eve said.

With their choices dwindling, they continued down the tunnel and entered a chamber created by widening the tunnel.

"What's this?" Alan asked, shining his light about.

"It was a ready room," Eve explained. "They used it to store drilling equipment, carts – things like that." She pointed to some wooden benches along one wall. "Let's rest awhile."

Alan continued scanning the walls and discovered an opening. "Where does this go?"

Eve sat down and leaned against the wall with her shoulders slumped. "It is a dead end. They made a second attempt to reach Frederick from here, but it, too, failed." She lowered her head and brushed a tear from her eye. When she looked up, she was more composed, but the anguish remained.

Alan noticed Tells breathing hard. The running had been rough on him. "You three rest," he suggested. "I'll look around."

He continued down the tunnel leading to the second cave-in. The shaft ran straight for several hundred meters before beginning a series of sharp bends. At each curve, the miners had left a pillar of rock intact to help support the walls and roof. If the rock stratum had not been so brittle, it might have held. Piles of rock lay along the floor of the tunnel, shaken from the roof by small tremors since the cave-in. When he saw the main roof collapse, he knew why rescue had been impossible. Tons of rock and slabs of stone blocked the tunnel, some weighing over a ton. As he examined the collapse, something about its odd symmetry caught his attention. He stared at the rubble for several minutes before finally realizing what was wrong.

"The right-hand wall went first," he said aloud. "Then the roof gave way. It doesn't make sense."

He poked through the rubble near the wall and spotted something protruding from beneath a rock. He picked it up and examined it, recognizing it as blasting wire, the wire that carried electrical current from a detonator to the blasting cap.

His chest tightened. "This was deliberate. Someone wanted to bring down the roof. That was why Verkhoen stopped any further attempts at rescue. He didn't want anyone to find this." He paused to let the implications sink in. "Eve's husband was murdered."

He stuck the wire in his pocket as evidence. If he managed to get out alive, he would see Verkhoen pay for his crime. As he started back to the others, he felt air brush his cheek. He scanned the roof but saw no airshaft. Shining his light along the floor, he spotted a two-meter-long crack several centimeters wide running along the floor. Pressing his cheek to the crack, he felt a rush of cool, moist air. He took off his belt and slipped it down into the fissure. It continued unimpeded until it reached the buckle. Shining his light down the fissure, he saw it widened the deeper it went. He knew it couldn't be a natural fault. There was another tunnel below him. An earthquake sometime in the last few years had cracked the thin shell of rock separating the two tunnels. If he could widen the opening, it might provide an exit.

He went back to the others and informed them of his discovery. Eve looked skeptical. "It must be the flooded tunnel."

"It was flooded several years ago. It might have drained since then. It's our only chance," he said. He set down his pouch and began removing dynamite.

"Wait a minute," Sandersohn cautioned when he saw the dynamite. "You don't seriously intend to detonate that stuff. It might bring down the entire tunnel on our heads."

"It's a possibility," he admitted, "but as I see it, the only other way out is the way we came, and it won't take long for those insects to get through that rotten door."

Sandersohn nodded. "I see your point."

"Look, I've handled explosives before. The fissure widens deeper down. All I need do is crack open the surface with a small, controlled blast."

He didn't add that dynamite was not very good for controlled blasts. He would have to guess at how much to use and hope for the best. He tied two sticks together, what he thought would be enough, inserted a blasting cap in one, and began cutting a length of fuse with his knife.

"Is that long enough?" Eve asked, eying with apprehension the short fuse he had measured out.

He held up the fuse. "This is fast-burning Visco fuse. It burns at twenty-four seconds per foot. That's thirty-point-five centimeters to you. I brought about ten feet of cord. That gives us a little less than four minutes of burn time. I want to keep some for later, just in case." He didn't mention his intention to seal the *Cerberus* shaft with his remaining dynamite. "Five feet gives me about two minutes. A few seconds one way or the other doesn't matter much."

He jammed the fuse into the end of the blasting cap and crimped it with his teeth.

"Stay here and take cover. The bends in the shaft should dampen the blast. After the explosion, wait a minute or two to make sure there's no aftershock, and join me." He dropped the pouch beside Eve. "Keep this here, but bring it with you when you come."

"What if this doesn't work?"

"We'll be dead and the bugs won't matter." He leaned closer to her and whispered, "If I don't come back, try the airshaft. Don't worry about the others."

She surprised him by kissing him on the lips. "Please come back."

It seemed more than a simple good luck kiss, and he enjoyed it. He smiled at her. "For more of that, I will."

She looked at him with a pleading smile, reached out, and touched his hand for a moment. "Be careful, Alan."

He nodded.

When he reached the fissure, he placed the bundle of dynamite just inside the fissure in what he judged as the weakest spot. He jammed it in place using a flat rock as a wedge. He ran the five feet of fuse as far as it would reach. To his eye, it looked pitifully short. He considered using the entire length of fuse, but he still wanted to seal the *Cerberus* shaft. He wondered how much distance he could cover in two minutes, dodging piles of rock and debris. He piled rocks on top of the fissure to contain as much of the blast as possible.

One detail he had omitted when describing his plan to the others – he had no way to determine if the tunnel contained a pocket of methane. If it did, the resulting explosion could sweep through the tunnel, killing them all.

"I'm ready to blast!" he yelled to the others. He ignited his Zippo lighter and lit the fuse. It burst into a furious flame that raced along its length at an alarming rate. He raced down the tunnel, counting backwards from one-twenty in his head.

At ten, he decided not to push his luck and looked for cover. As he knelt behind a pile of rocks he hoped suitable for the task, the floor of the tunnel heaved, slamming his head into the wall with enough force to draw blood. The sound of the blast roared down the tunnel, just ahead of a wave of hot air. A billowing cloud of dust and smoke followed, almost choking him. Rocks rained from the ceiling, bouncing off his head and landing all around him, but none big enough to cause more than a bruise hit him. He wished he had grabbed a hardhat from the emergency shelter. The roof and the walls groaned menacingly for thirty seconds but held.

He waited a full minute longer before leaving his shelter. The air was still thick with dust, making seeing difficult, but he hadn't brought the entire roof down on the fissure. For that bit of luck, he was grateful. He examined his handiwork. The tiny fissure was now a fracture several meters long and a meter wide. The flashlight couldn't penetrate the thick dust far enough to see the bottom, but cooler, moist, stale air rushed up to wash over his face. As he waited for the dust to clear, he heard the others approaching, coughing from the dust. Their hardhat lamps were three faint smudges in the darkness. By the time they arrived, the dust had cleared enough to see the floor of another tunnel less than three meters below. He saw no water.

He called to the others. "The tunnel is dry."

Eve appeared from the darkness, wiping dust from her eyes with her clenched hands. She left a white ring around her hazel eyes, giving her a raccoon appearance. He tried to hide his smile. Tells came next and stared down into the hole.

"I'll never be able to climb down there," he protested.

"I'll go down first," Alan said. "The others can help guide your feet to my shoulders, and I'll lower you to the ground."

Tells looked dubious. "If you say so."

Alan dropped through the hole. Once on the ground, he helped the less nimble Tells down. The overweight scientist moved clumsily, poking him in the eye with his foot; then almost fell on top of him, but after a little effort, he got him safely on the ground. Eve followed, clinging to him longer than necessary, but he didn't mind the close contact. Her breasts rubbed against him through her thin shirt, making it difficult to keep his mind on what he was doing. From her smile, he wondered if she had done it on purpose.

Sandersohn, nimbler than he looked, grabbed the edge of the fissure, dangled over the side for a moment, and dropped to the ground. "Which way?" he asked.

"The main tunnel is this way," Eve replied, pointing down the tunnel.

Alan examined the tunnel. He picked up a piece of rock and studied it by the light of the flashlight. "I thought you said this level had been flooded."

Eve looked at him queerly. "Yes, it was."

Alan tossed the rock aside. "I don't see any evidence of flooding here."

"Maybe it flooded farther down the tunnel."

"The floor is level. It wouldn't pool."

"Why would Verkhoen ...?"

"Can we discuss this later?" Sandersohn asked. "Let's get out of here."

Alan led the way, treading carefully over and around piles of loose rock that had fallen from the roof, some of it loosened by his blast. He searched the tunnel walls as they went, looking for some watermark or other indication the tunnel had been underwater, but it looked like the rest of the tunnel – dry. His light fell on an object ahead of them. He stopped.

"Wait here a minute while I check this out," he advised them.

As he neared the object, he had a sinking suspicion he knew what it was – a skeleton. Shining his light along the tunnel, he found four more, all dismembered, some with bones missing. He knelt beside one of the skeletons covered only with the tattered remnants of a jumpsuit. A dust-covered hardhat lay a few feet away. The skeleton was missing a leg and one hand. Like the other skeletons, the bones showed signs of gnawing. If not for their present situation, he might have written off the marks as post-mortem rat teeth marks. Now, he wasn't sure.

On the ground beside the body lay a small box that had fallen out through a hole in the decaying jumpsuit. He picked it up, looked inside, and found a tarnished gold ring, not something an ordinary miner would carry. He picked up the hardhat and wiped off a layer of dried mud concealing a metal nameplate – Frederick Means, Eve's husband.

"What is it?" Eve called out.

"I believe I've found your husband's remains," he said.

She was silent a long moment before answering. "No, that can't be. My husband died trapped in the tunnel above. Verkhoen assured me. This tunnel was flooded. That was why they couldn't use it to rescue him from below."

Alan was now beginning to have doubts about Verkhoen's honesty. First, the lava tube, and now a dry tunnel that should have been flooded. It sounded as if Eve was also suspicious. He held out the ring and saw the faint trace of an inscription etched inside the band covered by the oxidization.

"I found this."

Eve stared at the ring for a long moment before accepting it. She turned it over in her hand, squinting to read the writing. She scratched away some of the corrosion with her fingernail, read, "Were I your Adam and you my Eve," and gasped sharply. Fighting back a tear, she said, "Frederick said that to me once." She walked over to his body, looked down at the bones, and asked them, "Oh, Frederick! What happened?"

Frederick could not answer her question, so Alan tried. "I think they were trapped above and came down here just as we did through another crack, or perhaps they dug through trying to escape, but the insects found them."

Eve stared at him incredulous, "But, but that was four years ago."

"The miners must have punched through into the lava tube when they opened this shaft six years ago, just as *Cerberus* did." He made a rapid mental calculation. "Given the lava tube's twelve-degree slope, it should intersect this tunnel about two kilometers from where the *Cerberus* punched through. The miners lost six years ago probably suffered the same fate as your husband."

Eve groaned. Alan kicked himself mentally for suggesting insects had devoured her husband, though the condition of the skeleton made it likely.

"Yet Verkhoen tried again two years later, this time using my husband." She looked at Alan with equal parts of sorrow and rage on her face. "This tunnel wasn't flooded, was it?"

He shook his head. "No, I don't believe so. Verkhoen discovered the two miners' bodies six years ago but couldn't explain the condition of their bodies. He probably refused to let anyone examine them before burying them. Then, he deliberately concocted the phony flooding story and sealed the tunnel to keep anyone from finding out what had really happened."

"Why would Verkhoen lie? We could have reached my husband through this tunnel."

"He knew the discovery that the tunnel wasn't flooded would start an investigation into the previous deaths that would halt further digging in the area." He pulled out the piece of wire he had found. "I think someone deliberately collapsed the tunnel above using explosives. Someone wanted your husband trapped or dead and didn't want them rescued."

"Verkhoen," she hissed. "My husband warned me he was reporting Verkhoen's dangerous efforts to dig into the friable rock to the Board of Directors. Verkhoen is too vain to allow my husband to jeopardize his career."

"If it wasn't him, he had it done."

"Duchamps." She spat out the name as if it tasted foul. "Nothing happens in this mine that Mr. Lion Tamer Duchamps isn't aware of."

That had been Alan's thoughts as well when he first met the security chief. Eve's nickname for Duchamps intrigued him. "Where did that come from?"

"He likes to tell everyone his scar is from a lion attack, but the rumor is that a fellow officer in the SADF cut him in a knife fight. That's why they kicked him out."

"So the security chief is a disgraced former South African Defense Force officer. That might explain his bitterness."

"He's a right bastard, but it's Verkhoen I want to see in jail," she replied.

"I've got enough circumstantial evidence to turn the spotlight on him, but we need Duchamps' testimony to turn the key on his cell door."

She nodded, still staring at her husband's bones. To the others, he said, "Help me cover these remains, please."

Eve noticed her husband's iPad lying next to his body. She picked it up and brushed it off. The screen was cracked and the battery case punctured. A memory stick jutted from the USB port. "Frederick always used a backup," she said. She removed the memory stick and shoved it in her pocket.

When they finished with the makeshift graves, they stood silently over five small piles of rocks that barely resembled true graves. Eve spoke a few words. As she did, she unconsciously rubbed the ring that Alan had found between her thumb and index finger, but she didn't put it on. Alan wondered if having broken her ties with her dead husband years ago, she was afraid placing the ring on her finger would re-commit her to his memory.

Alan's mind was on Verkhoen. The Van Gotts CEO had been aware of the existence of the insects or at least the existence of something dangerous inhabiting the mine for six years; and yet, he had offered no warning. In fact, he had made a second failed attempt to reach the gold-bearing stratum from a new shaft. Had he murdered Frederick Means to assure his silence? He had no doubts that Duchamps was capable of such a reprehensible act. He had murdered Bill Bakkerman in cold blood after first forcing him to unplug the lava tube by moving *Cerberus*. Dozens would likely die before they could evacuate the mine.

So much death over a few diamonds.

After a few minutes, Sandersohn spoke up. "I don't mean to seem uncaring, but if Frederick Means and the other miners were killed by these creatures, another opening into the lava tube must exist. I suggest we leave before more of the creatures find us."

Alan nodded. "You're right. We should go." He looked at Eve. She brushed a tear away, placed the ring on her finger, and smiled.

"Yes, we should go now. I've had four years to grieve. It is good to see him finally at rest. Thank you for that."

They walked a kilometer down the tunnel. Alan hoped they were near the entrance. He didn't feel well. He looked down at his throbbing left hand. Blood and a cream-colored liquid oozed through the bandage. He peeled it back to examine the wound. The gash was red and puffy around the edges, and the flesh was very tender to the touch. He hoped he was not succumbing to some quarter-million-year old bacteria. He brushed his forehead with the back of his hand and found it was warm.

Abruptly, things got worse. A rock fall had sealed the tunnel. Piles of rock and debris blocked their way. He tapped on the rocks experimentally.

"It sounds solid. I don't think we can dig through."

"The door is only a few meters away," Eve moaned.

He felt her anguish. They were so close, but they were trapped. He didn't think it would be long before the insects found them. Doctor Tells leaned against the wall. His face was ashen, and he was breathing hard. Alan was concerned about him. He was an old man. The climbing and walking were taking a toll on him.

"What are our options?" Eve asked.

Alan could think of only one. "We have to go the other direction and hope this tunnel still opens to the lava tube. From there, we can make our way back to the *Cerberus* and out."

Sandersohn was aghast. "Go in there *with* these monsters? I thought we were trying to escape them."

Eve looked distressed at the idea as well.

"Look, I don't know what else to do," he said, exasperated that he was making all the decisions. "If the way to the lava tube is open, the insects could easily get to us here. Maybe, just maybe, most of them left the lava tube seeking, er, better feeding grounds."

Tells grimaced. "I don't know if I can make it, but I'm willing to try. We can't remain here. There is no telling when we might be rescued, and, confidentially, I place no trust in Verkhoen's searching for us."

Eve nodded. She had a very determined look in her eye. "I agree. We can't trust Verkhoen."

Alan shrugged. "As long as you know the risks. Once we get to the *Cerberus*, I might be able to change the odds in our favor with its laser."

"How many bullets do you have left?" Sandersohn asked.

Alan removed the magazine and checked. "About half a clip – maybe sixteen rounds."

Sandersohn turned and began walking back down the tunnel in the direction from which they had just come. "I hope it is enough."

Alan silently agreed.

The little troop followed the tunnel to its end and found the hole through which the insects had originally entered from the lava tube six years earlier. The opening was little more than a narrow crevice, a fault line traversing the soft Kimberlite conglomerate formation. The low roof forced them to squat, but in some areas, the roof dropped low enough to force them to squirm through on their bellies. It was hot, exhausting work crawling through the bowels of the earth. The effort was taking its toll on him. The hot air baked his lungs. The others were breathing equally as hard behind him. Doctor Tells, because of his age, especially suffered. He lagged farther and farther behind.

Alan's swollen hand throbbed constantly from the additional pressure of traversing the crack on his hands and knees. If not for the fact that he could not turn around in the close confines, he might have given up and returned to the mineshaft. After half an hour, the crack opened up wider, making it easier to negotiate. It intersected the lava tube halfway up the wall. He tumbled out and helped the others down.

The lava tube was more level and wider than where the *Cerberus* had entered it. When he saw the huge stalactites hanging from the ceiling, he decided they were in a cavern instead of the lava tube.

"Stay here," he told the others as he went to explore.

He walked deeper into the cavern, moving quietly to soften his footsteps. He traveled less than two hundred meters when he heard the sound of water dripping. He turned off the flashlight and crept forward. The cavern dropped off into a deep depression, a sort of basin. He estimated the cavern's diameter at over ten kilometers, an enormous volume of open space for so deep in the earth where the pressure of the surrounding rock fought to squeeze it out of existence.

Large patches of bioluminescent lichen on the walls and roof illuminated the cavern well enough to see that it was not the way out, but it was impressive. The roof of the cavern was a hundred meters above his head, supported by three enormous pillars of granite. Mounds of bioluminescent growth resembling fungi covered the floor of the cavern. From it, pale white horsetail ferns sprouted. Tall, spindly trees grew in tight clusters. They, too, were pale and colorless. From what source the plants drew their nourishment he couldn't venture a guess, though their lack of color suggested it was not from sunlight. Odd growths on the trunks might have been *epiphytes,* non-parasitical plants that fed on the air. It was possible they supplied nourishment to the host plants in a bizarre colonial organism arrangement. Eve would know. Perhaps he should fetch the others to witness the wonder of the underground world.

Languid pools of water dotted the floor of the cavern, some hundreds of meters wide. Other than the steady drip of water from the roof, the cavern was unnaturally silent, the air strangely empty of flying insects. No beetles, spiders, or other giant creatures were visible, though he did see many abandoned spider webs. Occasionally, the surface of the pools moved in swirling patterns, but whether from some creature beneath the surface or from the natural release of gases, he couldn't tell.

A few splashes of color mingled with the grays and greens, some of the earliest flowers. The attar of their scent mingled with the cloying odor of petrochemicals and decaying plants, and the mating and identifying stench of the giant insects.

He examined the rocks, mostly obsidian, feldspar, and granite – volcanic rocks. He was standing inside a gigantic empty magma chamber. Craning his neck upward, he could see the opening of the volcanic throat, now long plugged by solidified magma. The chamber and lava tubes had been a sealed environment until the *Cerberus* had broken through.

Vince was more right than he dreamed, Alan thought, smiling at Vince's fixation on Burroughs. He couldn't believe all the creatures had fled the lava tube or that none had returned. It made no sense. Then, he noticed something strange. Along one side of the cavern, near a series of small openings, thousands of giant snail and mollusk shells lay in piles many meters high. Bits and pieces of spider and beetle carapaces, legs, and mandibles lay strewn about as if periodically pushed from the openings. The smell of death and decay permeated the air.

In spite of the obvious absence of the *mandibulates*, he knew he wasn't alone. Another presence filled the cavern, dark, ominous, and foreboding. It scratched at the edges of his mind, attempting to enter his thoughts. Now he knew why the insects were so eager to escape the cavern. The cavern system had a top predator, an alpha feeder, and their numbers had sustained it for eons. He had no desire to meet it. He beat a hasty retreat to the others.

"What now?" Eve asked.

"We see if the *Cerberus* is in the tunnel," he said.

"If not?" Tells asked out of breath.

Alan studied Tells in the light of his flashlight. His cheeks looked hollow in spite of his pudginess. The scientist's age was telling on him. He wished he could stop and allow him to rest, but it seemed more critical than ever to get back as quickly as possible.

He sighed before answering Tells' question as honestly as he could with, "I don't know." He rubbed the back of his hand. He was certain it was infected, but he could do very little about it. He kept moving.

The unusual geology of the cavern and lava tube system fascinated him. He studied the formations as he walked. The lava tube branched off into many smaller tubes they had no time to explore. The lava tubes and magma chamber could have covered hundreds of square kilometers, providing pockets of biospheres for creatures other than the giant insects. Eve noticed his interest and began asking him questions. He suspected her attempt at conversation was to keep her from dwelling on her fears, or maybe it was to keep him from worrying about his hand. Either way, it helped pass the time.

"What are the rocks with the speckles of quartz in them?"

"Granite and diorite. Both are igneous rocks from intrusive lava flows."

"Intrusive? You mean they bothered someone?" She smiled.

He appreciated her attempt at humor. "No. Intrusive lava flows underground. It cools slowly, forming a crystalline matrix, creating tiny crystals in granite and feldspar. Extrusive lava cools more quickly above ground. It forms rocks like basalt or obsidian. If it ejects from a volcano violently, it mixes with air and gases to become pumice."

"So this cavern is granite."

"Most of it. It's riddled with kimberlite, the diamond-bearing igneous rock we saw in the lava tube. Kimberlite is an extrusive rock buried, along with the volcano, millions of years ago. This particular kimberlite is very brittle. That's the problem your husband tried to warn Verkhoen about."

"At times, after he died, I was so angry at him, pissed off at his selfishness."

Her eyes were damp with tears, but her anger was real, confusing him. "Selfishness?"

"That he cared more about the mine and the miners than he did me. I warned him about Verkhoen, but he wouldn't listen. I know he wasn't selfish. It just seemed that way on my darker days."

"I think the ring proves he loved you."

She glanced away. "Yes, it does."

A noise, like the slithering of a blanket across rocks echoed down the lava tube. Eve glanced up at him, frightened. "What did you see back there?"

He avoided answering but picked up the pace. When he saw the familiar hole of the *Cerberus* tunnel, he dared to hope they might make it out alive.

Sandersohn saw it too and said, "Thank God. I'm exhausted."

Tells, too tired to speak, simply nodded in agreement.

When they got closer, Alan's heart sank. He knew Duchamps had forced Bill to move the *Cerberus* back away from the opening. Now, someone had moved it forward again, blocking the tunnel. It had to have been Trace.

Then, he saw Verkhoen.

Give me a friggin' break, he muttered.

15

July 6, 2016, 3:15 a.m.   *Ngomo* Mine, 30 Level –
Things had gone unnaturally silent in the mine. The alarm klaxon had ceased its shrill, pulsating shriek, and over an hour had passed since Duchamps had last heard a scream. He ventured out of his hiding place and proceeded down the tunnel with caution, alert for any sounds of insects approaching. The four knapsacks of diamonds weighed approximately sixty kilos. At .2 grams per carat, that meant he carried twelve thousand carats of raw diamonds. Dragging the heavy bundles with one hand and keeping the R4 automatic in the other was difficult, but he feared the insect swarms he had released enough to keep it handy. He had two magazines left and hoped it was enough.

The silence in the mine was unnerving. The constant heavy throbbing of machinery and the pulsing hammering of the drills was absent. As he neared a junction of corridors, an army of spiders appeared from a side shaft, but they ignored him. Spider silk formed a cottony tunnel down one shaft. Sheets of it draped the walls and roof. The thick strands of silk reduced the tunnel lights to small blobs of dim iridescent haze punctuated by pools of darkness. It created a surreal Fun House effect, but there was nothing funny about the squirming, silk-wrapped bundles dangling from the ceiling like ripe fruit. He paled as he realized their contents. Several of the spiders fed from the bundles. He turned his head away in disgust.

He cursed his bad luck. He couldn't reach the elevator the same way he had come, and he didn't have enough ammunition to shoot his way through the spiders. He berated himself for not moving more quickly and beating the creatures to the elevator. He would have to go around. He had no other choice. He couldn't climb half a kilometer of airshafts carrying the diamonds, and he wouldn't leave them behind, not after the price he had paid to obtain them.

He chose a tunnel that would lead him back to the #3 elevator in a roundabout manner. Dragging the heavy load down the long tunnel, he wished he hadn't abandoned the electric cart so quickly. Twice, he shot beetles and spiders that ventured too close and a giant dragonfly swooping at his head. He passed dozens of bodies, some partially consumed by beetles and other horrors, some wrapped in silk, ready for collection by spiders. To the creatures from the lava tube, the mine provided a smorgasbord of delicacies. For millions of years, they had eaten each other. Now they had a new source of food, one of which they were making good use. *Everyone likes a change of diet every now and then,* he mused.

One bundle attached to the wall by a thick silken cord moved slightly. A partially concealed face he recognized stared up at him, one of his security guards. The man's eyes were wide with fright, but he couldn't speak and could wiggle only a few fingers. Duchamps took out his knife and cut the silk away from the guard's head.

"Hello, Mbimo," Duchamps said flashing a devilish grin. "Got yourself bitten, eh? Too bad, I've seen what they do with their prey."

Mbimo's eyes rolled and his lips trembled, as he tried to speak. Flecks of white foam dripped from the corners of his mouth. The paralyzing spider venom was slowly digesting his internal organs, liquefying them for the spider's leisurely consumption. He couldn't save Mbimo if he wanted. Death was inevitable from the first bite.

"Don't bother, old boy. I know what you want. You want me to release you, don't you? Well, sorry I can't oblige. I've just resigned from my post as head of security." Scratching, scuttling sounds came from down the tunnel behind him. "They're coming for you now. I have to go."

Mbimo uttered a pathetic squeak of protest.

Duchamps put away his knife and pulled out his pistol. "Okay. You weren't such a bad bloke. I'll make it quick for you." He placed the gun to Mbimo's head. The hapless guard, knowing what was coming, closed his eyes and ceased struggling. Duchamps pulled the trigger. Blood splashed his hand and face. "That ought to piss the bugger's off," he chuckled.

The loud report of the gun would draw more insects. He dragged the knapsacks down the tunnel as quickly as he could. He passed a few more corpses but no more insects. By the time he reached the elevator, he was exhausted. His shoulder ached from his heavy load and his hands were raw and blistered. He needed to rest, but he didn't have the luxury of time. If the company brought in outside help and mounted an offensive against the creatures, they would find him under somewhat less than honorable circumstances.

The #3 elevator appeared safe. Pools of blood and bits of flesh, as well as the occasional dead insect, indicated a recent battle, but he saw no large concentrations of the creatures in the vicinity. The #3 elevator went only as high as 20 Level. From there he would have to use the main elevator or face a long climb. He hit the button and waited. He grew nervous when the sound of insects echoed down the tunnel, but he heard the cage descending and looked up the shaft. The cage lift was only two levels above him. He was certain it would beat the bugs. He smiled when the elevator stopped. *Almost out of here.*

His smile vanished when he slid aside the cage door and took a step into the elevator. A creature he had not seen before, a grayish millipede three meters long, reared from the darkness at the rear of the cage. Its dozens of legs ended in sharp pincers. Long, flesh-rendering mandibles opened to reveal rows of needle-thin teeth lining the mouth. Its hiss reminded Duchamps of a cornered cockroach.

"Damn," he said, raising his rifle. The creature moved surprisingly fast and was on him before he could pull the trigger. Razor-sharp pincers the size of cattle horns ripped into the sides of his chest. The only thing that prevented them from meeting in the middle of his heart was the steel pipe to which the pulley for the cage door attached. In spite of the obstacle, the millipede's jaws clamped down on his forearm like a vise. He dropped his rifle, as pain exploded in his arm, racing to join the agony of the creature's pincers. The pain faded quickly to a dull, throbbing ache, as the millipede's numbing venom coursed through his body. He brought up his pistol, emptied the clip into what he hoped was the millipede's abdomen, and staggered backward when it loosened its grip on him.

He suspected he had not hit a vital organ. It shrugged off the bullet wounds and slithered toward him again. He dropped the useless pistol, slid down the cage door to the floor, and picked up the rifle. It felt heavy in his hands. He forced his finger to pull the trigger, placing three quick bursts into its head. The millipede curled into a ball and died on the elevator floor, oozing a foul-smelling liquid from its wounds.

He examined his own wounds. There was surprisingly little blood from the wound in his arm, but it was rapidly growing numb, and he was woozy. The steel bar had saved him from the pincers. He probed one of the twin holes in his chest with his finger. It went in to the last knuckle before hitting bottom. It was deep, but the pincers hadn't pierced a lung or an artery. He hoped he had killed the creature before it pumped enough venom in him to kill him.

He noticed the elevator was descending. He had hit the button as he fell. He slapped the up button, but it didn't respond. Then he noticed the blinking red System Locked light on the panel and cursed. He had no choice but go where the elevator was taking him, on a one-way ride to hell.

16

July 6, 2016, 3:30 a.m.   *Ngomo* Mine, the Shack −
Trace arrived at the Shack just as security was removing Bill's body on a litter. His face was covered, but blood soaked through the thin, white sheet draped over him. Trace stopped the two men carrying him and drew back the sheet. Seeing his friend's bloodied head, he shook with rage.

"Who killed him?" he demanded of one of the security guards accompanying the attendants.

The guard glanced at his companion and looked back at Trace. "We believe Captain Duchamps forced your friend to move your machine and allow the creatures to enter the mine. He is after the diamonds."

Trace listened, but he couldn't comprehend what the security man was saying. "But, why release the creatures? They'll kill the miners."

The guard was bitter at Duchamps' betrayal. "Yes. Now we must kill the creatures and save the miners. We have no time to apprehend Duchamps. That must come later, after the miners are safe. Then, he will face his punishment."

From the resentment in the guard's voice, Trace wondered if Duchamps would have his day in court, or face the revenge of his betrayed co-workers. He should have been appalled at the idea of swift justice by a mob, but he hoped the latter.

"Where is Alan? Does he know about this?"

"Yes. He informed us of what had happened. He went into the mine after Doctor Means and her companions."

Trace was stunned. "Into the mine …? We gotta go after him."

The guard stopped him. "No. You must repair the damage and move your machine. You must plug the tunnel to prevent the release of more of these creatures. We cannot send anyone that deep into the mine. The miners' safety comes first."

As much as he resented the guard's refusal, he knew he was right. He could offer no help in the mine. His job was in the Shack. He watched them carry Bill's body away before entering the control trailer. The tiny room reeked of the coppery stench of violent death. Partially congealed blood pooled on the floor and the desk. Streaks of blood smeared the walls. The amount of blood in the room staggered him. He couldn't comprehend that a human body could contain so much blood.

Bullet holes riddled the *Cerberus* monitor control panel. The damage was irreparable without the spare parts they had neglected to bring with them. They had considered the likelihood of needing them only a remote possibility. The bullets that had ripped holes through both Bill and Vince's laptops had also severed the connections to the control panel. He checked the filing cabinet and was pleased to find his laptop intact. Duchamps had not had time to search the Shack thoroughly. With luck, he could jury rig a control system.

He stood and stared at the depressing sight of the desk covered in Bill's blood. Fighting to maintain his emotional control, he took a handful of paper towels, wiped the desk off as best he could, and tossed them in the garbage can. He laid several layers of paper towels over the remaining bloodstain. In spite of his concentration at the task, he felt his eyes growing moist. He sighed, took a deep breath, and continued. Bill would have understood. Grieving could come later. The important thing now was to reseal the shaft.

He set his laptop on the paper towels and chose the only chair unsullied by blood. He felt decidedly awkward and uncomfortable, as if he were defiling a grave. He connected his laptop to the *Cerberus* video feeds and powered up his computer, relieved to find they still functioned. Switching on the floodlights, he saw the lava tube was empty. The drilling rig now rested several meters away from the opening. Trace ran the machine through the diagnostics program. Everything checked out, but when he tried to move it back into position, he discovered the joystick was broken. Without it, he couldn't move the *Cerberus*.

He thought furiously. What would Vince have done? He choked up for a moment thinking about Vince, so young and naïve, believing in his beloved underground world of Pellucidar. If he were alive, he would have had the last laugh. The creatures in the lava tube proved that life, and not just extremophiles or insects, could survive deep underground. Now, people would begin to wonder what else might lie beneath their feet.

Deciding on a course of action, he began dismantling the tether box, the terminal connection for the fiber optic cable linking the *Cerberus* to the control panel. Cannibalizing parts from the tether box, he began the tedious task of connecting the cable directly to his laptop. In less than an hour, he had the tread controls operating again. He cranked the *Cerberus* and slowly moved the massive machine into the hole, turning it sideways at the last minute to wedge it against both walls to ensure no more of the creatures could enter the mines. Now, they just had to eliminate the ones already there.

Most of the *Cerberus* functions still needed repair. Hours of work yet remained. He focused on his job. Later, glancing up from his work to wipe sweat from his brow, he witnessed scores of frightened miners pour from of the main elevator and scatter across the grounds into the darkness. After a while, the mass exodus became a dribble, and then stopped altogether. He didn't know how many miners remained below, but he feared they were either trapped or dead. He had witnessed firsthand how fast and deadly the creatures were. Unarmed miners had no chance. Even armed security guards would have a difficult time if confronted by large numbers of the creatures.

He couldn't decide what to do. The hole was sealed. The job of restoring the *Cerberus* controls was taking longer than he had anticipated. He wanted to go below and find Alan, but the thought of descending into the hell he knew awaited below ground frightened him more than he cared to admit to himself. He had never considered himself a coward. He had survived a few bar brawls, even instigated a couple. A few bumps and bruises, a cut or two, and the cost of a few beers to make amends had been the extent of them. He had never once feared for his life. Even the two auto accidents he had survived had happened too fast for fear to become a factor; however, when he watched the creatures in action outside the Shack window, his flesh crawled.

His quandary became a moot point when five, three-meter-long millipedes scampered from an elevator shaft. They scurried across the parking lot like multi-legged surfboards, pursued by a dozen gun-wielding security guards. Two of the creatures died in a blaze of gunfire. The others retreated to a small metal building marked *Explosives*. Trace watched in awe, as one of the guards lit a road flare, crept close to the building, and tossed it through the open door. He quickly retreated for cover, but the blast caught him midstride, tossing him end-over-end like a ragdoll. He landed ten meters away and didn't move.

Trace fell off his chair as the concussion of the tremendous explosion swept across the parking lot and struck the trailer, lifting the wheels on one side off the ground. It canted precariously for several gravity-defying moments before resettling with a thud and bouncing a few times. The refrigerator door opened, spilling ice, cans of soda, bottles of water, and containers of old food across the floor. The explosion chewed a tremendous crater ten meters in diameter, obliterating the explosives building and any creatures it had harbored.

Men rushed to the stunned man. Amazingly, he slowly got to his feet and shook his head. Trace was astonished the man had survived such a blast. Unfortunately, the link to the *Cerberus* had not. His screen was dead, as were all the connections he had so painstakingly soldered. He sighed, picked up the soldering gun, and went back to work.

He tried to ignore the distractions as he worked feverishly, but the sight of several giant spiders climbing out of a ventilator shaft and attacking four soldiers diverted his attention. The spiders didn't get far, as two SAPS Special Tactical Force members wielding flame throwers moved in and incinerated the escapees. The South African Police Service equivalent of SWAT teams had arrived earlier in two *Casspir* armored personnel carriers. Each member of the team carried a Heckler and Koch MP5 submachine gun and displayed a practical knowledge of its use. He felt a little more confident now that they were on the scene.

Movement on the video feed attracted his attention. He hoped it was Alan, but was disappointed to see it was Verkhoen. The Van Gotts' CEO beat on the camera lens and screamed something inaudible, but his wild eyes expressed his panic. He wanted out of the lava tube.

Trace pressed the control to start the electric motors operating the *Cerberus'* tracks. A sizzle of electricity and the ozone smell of a short circuit filled the room.

"Damn," he swore. One of his hastily soldered connections had failed.

Verkhoen continued pounding on the camera. His men stood around him, staring at him. More people appeared upslope of the *Cerberus*. He panned the camera. This time, it was Alan, along with Eve Means, and two others. Alan spoke into the camera microphone, but Trace had no way to reply. Even the motor controlling the camera was out. He watched Alan connect his laptop to *Cerberus'* outboard USB port.

"He's trying to access remote control," he mumbled to himself.

He pulled up the computer's diagnostics screen. The troubleshooting program continued searching the system for problems. He had no way to shut it down or bypass until it completed the cycle. He registered Alan's disappointment as he discovered the same thing. Alan pointed downslope.

Unable to do anything to help them, he flashed the floodlights off and then back on to indicate he understood. Disheartened by his inability to do more, he watched Alan and the others leave. He sighed, picked up his soldering gun, and went back to work.

17

July 6, 2016, 4:30 a.m.   *Ngomo* Mine, the Lava Tube –
Klaus Verkhoen had lost control of the situation, something
contrary to every fiber of his being. He had been raised his father's
son – ruthless, decisive, and motivated. The elder Verkhoen had built
a global corporation from his shares of a barely profitable mining
concern by cornering the gold market, and he had done it by using
men, black or white, to his advantage without apology or regret. He
had been one of the first Rand Barons, the white social elitists of
South Africa, and had built an empire. Klaus Verkhoen was
struggling to hold on to it.

The increased cost of labor, the drop in world gold prices, and the
need to dig ever deeper for gold-bearing ore threatened to break the
company. The mine produced over 12,000 kilograms of gold last
year, valued at 5.6 billion ZAR, worth 456 million US dollars, and
yet had shown a profit of less than 800 million ZAR. His efforts to
find more gold by following the seam deeper than anyone had ever
tried had ended in failure. If the stockholders had learned of the
strange condition of the bodies of the two miners, the company
would have gone bankrupt. He had bided his time, and four years
later tried again with a second tunnel against his chief engineer,
Frederick Means', advice. When Means threatened to report his
analysis of the dangers involved to the Board, he had turned to his
chief of security, who in Duchamps' inimical style, had blasted the
tunnel and killed everyone involved.

Now, Duchamps had double-crossed him. He should have seen it
coming. He had ridden Duchamps like an unruly stepchild, cowed
him into submission, channeled his propensity for violence into a
Van Gotts tool, but he had failed to break him. Duchamps had

patiently waited years for his chance for revenge. The discovery of the diamonds had provided the impetus, and the insects had provided the means. The theft of the diamonds was secondary to the revenge. Though Verkhoen loathed admitting it, Duchamps was like him in many ways.

When security advised him of the Hoffman engineer's death, he immediately knew Duchamps was behind it. Releasing the creatures while he made good his escape with the diamonds would be Duchamps' ultimate act of revenge. Even meek, quiet Evelyn Means had betrayed him by contacting the World Heritage Foundation and posting a video of the creatures on YouTube. Now, he stood to lose his diamonds and his mine. At least Means and her cronies were trapped in the mine with the creatures she so wanted to preserve. He hoped they dined on her luscious little body, as they had her husbands'.

Verkhoen knew he had to chance entering the mine. Duchamps could not have taken all the diamonds. He needed to remove them before the opportunity passed. At the same time, he would see Means and the others did not live to interfere with him again. This time he would take matters into his own hands.

Accompanying him were six security guards, each with a packet of twenty, two-hundred-rand notes in their pockets, about seventeen-hundred American dollars, a month's wages. He was acutely aware this would leave the trapped miners unprotected, but he needed the guards' firepower to retrieve the diamonds and escape alive. He had seen the video of the creatures attacking the hapless miners, but their deaths did not move him. He left the remaining security personnel on the surface to prevent any of the creatures from escaping. The last thing he needed was the SADF to take charge.

Before descending into the mine, he locked all the elevators. Now, they would only travel down unless he entered the proper code. He and the guards passed numerous mutilated corpses on the way to the new shaft, but encountered no insects until they neared the pit. Seeing the abhorrent creatures close up was unsettling, his childhood revulsion at bugs magnified a thousand times. He was pleased they weren't immune to automatic rifle bullets.

He reached the lava tube without incident and located the diamond seam. His eyes grew large when he saw the priceless crystals embedded in the walls, as well as nodes of nearly pure metals – gold, copper, and palladium. He glared at the empty pockets where Duchamps had pried his precious stones from the rock. His quickly realized his estimate to Hoffman of their value had been extremely pessimistic. He saw ten times the number of diamonds he had imagined. Given their color, clarity, and size, the wealth they represented was inestimable.

As four of the guards chipped raw diamonds from the walls, some as large as five-hundred carats, the remaining two guards filled large Samsonite travel cases. Over the loud echoes of the hammering, another noise caught his attention, a mechanical one.

"You," he yelled, pointing to one of the guards, "go see what that noise is."

The guard glanced at his compatriots for support, but they avoided his gaze. He licked his lips and shuffled his feet. "Me, Mister Verkhoen? Alone?"

"You've got your rifle. Now go."

With the choice of facing monsters or Verkhoen's anger, he chose the monsters. He trotted back up the tube.

Verkhoen turned to the other guards, who had stopped working and looked around nervously. "Hurry," he yelled. "We don't have all day."

Like them, the eerie silence of the lava tube was getting to him. He knew the rifles were effective against the insects, but his mind conjured imaginary creatures from childhood fairy tales told to him by his black nanny lurking in the darkness.

Five minutes later, the guard ran back, yelling, "The machine is back in the hole. We are trapped."

"Trapped? That is impossible," he replied, shoving the man aside.

Feeling the first tingling grip of dread, he went to investigate himself. His fears magnified when he saw the *Cerberus* was indeed once again blocking the tunnel, sealing him inside the lava tube with the giant insects. His entomophobia seized him fully, expunging any thoughts of the diamonds or of saving his company. The idea of insects, of any size, touching his flesh or crawling over his body, sent him into a panic. Someone had moved the machine to seal them in, to seal him in. Furious, he beat on the camera with his fists, yelling at the top of his lungs to attract their attention, but nothing happened.

"What do we do, boss?" one of the guards asked.

Everyone had abandoned the diamonds and followed him to the tunnel. Now, they stared at Verkhoen's bizarre behavior, growing more frightened by the second. He knew he had to regain control of his emotions, or they would leave him and fend for themselves. He considered his options, which were few. Unless someone moved the *Cerberus*, he had no way out of the lava tube.

A guard yelled, "Look!" and pointed up the tube.

The faint glow of a light grew brighter as its source neared. Someone else was in the lava tube. They had come to rescue them. He sighed in relief.

"Hello. Who are you?" he cried out.

"Alan Hoffman."

Verkhoen chuckled at the cruel twist of fate that had thrown the two men back together. He waited until Alan, Eve Means, and two other men arrived. One of them, the eldest, was on his last legs, breathing hard and barely limping along with the help of the younger man. When they stopped, the old man studied Verkhoen with the steady gaze of a careful observer. In spite of his age and deplorable physical state, the old man appeared relaxed and more at home in the lava tube than he did. He looked at Eve, noted her chilly stare, and then addressed the older man.

"I take it you are Doctor Tells."

Tells nodded. "I am. You need not introduce yourself. Your decision to wear your expensive business attire instead of a coverall or jumpsuit announces you as Klaus Verkhoen. Your infamy precedes you."

Verkhoen frowned at the mention of his suit. While it was true he always wanted to look his best, he wore the suit because he hadn't had time to change. It was filthy from mine dust, and the creases in his pants had gone limp because of the humidity, but what was one custom-tailored suit compared to the wealth of diamonds they had salvaged; however, he did take umbrage at Tells' last remark. He cocked his head to one side and asked, "Infamy?"

"We have seen evidence of your handiwork, Mister Verkhoen."

"Not mine. I had no hand in this. How did you get here?" he asked.

Eve approached until she stood directly in front of him. She glared at him with undisguised hatred. Her hands jerked uncontrollably, as if she wanted to strike out. He waited for her to slap him, but she surprised him by taking a deep breath and stepping back. Her voice trembled with rage, as she replied, "We came through the tunnel you swore was flooded when Frederick was trapped. We found Frederick's remains." She leaned forward, jabbing a finger into his chest. "You lied to me."

"No, I did not," he countered. "The water must have drained away. I regret the death of your husband. It was an unfortunate accident."

"Was it an accident?" Alan asked.

Verkhoen looked Alan in the eye. The American's cold tone left no doubt his seemingly innocuous question was more of an accusation. "What are you implying?"

Alan shook his head. "I'm not sure. Frederick Means' death looks suspicious. I found blasting wire in the tunnel he was digging."

Verkhoen tried to hide his relief. Hoffman had no proof, only vague suspicions. "Then your problem is with Duchamps, not me. He is the one who betrayed all of us by releasing the creatures."

Alan glanced at the cases Verkhoen's men carried. "I see you risked everything for the diamonds. Weren't you at all concerned with the miners?"

"These stones can save my company, Hoffman. The mine provides jobs for hundreds of men. The mine is more important than a few workers." He offered Eve a defiant scowl. "I will let no one take them from me. No, the miners do not concern me. Their blood is not on my hands. Duchamps released the creatures, not I."

"He's your dog. You let him off the leash."

Verkhoen grinned at Alan's fitting metaphor. "He has proven to be somewhat of a problem dog."

"We have bigger problems, Verkhoen," Alan said. "We came from farther up the lava tube through your sealed and flooded mine shaft. We can't get out that way. We need to find a way out of here. Now."

Verkhoen waved his hand at the *Cerberus*. "Your man blocked the hole, but he will not answer. It is the only way out." He looked at Alan more closely and realized the American looked frightened. "What did you find? More giant insects?" he shuddered at the thought of more giant insects.

"No, the upper level of the lava tube was completely empty."

Verkhoen grew frustrated by Alan's cryptic tone. "Why? Is there a problem? I do not understand."

"Think, Verkhoen. These creatures have been sealed in this lava tube system for eons. It's been their home since the Cambrian Period. They have developed an ecosystem that works. Now, suddenly, they abandon it. Why? I think there's something in here they wish to escape, something higher up the feeding chain."

Verkhoen grabbed Alan's sleeve. "You must contact your man or figure out how to move the *Cerberus*. We are trapped here." Verkhoen realized he was nearing panic and tried to control the fear sweeping through him, but images of the dead men he had passed in the mine kept popping into his head. He didn't want to suffer a similar fate. Now, Alan informed him there could be something worse in the lava tube.

Alan pried Verkhoen's fingers from his sleeve and looked into the camera. "Trace, if you can hear me, move the *Cerberus*."

Verkhoen waited impatiently, but again nothing happened. "I tried that. He can't hear you, or he's dead."

Alan glared at him, and then removed his laptop from his bag. Verkhoen watched with renewed hope, as Alan connected his laptop to the *Cerberus*. Hope faded after a few minutes when Alan's face clouded.

"What's wrong?" Verkhoen demanded.

"It's in diagnostics mode from the other end. Trace must be trying to repair the damage Duchamp caused. I can't get in." Alan glared at him as he mentioned Duchamps, but Verkhoen dismissed it as a veiled accusation.

"What do you suggest we do?"

Alan disconnected his computer. "If we're caught out in the open, we'll die. I suggest we move down the tube past the diamonds. There's a place that might offer some protection."

Verkhoen seized on the idea of a safe place and nodded. "Yes! Yes! A place we can defend against these monsters and wait for rescue."

Alan glared at him and pointed past the *Cerberus* toward the mine. "Rescue? There are hundreds of miners out there in that stony labyrinth dying. What makes you think they'll come looking for us? Did you inform anyone where you were going? Eve didn't. I didn't. We're trapped here until we can figure a way to get out."

"Your man will fix the machine. In the meantime, we need cover."

Verkhoen rallied his men and explained the situation to the ones who didn't understand English. Watching him break had diminished their faith in him. They began grumbling in protest at his suggestion. They wanted out of the lava tube and knew the machine blocked the only access. He couldn't allow them to stand around and argue, and he couldn't leave them. He needed their firepower.

Exasperated, he turned and began walking back down the lava tube. He said, "Come with me, and I will give each of you an additional fifty thousand rand." Their grumbling abruptly ceased and they followed.

Greed has its uses, he thought.

* * * *

They rested in the grotto Duchamps had found the day before. Verkhoen selected two men to stand guard outside the opening. They hesitated at first, but quickly wilted in Verkhoen's intimidating presence. To save batteries, only one flashlight illuminated the entrance to the cleft. The colorful bioluminescent lichen covering the walls and roof reminded him of the black light day-glow posters on his bedroom walls as a child: a dark, silent elf woods washed by silver moonlight; a vast, pulsating nebula against the ebony backdrop of space; and a half-naked warrior princess Dejah atop an eight-legged Martian *thoat*. Under ordinary circumstances, it would have been relaxing, but circumstances were far from normal, and Alan was wound too tight to relax.

He leaned against a smooth boulder trying to decide what to do. His pain made thinking difficult. His hand now throbbed constantly and was tender to the touch. The redness and swelling was moving up his arm. He feared whatever prehistoric microbe or poison affecting him was fatal. Trapped in the bowels of the earth was not the way he had pictured himself dying.

Eve noticed his discomfort and came to sit beside him. Her presence made him want to redouble his efforts to save them, to save her. Somehow, over the last two days, she had wormed her way under his skin, and he found he enjoyed the forgotten sensation. He had thought discovering the remains of her husband would change her, but she had long ago made her peace with his death. She had found closure, but only in his death. Now, she wanted closure with Verkhoen. So did he.

"What's wrong, Alan?"

She spoke quietly to not disturb the others. The pallid light from the lichen softened her features, giving her a ghostly appearance. Her eyes, once so bright, were now just dark depressions above her pale cheeks.

He showed her his hand. "I think it is infected."

She looked alarmed as she took his hand and gently examined it. "We have nothing to fight the infection, but I do have a bottle of pain relievers in my pocket, acteominephin. It might slow the fever." She took out the bottle and offered Alan two capsules. "I often have headaches," she admitted reluctantly. He swallowed them dry. They were very low on water. Verkhoen's men had brought none, and he and the others had shared theirs with the security men.

"Thanks," he said.

"What did you see back there?" she asked. "Whatever it was, it frightened you."

He hesitated, not wishing to alarm her. "I saw nothing except evidence something higher up the food chain eats the mandibulates and everything else in the lava tube system. However, I felt … something. It was as if something was trying to read my mind. It felt … alien."

She chuckled. "Alien, like from outer space?"

He smiled, glad she could still joke. "No, just like nothing I could ever imagine." He didn't mention that his first thought had been the telepathic *Mahar*, rulers of Pellucidar, elicited by Vince's references to the Burroughs' novel.

"I couldn't imagine these giant insects even though I knew they had existed, eons ago, in another world. Even if we get out of here, the creatures are out there, in the mine. We have to go through them."

"We have Verkhoen's armed security men."

She turned away from him and pursed her lips. When she turned back, her face was cold, devoid of expression. "We cannot trust him. He killed Frederick."

"I think so, too. I'll keep an eye on him. Now, you must rest. It has been a long day."

She didn't protest. She leaned into him and rested her head against his shoulder. He breathed in the smell of her hair, her perfume, and smiled to himself. He wrapped an arm around her, and she draped her arm over his leg. A few minutes later, he heard her gentle breathing as she slept.

He was concerned about Verkhoen as well. He had no doubts the CEO had ordered Frederick Means' death four years ago and would have no qualms with killing his widow to shut her up. He had known about or suspected the existence of the diamonds long before contacting Hoffman Industries. The *Cerberus AT10* had provided the means to reach them safely. His hoard of diamonds would lose much of their value if word got out about their discovery. Only by quietly placing them on the market a few at a time could he hope to reap the rewards he sought.

Alan was concerned about what he had felt in the cavern. The mandibulates showed a greater than normal intelligence and organizational skill. One way to develop this trait over the eons was the constant need to outwit an even smarter enemy. What he had felt had been alien, but intelligent, and thoroughly evil. He had never believed in evil except as bad to the nth degree, but he knew this creature was the epitome of evil – heartless, cruel, deadly, and coldly calculating.

He yawned. He was tired and his fevered mind was playing tricks on him due to the stress. Maybe all he had felt in the cavern was his own doubts of his ability and frustration at what fate had dealt him. He glanced over at Verkhoen. The normally dapper CEO was sitting apart from his men; head hunched over his knees, arms folded clasping his chest, as if trying to absorb the light cast by the single flashlight, sobbing quietly. His hair was mussed and dirty. His three-thousand-dollar suit was dirty and wrinkled. His men stole worried glances at him. They were losing confidence in their boss.

Sandersohn halfheartedly studied the bioluminescent lichen, while Doctor Tells lay on his back asleep, snoring loudly. The elderly scientist had pushed himself past his limits already, but Alan feared the worst was yet to come. They had to make their way through the mine to the surface.

Eve moaned and jumped. She looked up at him frightened but

seeing his face, she closed her eyes and quickly fell back to sleep. He pulled her closer. It had been a while since he had bothered feeling anything for a woman; he hadn't the time. The *Cerberus* had taken every waking minute. The few dates he had managed had been purely recreational, no emotional involvement allowed in the sex afterwards. Eve was different. She was determined and not easily frightened. Few women could have coped with seeing their husband's bones as she had or faced giant prehistoric monsters. Throughout the ordeal, she had shown remarkable courage. He couldn't allow anything to happen to her.

A chill swept over him though there was no wind. He felt that seeking mind again reaching out, probing, so utterly alien he had no way to connect to it, no method of interpreting the dizzying images flittering through his mind. Simultaneously, the cave lichen went berserk, emitting sporadic bursts of frenzied light. Sandersohn dropped the lichen he held in his hand as if burned, staring at it uncomprehending. The guards began muttering. Even Verkhoen roused from his stupor and looked around.

Eve sat up with a look of puzzlement, holding her head in her hands. "I feel something, like a tickle in my mind."

"Try to ignore it," he suggested, though he was having difficulty following his own advice. His mind itched as badly as his wounded hand as strange thoughts brushed his thoughts, tasting them like a lion tasting the fresh blood of its kill before devouring it. *My God, Vince was right*, he thought in dismay. *We're in the African equivalent of Pellucidar.*

One of the guards in the lava tube ran in, yelling to Verkhoen, "Something is coming."

The second guard still outside the grotto opened fire with his weapon just outside the mouth of the cleft, the reports thunderous in the small space. A few seconds later, the firing stopped, following quickly by a man's terrifying shriek. Alan jumped to his feet and stared toward the lava tube. He saw it now, a movement in the shadows. *No,* he corrected himself, *it was the shadows moving.* All flashlights snapped on, the beams searching for the intruder. The scene reminded him of a movie with prison searchlights looking for an escaped prisoner. They converged on the entrance, their beams disappearing when they struck the dark creatures flowing toward them.

They spilled across the rocks, a deadly mass of giant, jet black millipedes. The cave lichen exploded in one last burst of light, and then went dark. Alan wasn't sure, if they had doused their internal light to hide from the creatures, or if the creatures had sucked the life from them. The guards began firing at the creatures, but the bullets passed through their spongy flesh causing no apparent damage.

One man, braver or more foolhardy than the others, stepped too close to the creature, firing straight down at the black mass of millipedes his feet. One reared to its full four-meter height, towering over him. It lunged forward and enveloped him in folds of chitinous flesh. He dropped his weapon and began screaming, beating at the creature with his fists. His screams became more frantic as the creature's pointed feet began piercing his flesh. The creature's mandibles injected powerful digestive enzymes into the guard's body, dissolving his organs so quickly the guard seemed to melt. He jerked once, hard enough to snap his spine. The sound echoed over the sound of his screams, a tree limb snapping from the trunk in a strong gale.

He didn't fall immediately. The ebony monster wound around him supported him. Black fluid began to exude from his open mouth and eyes. Slowly, like a sand castle tower devoured by the rising tide, he fell forward to the floor. A seconds creature joined the first, absorbing the guard's fluids, his blood, into their bodies. When they retreated, only a viscous fluid remained.

Alan was horrified. These creatures were what had devoured the mollusks, snails, and giant insects in the swamp, leaving only shells and bits and pieces of hard carapace; the reason the insects had fled into the mine, seeking not food, but escape. What manner of creature they were, he didn't know. They resembled millipedes, but their segments were so narrow, fit together so tightly together, they moved like reptiles. Their brains, which could not have been large because of their thin bodies, had evolved over the eons, changed by the tremendous pressure of evolution. Their intelligence was not much greater than their mindless prey, but their real advantage lay in their ability to mesmerize their prey using their ability to project their thoughts, to freeze their prey into helplessness.

As a biologist, Eve might have told him more about the creatures, but now she stood behind him, screaming. He could barely hear her over the staccato burst of machine guns and the yelling of the guards. The creatures slowly edged into the grotto, unsure of its adversaries, but having found the taste of humans to their liking, sought ways around the stinging bullets. Several of the creatures climbed up the wall and spread across the roof. Attaching themselves to the roof by their rear feet, they dropped like flypaper, snaring men in their folds and snatching them from the ground. The guards dangled like human yo-yos, bobbing up and down and screaming as the creature slowly consumed their flesh. One man so ensnared continued firing his machine gun, spraying both the creatures and a second guard with stray bullets.

Alan stood staring, mesmerized by the creatures' movement, watching one slither toward him in slow motion. A shiver raced up his spine from the sudden cold enveloping him. He knew he was in danger, but his mind balked at obeying his command to run. He was a human and the monster was just an insect. To think that it was more powerful than he irritated him, but he could not break free of its hypnotic pull.

Eve stopped screaming and jerked at his arm. He turned to look at her.

"Run," she yelled.

Her words had no meaning. *Run where? From what?* He peered into her eyes, saw the sheer terror in them, and wondered why he felt no such fear. Then, with a shudder of revulsion, he realized the creature was touching his mind, holding him immobile while it attended to other prey. It knew of men, of their numbers outside its small world, and felt an eagerness to leave the cavern. With a start, Alan realized the creatures had sustained themselves through the eons by carefully controlling their appetites, allowing the mandibulates and other creatures to reproduce, consuming only the weak and dying, culling the herd. They had fed, sparingly, but over the eons had never quenched their insatiable appetite. They were starving. They were eager for a feeding frenzy.

He turned to Eve. "We have to go," he said.

She nodded. He gathered Sandersohn and Tells and urged them to follow.

"Where to?" Sandersohn asked.

"Back to the *Cerberus* and pray Trace has fixed the problem."

They edged around the creatures, as they moved deeper into the grotto. He saw only two men standing, one of which was Verkhoen, who amid the turmoil and carnage, still had not abandoned the light of his flashlight. He noticed them leaving and chased after them with panic in his eyes. "Don't leave me," he yelled. Amazingly, he stopped to pick up the case of diamonds. A single surviving guard followed him from the cleft.

It was a frantic run to the *Cerberus*, a mad dash Alan wasn't sure they would win. Sandersohn helped Doctor Tells, but the overweight, aged scientist faltered often, stumbling badly every few steps. Alan had no time to herd the survivors together. They had foolishly entered the mine to observe the insects and had instead become part of the food chain. He couldn't be responsible for everyone's foolhardy decision. His only concern was Eve. Her desire to learn what had happened to her husband drove her. He could overlook that kind of foolishness, could understand it. His decision to accept Verkhoen's offer placed him in the same category. He clung to her hand, half-dragging her as he raced ahead. The others would have to fend for themselves.

The *Cerberus* lights were on, blinding them all. Trace had managed to fix that problem, at least. Covering his eyes with his wounded hand and clinging to Eve with his other, he ran to the camera and yelled into the microphone.

"Trace! Move the *Cerberus*. Let us out."

Nothing happened.

"Trace," he screamed in a panic. The camera light was on, but he had no way of knowing if Trace was even in the Shack, or if he had been able to repair all the controls. If any of the creatures had escaped the mine, the authorities would have evacuated the entire mining complex. The alternative, that Trace was dead as Verkhoen suggested, he could not accept. He fumbled with his laptop. Maybe Trace had witnessed his efforts earlier and had engaged the remote access.

He rued the day he had written the diagnostics program. At the time, he hadn't worried about the troubleshooter's slow pace. Being thorough was more important than speed. He had never imagined the need for an override. He had never anticipated an attack by goddamned creatures from hell.

"Hurry," Eve urged, looking intently back down the tube. "They're coming."

He already knew. The creatures' presence once again brushed his mind. There was no individuality. They were a hive mind, a collective stronger together than as individuals. This, too, was part of their evolutionary advantage, what had made of them apex predators. He glanced at the others. Sandersohn and Tells had stopped running and stared behind them, gazing into the shadows. He wondered if the creatures had touched their minds as well, paralyzing them as it had him earlier. Verkhoen brushed past the pair without a backward glance, clutching the diamond case to his chest.

"Sandersohn! Tells! Get a move on," Alan yelled, breaking the spell over them. He cursed aloud. The computer still refused him access. He couldn't control the *Cerberus'* movement or the laser array. They couldn't escape or defend themselves. They were sitting ducks. He had no illusions about their chances if they couldn't escape the lava tube. He was ready to give up hope; then, Eve squeezed his hand. Her determination, her strength flooded into him. He made a bold decision. He disconnected his laptop.

Eve stared at him aghast at his actions.

"Come on," he said, urging her upslope of the lava tube.

She resisted. "Where are we going?"

"The only place where we might have a chance," he replied.

18

July 6, 2016, 6:05 a.m. *Ngomo* Mine, the Lava Tube –

Alan hurried Eve, Tells, and Sandersohn up the lava tube. He wished he didn't have to risk their lives in his mad plan to destroy the ebony nightmares and seal the tunnel, but events had taken the choice from him. If he could lure the creatures into the magma chamber, the others might escape through the crack back into the mine. It was their only chance. He didn't hold out such hope for him.

Verkhoen stumbled along behind them, assisted by the sole surviving security guard. Why the man helped the boss he despised, he didn't know, unless Verkhoen had sweetened the pot with more money. He didn't know how fast the ebony creatures could move, but he suspected they were faster than Tells could manage. The only reason the creatures had not overtaken them was that they were toying with them, like a cat with a mouse. The creatures could pounce on them at any moment from the darkness.

No sooner had he thought of the creatures, than he felt their dark presence in his mind, hunting them, trying to weave a spell over them. Verkhoen stiffened and shoved the guard away, clutching his precious case with one arm, and cradling his weapon with the other. The others felt it as well and stopped running.

"Keep moving," he yelled, trying to break through the creatures' hypnotic spell. He shoved Sandersohn in the back to get him moving.

The guard stood, pivoting his entire upper torso, as he swung his flashlight and his weapon back and forth across the width of the lava tube behind him, searching for a target. After a full minute passed, he relaxed his stance, glanced at Verkhoen, and shrugged his shoulders. He had forgotten to think in three dimensions. As one of the creatures fell on him from the roof of the tunnel, he managed one quick burst with his rifle before disappearing into the black shroud of death. He didn't even have time to scream.

Watching the guard die, Verkhoen lost all semblance of rational thinking. He backed against the wall of the lava tube, hugging it as if the rock would absorb him and hide him from the creatures. He began jabbering in a mixture of Afrikaans, English, and Zulu, wailing, "*Intulo! Intulo!*"

The creature stopped consuming the guard and regarded him with its cold, dark eyes.

Alan picked up a large rock and tossed it to the opposite side of the tube, hoping to distract it. At the same time, he yelled to Verkhoen, motioning for the terrified CEO to run toward him.

"Verkhoen! Come on."

Verkhoen stared at Alan without comprehension; then, he began running back down the lava tube toward the *Cerberus.*

"No, you fool," Alan shouted. "Come with us."

Verkhoen ignored him, disappearing into the darkness still babbling.

"Stupid son of a bitch," he muttered.

The millipede returned to its grizzly meal. He hoped it took the creature a while to digest its human prey, giving them a chance to place some distance between the creatures and them.

* * * *

By the time they had covered the two kilometers back to the crack in the wall, Alan knew they could never escape the creatures that way. Doctor Tells was exhausted, barely able to remain on his feet. They had all pushed themselves beyond their limits, but the aged doctor had no reserve left to draw upon. He could go no farther without rest. Alan knew Eve would never abandon her colleague, not even to save her own life. It was an admirable trait in theory, but it would cost her life in practice.

Alan had changed his mind about Sandersohn. At first, he had thought him supercilious and a whiner, but he had discovered that the young, outspoken paleozoologist possessed a remarkable capacity for compassion his acerbic demeanor belied. He watched over his older companion like a mother hen.

Alan walked over to Tells to assess his condition. "Doctor Tells, how are you holding up?"

Tells was perspiring heavily, pale, and gasping for breath, but he smiled. "If I survive, this will make an interesting chapter in my new book."

"We'll make it," Sandersohn said, holding onto Tells. He glanced at the narrow, twisting crack in the wall; arriving at the same conclusion Alan had pertaining to Tells. "Which way now?"

Alan didn't respond. He was hesitant to reveal his bold, perhaps foolhardy plan. Instead, he asked, "Do you have any idea what those creatures are?

He shook his head. "No, there has never been any fossil record of it, but there wouldn't be, would there? They resemble millipedes, but I suspect the similarity ends there." He shook his head. "The others – the *mandibulates*, the *arthropleura* millipedes, the *meganeura* dragonflies, even the mollusks and snails you saw – are evident in the Pennsylvania Epoch sedimentary layers of the Late Carboniferous Period, about three-hundred million years ago. Whether this creature, this meta-millipede, is from that period or much older, I cannot say. I do know, from what I've seen that this creature could have been responsible for the disappearance of whole orders of species, such as the Permian-Triassic extinction."

"If this creature has survived the changing of the continents," Doctor Tells broke in, "it could be responsible for the mass elimination of many species. There have been five major extinction events through history – the Ordovician-Silurian, in which over fifty percent of all life forms vanished. Before the Ordovician, there were no creatures with skeletons or hard shells, so there would be no fossil record. Next, the Devonian, in which most fish and many species of trilobites and reef-building organisms vanished. The Permian-Triassic two-hundred-fifty million years ago, of which Doctor Sandersohn spoke, saw the elimination of seventy percent of all terrestrial vertebrates and ninety-six percent of all marine species. Most insect species did not survive it. The Triassic-Jurassic extinction saw the end of the large amphibians and archosaurs. The last, the Cretaceous-Tertiary, heralded the end of the dinosaurs and the advance of mammals."

Alan marveled that Tells, moments earlier on his last legs, seemed to perk up as he spoke, putting his misery and fatigue aside for scientific debate. "I thought an asteroid killed the dinosaurs."

"Asteroid, disease, severe climate change, or our ebony friends – who knows? Considering what we have witnessed, I suggest our meta-millipedes are quite capable."

Sandersohn interrupted. "You still haven't said what your plan is."

Alan sighed. He couldn't postpone it any longer. "I intend to draw the creatures into the swamp and blow them up with dynamite."

Eve was aghast. "You only have a few minutes of fuse left. You could never ..." Then, as the implication hit her, she stared at him. "You were going to sacrifice yourself."

He didn't want her to think him heroic or foolish. "We can't let these things get out of here, no matter the cost. However dangerous the insects are, these creatures are infinitely worse."

"My good man," Tells said. "I am an old man and unlikely to make it out of here under any circumstances. Show me what you intended to do and lead these people to safety. If I learn one new thing at the moment of my death, I will consider dying a small price to pay."

"My idea, my responsibility," he answered.

"No," Eve said. "I'm not going back into that hole again. I'm going with you. I want to see the swamp. I am a biologist."

"I'm not going back alone," Sandersohn said. "I guess I'm playing tourist as well."

"Damn it all!" Alan snapped, frustrated by their obstinacy. "Is everyone here crazy? If my idea doesn't work, and in all likelihood it won't, we'll all die a horrible death."

"One for all," Tells said, chuckling slightly.

Alan shook his head. "We're not Musketeers. I can't make you leave, but I had hoped you, Eve, were intelligent enough to at least make the attempt."

She squeezed Alan's hand. "I lost one man four years ago and wished every minute since that I had been with him at the end. I won't go through that again."

Looking into her eyes, he allowed her to persuade him, though he knew he would regret it. "You win. We don't have much time."

"You cannot kill *Intulo*. It is a god."

Startled by the strange voice, Alan turned so quickly he almost fell. He didn't understand the language, but he recognized *Intulo* as the word Verkhoen had repeated when he saw the ebony creature. The speaker stood in the shadows of a small alcove in the tunnel wall. He stepped out, revealing a tall, thin black man wearing a tattered, white t-shirt and blue pants. Long gashes streaked his left arm, which he held limp at his side. His curly black hair lay melted against his scalp on one side of his head, and a livid burn marked his right cheek and neck.

"Who are you?" Alan asked.

The man stared at him.

"He's speaking Zulu," Sandersohn said. "I'll try to find out who he is, although my Zulu is a bit rusty." He faced the stranger. "*Sabuwona.*"

The man nodded.

"I told him 'I see you'. It's a traditional Zulu greeting. *Ngubani ijama lakho?*"

"Ntulli Masowe."

Alan's anger rose as he recognized the name. "You were with Vince," he growled, taking a step toward the missing security guard they had all thought dead. "Did you kill him?"

Sandersohn stepped between them, translated Alan's question, and relayed Masowe's reply. "No, the scorpions killed him, as they almost did me."

Alan wasn't sure he believed him. "How did you survive?"

"He ran faster than the creatures."

"You left Vince there to die," Alan accused.

At this Masowe shook his head. He seemed genuinely offended by the accusation. "No, he was already dead," he answered in English, surprising both Alan and Sandersohn. "The explosion and sheet of flame when I fired my pistol stunned the creatures attacking me long enough to get away. They chased me, but I left false blood trails until they gave up."

"What did you mean *Intulo*?" Tells asked. "According to Zulu legend, *Intulo* is half-man/half-reptile."

Masowe laughed. "*Intulo* is a dark god, a bringer of death. As a god, it can take any form it wishes."

Eve leaned closer to Alan. "I think he's feverish from his wound."

He whispered in return, "Maybe he's just crazy. He's been down here in the dark with these things for three days." He turned to

Masowe. "How have you managed to survive down here?"

Masowe pointed toward the magma chamber cavern. "By hiding in *Uhlanga.*"

"The swamp?" Alan asked.

Masowe nodded. *"Unkulunkulu,* the Ancient One who created the Zulu people, lives in *Uhlanga.* He protects me."

"Every African culture has its creation myth," Tells said. "The Bushongo Bantu believe in *Bomba,* who vomited up the sun. The Ethiopians have *Wak,* who lives in the clouds."

Masowe took a menacing step toward Tells, snarling. *"Unkulunkulu* is God," he said. "He is no myth."

Sandersohn raised his rifle. Masowe glowered at him but did not retreat. Alan raised his arms in the air. "No one wants to harm you. Can you show us where you hide in the swamp?"

Masowe shuffled his feet, staring first down the tunnel toward *Intulo,* and then toward the swamp. He nodded. "But *Unkulunkulu* will not protect you. You are *nomlungu,* white men."

"We'll take our chances," Sandersohn quipped.

Without waiting to see if they followed, Masowe set off at a fast trot toward the swamp.

Alan shrugged. "We don't have much to lose."

He helped Sandersohn with Tells, who was indignant at their insistence in assisting him. "I can manage," he said in a chiding voice.

"We don't want you to get lost," Alan replied.

When they caught up with Masowe, he stood on the lip of the slope leading down into the swamp. Alan saw no living creatures or edible plants.

"How do you survive? What do you eat?"

"Isibankwa esincane." He smiled and pointed to a pile of rocks. Looking more closely, Alan spotted the slight movement of small reptiles."

"Amniotes," Eve said with wonder in her voice, "some of the first reptiles hatched from eggs. They must have entered the cavern system hundreds of millions of years after the insects."

Tells took a deep breath. "Taste the air. One theory for the gigantism of Carboniferous insects of the Pennsylvanian Epoch is its markedly higher oxygen content. The swamp plants might account for the increase." He pushed away from Sandersohn and Alan. "I feel invigorated. Please allow me to enter *Uhlanga* alone."

19

July 6, 2016, 6:30 a.m.   *Ngomo* Mine, the Shack –
Trace worked feverishly, but took no shortcuts. He and Alan had
designed the fiber optic cable connecting the *Cerberus* computer to
the tether box to be both flexible and durable for the rough handling
they expected the machine to endure. However, the circuitry relaying
the myriad of signals from the micro-servers in the control panel to
the tether box was not. They were in essence, the ganglia and axioms
of the machine's brain, serving the same function, except they
controlled hydraulic pumps and micro-actuators instead of muscle.
The spider web network of delicate, fragile wires would not tolerate
rough handling. It was delicate work.

At last, the job was finished. He panned the camera but saw
nothing within range of the *Cerberus'* lights. He still had no audio,
but that could have been a physical problem on the *Cerberus* end. He
sat watching for half an hour. Finally, fearing to leave the Shack in
case Alan needed him, he used the password Bill had given him for
the mine's security cameras. Many of the cameras weren't working,
but by switching from level to level, he discovered the mine was a
ghost town. He saw no miners. Drills, mining locos, lunch pails, hard
hats, and explosives carts, all hastily abandoned. He saw no security
personnel. The military had met fierce resistance deeper in the mine
and pulled back to the upper levels to regroup. They stood around in
confused groups near elevators and ventilation tunnels waiting for
orders.

He saw scores of corpses and partially dismembered human
skeletons, enough to give him an idea of the bloodbath below the
ground. The insects had caught the miners unaware and wreaked
havoc on them. Jackhammers, picks, shovels, and bare hands proved

no match for the creatures. The various species of insects had staked out individual territories. The beetles remained in the lower levels, while the spiders had taken up residence in 60 Level and above. Millipedes preferred the airshafts. The scorpion-like *mandibulates* haunted the first and second levels, but they were few in number. As he watched, one of the creatures dashed from an airshaft. It disintegrated beneath a hail of SADF automatic weapons' fire. The young soldiers seemed relieved to have a target to shoot at.

At a brief flicker of movement on the *Cerberus'* monitor screen, he abandoned the security cameras. A shadow fell across the screen. He panned the camera and adjusted the focus. The ebony creature slid from the shadows and undulated across his field of view before disappearing upslope of the lava tube. It moved with such speed, he had no time to start the laser array for a shot at it. He hoped it was moving away from Alan and the others.

He continued his repairs, but uncertainty about Alan's situation plagued his mind. When he glimpsed a tall figure on the monitor screen emerging from the shadows, his pulse raced. *Alan,* he thought. He dropped his tools and tried the audio. The sound of heavy footsteps reached him before he was able to identify the person. He called out over the speaker, "Alan. It's good to see …"

Verkhoen poked his face into the camera. His face and shirt were drenched with perspiration, and his chest heaved with heavy breathing, as if he had been running. His pallid complexion and wild, restless eyes spooked Trace. "Let me out!" he yelled. "It's coming."

"Where's Alan?"

"Dead."

The single word, delivered so dispassionately by Verkhoen confirmed his darkest fear. A dark, sinister cloud enveloped his mind, threatening to overwhelm him. "What happened?"

"The creatures," Verkhoen shouted, staring back up the lava tube. "Move this thing and let me out."

Trace hesitated. Why was Verkhoen alone? "What about the others?"

Verkhoen stared directly into the camera, but his eyes remained unfocused, jerking spasmodically from side to side. They were the eyes of a man driven half-mad by fright. His voice rose in volume until it became a shrill screech. "Dead," he moaned. "Dead. They're all dead, all dead, all dead," he repeated.

Trace groaned in anguish. Alan had risked his life to save Eve Means, and now they were both dead. Alan, Bill, Vince – the only people he cared about were all dead.

"Move this thing!" Verkhoen yelled. He was frantic, pounding on the camera with both fists, causing the image to shake. He was afraid Verkhoen would break the lens. As much as he despised the man, he had to let Verkhoen out. He couldn't let the creatures kill him too. He backed the *Cerberus* away from the opening. It was still moving as Verkhoen squeezed through the narrow gap he created. Trace panned the camera to watch Verkhoen race down the tunnel. Then, feeling he could do no more, he resealed the opening.

He leaned back in his chair, drained of all sense of purpose. The price of success had been much too high. What would he say to Alan's parents? He gazed at the scene of carnage that had been the control trailer. South Africa had seen too much bloodshed in its sordid past. It seemed to be a trend carrying into the future as well. Shipping the ill-fated Shack back to Nevada might introduce shades of the past. It was up to Alan's father, of course, but if it were his call, he would burn the Shack to the ground, scatter the ashes to the wind, and leave South Africa with only his laptop and toothbrush. *And a signed contract from Verkhoen for three Cerberus AT10s*, he added.

20

July 6, 2016, 6:00 a.m.   *Ngomo* Mine, 60 Level –

Duchamps stumbled as he stepped out of the elevator. His legs were growing numb, and a gray mist filled his vision. *Almost as thick as the fog in my brain*, he thought, joking at his sardonic joke. The millipede venom, poisonous or not, was affecting him in peculiar ways. He could barely lift his arms much less carry the diamonds. He glanced back at the elevator and his four knapsacks of stolen riches. They were useless to him now. Verkhoen had gotten his revenge by locking down the elevators, trapping him with the creatures he had allowed to escape. The irony was not lost on him.

He shambled to an emergency station beside the elevator and fumbled with the catch to open a first-aid kit attached to a wall. He rifled its contents, shoving most of them to the floor, until he located a single-dose hypo of adrenaline. He jammed it against his arm and pressed it home. The adrenaline hit his system quickly, forcing back part of the gray mist. If the millipede venom was poisonous, the adrenaline wouldn't save his life, but it might keep him functioning long enough for rescuers to find him and transport him to medical treatment. Survival had now become more important to him than riches.

He had no doubt the SADF or the SAPS would come eventually. He had been instrumental in setting up the protocols for the army and police in case of a mine catastrophe. He had planned to use the confusion of their arrival to mask his escape. Now, he needed them.

He poured hydrogen peroxide over the gash in his chest, fighting to keep from screaming at the pain and attracting unwanted attention from insects. Once the burning subsided, he placed a gauze pad over the wound and taped it in place. With shaking hands, he did a poor job at it, but it would have to do for now.

He needed to get his bearings. He was back on 60 Level, two-hundred meters deeper in the mine. He laughed at the irony. He was back where he had started. He couldn't use the elevators to escape the mine. That left one of the airshafts. The climb would be impossible hauling sixty kilos of diamonds, especially in his weakened condition. He could barely walk. He would have to stash them some place safe and devise a way to return for them later. He chose several of the more valuable stones and stuffed them in his pockets for traveling money to get him out of South Africa.

He tried dragging the knapsacks, but his hands couldn't maintain their grip. He connected the bags end-to-end by their straps and looped one of the straps over his chest. He leaned into his makeshift harness like a lead dog in a dogsled team. It took all his strength, but he dragged the knapsacks a short way down the corridor to a caged area used to store used pumps and lengths of pipe. He came close to passing out from the effort. His hands were growing number and each breath hurt his chest.

He fell to his knees in front of the chicken-wire enclosure, fighting the lethargy draining his willpower to continue, as he gasped for air. He surveyed the enclosure, searching for a safe hiding place for his diamonds. Most of the pumps were rusty and beyond repair. Like the stack of used pipes removed during water line refits, they awaited pickup for the recycling plant. He wasn't worried about discovery. Most of the junk had lain there since he started working at the mine fifteen years earlier.

Choosing a pump farthest from the door partially stripped for parts, he removed the diamonds from the knapsacks, and shoveled them with his hands into the empty impeller housing, filling it to the level of the intake pipe. He stuffed the empty knapsacks on top of them and piled rusted metal parts against intake opening. Satisfied they would avoid a cursory search, he left.

The nearest airshaft with an emergency ladder was almost a kilometer away. The mine was crawling with killer giant insects, and he had only a single magazine of ammunition left. If he couldn't find a discarded weapon along the way, he would never make it. He kept one hand on the shaft wall as he walked to keep from falling. The shaft was strangely silent. A few times, he heard small sounds farther down side tunnels and stopped moving to avoid making a sound, but he met no survivors or insects. Evidence of their carnage abounded: human bones but no whole skeletons; a few obscenely shrunken, silk-wrapped mummies; pools of dried blood. His curiosity at the alarming number of pieces of chitinous insect carapaces passed quickly. Whatever had killed them didn't concern him. Dead bugs were good bugs.

He reached the airshaft without incident. He stared into the darkness above his head and cringed. When he reached inside, his hand slipped off the first rung. He tried again, but his hands wouldn't cooperate. The millipede toxin was coursing through his body. He knew he would never be able to climb up the shaft. He sat down in front of the airshaft vent with his back to the wall.

Through the mist of his vision, he saw a human figure moving toward him. He didn't care if it was a frightened miner or the SAPS come to arrest him. He called out.

"Help me."

The shadowy figure answered, "Where are my diamonds, Duchamps?"

Duchamps hung his head in defeat. Verkhoen had beaten him after all. He stared up his ex-boss, trying to focus on his face through the mist of his failing vision. Verkhoen had a R4 rifle pointed at his stomach. He noticed Verkhoen was no longer the pristine clotheshorse. Instead of the usual jumpsuit that most people wore in the mines, Verkhoen's wrinkled, dirt-smeared suit pants and ripped, bloodstained white shirt made him look like a vagabond tramp. His tie and suit coat were missing.

"You look like shit, Verkhoen," Duchamps chuckled. "Are you lost?"

"You stole my diamonds, Duchamps, and then you tried to shut down my mine. Give me my diamonds."

Duchamps laughed. "I'll tell you where they are if you want them, but you'll have to fight your way through a mess of giant, slimy insects to get to them."

He knew about Verkhoen's phobia and wanted to watch the ruthless CEO squirm at the thought of insects. To his surprise, Verkhoen smiled at him.

"There are worse things down here than the insects, Duchamps,

174

much worse."

"What things?"

"The devil himself. I know. I've seen him. He's coming for you, Duchamps."

Verkhoen's strange manner made him nervous. He glanced up the airshaft but saw nothing. He nodded at the case sitting at Verkhoen's feet. "I see you brought along a few sparklers." He patted his pocket. "I have a few more. If we join forces, we can help each other out of here. Once we're topside, we go our separate ways. You keep the diamonds and the mine, and I don't tell the authorities what you've been doing. Just let me keep these few."

"I could simply shoot you and take all the diamonds," Verkhoen replied. "No one would care."

"If you shoot, you'll attract a horde of insects and spiders."

This time, his mention of insects had the desired effect. Verkhoen glanced about furtively. His hands shook. He was on the edge. Duchamps knew if he pushed just a little harder, the former tyrant would fold like a beach umbrella in a gale.

"Are you more afraid of this creature you mentioned or of Alan Hoffman?"

Verkhoen's hand steadied. His eyes narrowed and focused on Duchamps. Duchamps realized too late that he had pushed Verkhoen too far. The smile that creased his lips was more vicious than the snarl of an enraged lion.

"Then I must give the bugs something to hold their attention," he said, and then squeezed the trigger.

A searing pain exploded in Duchamps' right side. He glanced at the bright red blood staining his shirt and running down his pants leg and recognized arterial blood. "Shit," he mumbled. He stared at Verkhoen in disbelief.

Verkhoen cupped his hand to his ear and cocked his head to one side, grinning. "I hear them, Duchamps. They're answering my dinner bell. They're coming for you"

"You bloody bastard."

"You can keep the diamonds in your pocket to pay for the ferry ride across the River Styx. I'll be back for the others. You hid them somewhere. I'll turn my mine upside if I have to find them. They belong to me. But first, I have to clean house."

Guessing Verkhoen's plan, Duchamps stared at him incredulous. "You intend to flood the mine."

"The rushing water will sweep these creatures back to hell, and erase any incriminating evidence. Don't worry. You won't drown. I think you'll be dead long before the water reaches you."

The sound of insects echoed from down the tunnel. Duchamps panicked. "Shoot me, Verkhoen," he pleaded. "Don't leave me here for these monsters."

Verkhoen place a finger to his lips. "Hush, now, and maybe they won't find you." He burst into a big grin. "No, wait, they can smell blood. Maybe you should stop bleeding, Duchamps."

"I hope you die slowly, Verkhoen."

"That's the way you'll die, Duchamps." He paused. All traces of rancor vanished, replaced by a deep, resonating fear that showed in his eyes. "Unless the black nightmare creatures reach you first." He shook his head. "I wouldn't wish that on even you, Duchamps."

He crawled inside the vent and began climbing the ladder with one hand, holding onto the case with the other. He leaned over and looked back at Duchamps. "You shouldn't have broken your leash, Duchamps. You let this mad venture of yours screw you up the ass."

"Fuck you, Verkhoen!" he shouted.

The skittering grew louder, coming from both directions. He raised his rifle and laid it across his lap. He had only a handful of bullets left, not enough, but the thought of killing himself didn't enter his mind. That was giving up. He would fight the bastards until they tore him apart.

The lights began flickering, and then went out. The mineshaft instantly became as dark as the inside of a nun's habit. He laughed. "*Bliksem*," he said in Afrikaans. "Fuck it."

21

July 6, 2016, 8:45 a.m.   Magma chamber, Ngomo Volcano –
Masowe showed them a winding path down the side of the magma chamber. Small lizards and smaller versions of the giant insects scurried between crevasses in the rocks. Partially dissolved or shattered insect carapaces lay scattered over the steep slope, discarded remnants of past meals. Late to the feast but eager to participate, tiny scavengers crawled over the husks seeking any remaining tidbits of food. The ground teemed with cockroaches, some as large as the palm of Alan's hand. Unlike their darkness loving, beneath-the-oven-scurrying, topside counterparts, these roaches had no fear of man. They scampered around and over Alan's boots. Disgusted by their presence, he kicked at them. They dodged his flailing boot but otherwise ignored him.

Small pools of water connected by narrow channels formed a large lagoon. Clouds of insects the size of dust motes swirled over the water's dark surface. Occasionally, a large flying insect or an even larger dragonfly would glide through the formation, scooping up mouthfuls of insects like a whale through a school of fish, temporarily leaving a clear wake in its path that quickly filled in. The water moved sluggishly, like molasses on a frigid day. Alan suspected the liquid was more proto-petroleum than water, heavily laden with a stew of organic compounds and dissolved gasses. Churned by the movement of unseen denizens below the surface, ripples spread in concentric circles, holding their shapes for a disconcerting length of time. Bubbles of methane gas ballooned from the surface, becoming unnaturally large before bursting and releasing their contents.

Interspersed among the ponds, clinging to the ribbons of dark earth between them, tall trees looking remarkably like the scrub junipers and pinion pines found on the slopes of the Sierra Madres harbored a host of insects and lizards scampering among their foliage. Their noise died as Alan's group approached.

The air grew warmer and more humid as they descended, becoming a sweltering sauna. He had once visited Okefenokee Swamp in Georgia. There as here, the hot, humid air trapped by the dense tree canopy, or in this case the cavern roof, created an inhospitable environment. The air smelled the same as well – ripe with the heavy, earthy stench of rotting vegetation and reeking of swamp gas.

"The swamp is a cauldron," he said to the others, "probably heated by a second, deeper chamber filled with molten magma."

He noticed no one was listening. Sandersohn calmly scribbled notes on his iPad as he walked, while Eve stopped every few dozen steps to snap photographs with her cell phone. There was no sense of urgency in any of them. Bedazzled by the thrill of discovery, they had forgotten what followed them. *Or what lies ahead*, he reminded himself.

The higher oxygen content of the magma chamber invigorated him, urging him to walk faster in spite of the oppressive heat. He resisted the impulse and remained with the others. Despite his weakened condition, Doctor Tells refused any assistance. He rested his weight on boulders and fallen plants to maintain his precarious balance on the steep path. His pace was excruciatingly slow, especially for Masowe, who stopped often to look back and scowl.

"Where are we going?" Alan asked Masowe.

The security guard pointed to a grove of trees. "There. Beyond the trees is a cave. We will be safe there."

Alan studied the trees more carefully. Now he could see the conifers bore only a faint resemblance to the ones with which he was familiar. Others looked more like giant ferns. Sandersohn walked up beside him.

"The tallest plants are *lepidodendrons*. Some of them are thirty-meters tall. The ones that look like Christmas trees are *cordaites*, a primitive conifer. The giant horsetail ferns are *calamites* and the smaller ones are *filicales*. They remained relatively unchanged to the present day. The vines are *phenophyllales*. They're beautiful, aren't they?" he added.

"It reminds me of a photo of a northern Australian forest," Alan replied.

Sandersohn smiled. "You're not far off. The Gondwana Rain Forest in Australia contains plants very similar to fossil records of plants living when Gondwana was a continent. To see them as they were is ... awe inspiring."

"Like Daniel Boone once said, 'I hardly ever looked at a tree except to see if there was an Indian behind it or a bear in it.' I'm more worried about what we might find."

Sandersohn glanced behind him. "Yes, I see. Those ... creatures confound me. They are impossible, yet they exist. One can readily imagine what other exotic wonders nature created, which did not survive the upheaval of the continents or leave a fossil record."

"You call it an exotic wonder. I think it's a monster from hell."

"It is *Intulo*," Masowe called out, "a demon."

"I won't argue the point," Alan replied. "The problem is surviving until we can deal with it."

Sandersohn looked at him questioningly. "How do you propose to deal with them?"

Alan sniffed the air. "Smell that? Methane. The lagoon is full of it, as well as other flammable chemicals. A layer of combustible gas covers the entire bottom of the magma chamber. The higher oxygen content of the air will magnify the force of even a small explosion. I propose to seal the creatures in here with dynamite if not kill them outright."

Sandersohn shook. "You're mad. You'll kill us all."

"We're dead anyway. Those things are toying with us. They could easily have killed us all by now. We'll never get past them."

"I refuse to believe there is no hope," Sandersohn insisted.

"You were pretty damn certain we were dying earlier," Alan said.

Eve placed her hand on the distraught paleozoologist's shoulder. "We can't allow these monsters to escape, even at the cost of our lives. I proposed this venture thinking I was doing something noble. I should have known my personal motives would bear bitter fruit. I wanted to destroy Verkhoen in revenge for my husband's death. Now, I've helped unleash creatures that could kill hundreds and another group of monsters that could eradicate all mankind. I'm prepared to pay whatever price necessary to correct my mistakes." She glanced at Alan and smiled.

"You didn't let them out," he said. "We can hold that bastard Duchamps accountable for that. Verkhoen's not much better. He's more interested in saving his company and his ass than in correcting nature's oversight. I'm determined to cause another E.L.E., an extinction level event that will do what evolution couldn't."

Tells sat down on a boulder to rest. He glanced around the magma chamber. "What will you call your newly discovered volcano?"

Tells' question caught him by surprise. "What?"

"As its discoverer, you retain the privilege of naming it."

"Masowe discovered it, but I guess Ngomo Volcano is as good a name as any."

Tells nodded. "It is an apt name worthy of placement on the maps."

"If we don't get out of here, no one will know about it," he reminded the doctor.

"Hurry," Masowe urged.

This time, Tells accepted Alan's hand to help him up and leaned against him for support as they continued down the path. The path wound around the slope of the chamber, avoiding the water, finally reaching a wide shelf of glassy obsidian. The obsidian had fractured over time, leaving shards of volcanic glass thrusting upwards like daggers. Picking a safe course through the dangerous maze took time. Beyond the shelf, an opening in the cliff proved to be a shallow cave. It was to this Masowe led them.

Inside, a mat of dried lichen beside the ashes of a fire was Masowe's bed. Bones of small lizards from his last meal lay scattered around the ashes. Alan helped Tells to a raised flat outcropping, where he lay on his back to catch his breath. Masowe squatted beside the entrance, staring into the distance. Alan chose a spot on the ground beside him. As he watched, a disturbance on the shore of the lagoon attracted his attention. A large lizard had strayed too close to the edge and mired in the mud. The lizard's pathetic bleats became more frantic, as the dark sludge encased its hind legs, drawing it deeper into the bog.

"That lizard is a *hylononus*," Sandersohn said in his lecture voice. "I believe Masowe can attest to their taste. The bones of its relatives are scattered around his campfire. I noticed other lizards larger than humans as we descended the slope, *ophiacodons*. It is good he hasn't tried to make a meal of them lest the tables turn and he becomes their dinner."

Before Alan could respond, to his astonishment, the mud moved. Terror gripped him, squeezing the air from his lungs. His pulsed thundered in his ears. It was all he could do to keep from running away screaming; the ebony creatures had returned. Then, noticing Masowe's lack of apprehension, he took a closer look at the creature and saw that it was too small to be the ebony monster. It was barely larger than a beach towel.

"The meta-millipede has offspring," he gasped as realization struck him. He was both amazed and frightened by his discovery.

"Yes, there are many of its babies living in the water," Masowe said. "They prefer the water to the land; nevertheless, they venture out upon it when hungry."

Now, he had more reason than ever to seal the tunnels. Just the handful of the creatures they had seen could devastate the outside world. Hundreds could wipe mankind from the face of the planet. God or nature had been kind to seal the monsters in the cavern below the surface so many eons ago. It had taken the greed and audacity of humans to release them.

Eve had noticed the immature creatures as well. Her hand pressed against her open mouth, and she sagged against a boulder for support. He wanted to go to her, to reassure her, but the gesture would have been meaningless. She was well aware of the danger they faced. If the babies were here, then mama must be nearby.

"Is *Intulo* here?" he asked Masowe.

Masowe closed his eyes for a moment. "No," he said with finality. "I sense it is far away in the mine."

Alan's relief that the creature was not nearby withered with the realization that all his plans were for naught. "My God," he moaned. "It's loose. I'm too late."

"Perhaps not," Sandersohn said. His gaze remained fixed on the struggle between *hylononus* and baby monster, a battle the lizard could not hope to win. Its death was as inevitable as the eventual extinction of its dinosaur descendants.

"What do you mean?"

"Fascinating."

"Get to your point," Alan urged him.

"Most creatures maintain a bond of some kind with their offspring. If these creatures are as intelligent as we think, they will also."

Intrigued, Alan asked, "How does that help us?"

"If we threaten the babies, mama might come to the rescue."

Masowe stared at them. "You cannot deceive *Intulo*."

Exasperated, Alan confronted the Zulu. "It's no god, Masowe. Does God have babies? It's a creature no one has ever seen before, but it's no god."

"It created them from its flesh, like your Christian God."

"God made man, not more gods. There can only be one God. God can't create gods."

While Masowe pondered the theological dilemma he had put forward, Alan turned back to Sandersohn. "Drawing them back by threatening the young makes more sense than using us as bait, but I'm afraid my original plan won't work. Even if I ignite the methane and cause a cave-in, it won't bring down the roof. The rock is dense granite and obsidian, not kimberlite as I hoped. Sealing the tunnel the *Cerberus* dug isn't enough, and there's still the crack in the wall we came through." He pointed to the series of openings in the cliff. "Any one of these caves could intersect other mine shafts. A tremor could create a new opening, releasing these horrors on an unsuspecting world."

"What do you propose?"

"I have to gain access to the *Cerberus* and bring it here." He pointed to one of the pillars holding up the roof of the magma chamber. "The *Cerberus'* lasers can direct enough heat to the base of the pillar to weaken it. The weight of the rock above should bring down the entire roof."

Eve walked over to him. Her initial shock at seeing the young *Intulos* had worn off, but her pained expressed mirrored her fear. Her voice trembled as she said, "You can't go back to your machine, Alan. Those ... things could come back at any moment."

He had considered that possibility, but he had been willing to sacrifice himself earlier. Nothing had changed. In fact, the necessity had become more urgent. "I have to take a chance. Don't you see? If

I can draw the creatures to me, the rest of you can escape through the crack and back into the mine."

"You will die," she said.

Regret filled her voice. Alan's resolve wavered. He wished things had unfolded differently. Eve was someone he might have come to love. *Sometimes love*, he reminded himself, *just isn't in the cards*.

"No," Masowe said. "He will not."

Masowe's certainty confused him. "Why not?"

"If the creatures are not *Intulo*, if they are monsters as you say, then this place is not *Uhlanga*. Bring your machine here. Show me how to operate it. I will remain here. *Intulo* is a creature of Zulu legend, and I am the son of a Zulu *sangoma*. It is my place to destroy it." He grimaced as he tapped his finger against his temple. "It is in here, inside my head. It toys with me. I must free myself of it."

"You should reconsider your offer," Alan said. "I'll do it."

Masowe hung his head. "I know you think I am mad. Perhaps I am or was for a short time, but I am thinking clearly now. How can I continue with my life with the memory of the creatures inside my mind, scarring it as my body is now scarred?" He shook his head. "I am descended from warriors. Let me die as a warrior."

Alan stared at the Zulu security guard as he considered his plea. He, too, had felt the shadow of the creature in his mind. How much darker was its presence in Masowe's? When he looked back at the lagoon, more of the immature creatures had joined the first to engulf the lizard completely. Its struggles ceased. A few minutes later, they returned to the water, slipping below its sluggish surface, leaving nothing behind.

"All right. You discovered this place. You deserve the opportunity to determine its fate. When we've rested, we'll accompany the others to the crack, and make sure they make it out before we continue to the *Cerberus*. If I can gain control of its systems, I'll show you what to do on the way back. If not," he shrugged, "we die."

Masowe smiled. "We will die as warriors."

"I won't leave you," Eve insisted.

"Yes you will. You have to guide the others through the mine to the surface. You're the only one who knows the way. Sandersohn." He handed Sandersohn the R4 rifle. "Take this. You might need it."

Sandersohn took the rifle and nodded. "Help Doctor Tells. Be gentle with him but keep him moving. You might not have much time."

"What about you?" he asked.

"Once I show Masowe what to do, I'll join you somewhere along the way, but don't wait for me. I'll catch up. The insects will be around the elevators looking for a way out. Eve, is there another, safer way out?"

"The ore conveyor belt on 70 Level. It leads to the old mining pit. It and the skip elevator on 65 Level are the only other two exits."

"Try for the conveyor on 70 Level. It's closer."

Eve fell to her knees beside Alan and wrapped her arms around him, sobbing into his shoulder. "Oh, Alan," she whispered. "Don't do it, please."

He returned her embrace, wishing he had time to linger with her in his arms. After a few moments, he pushed her away, clasping her hands in his. "Don't worry about me. I'm a Nevada boy. I'm as fast as a jackrabbit and tougher than an armadillo. I'll see you outside."

She wiped her eyes and nodded.

"I have a small medical kit in my bag. See if you can tend to some of Masowe's wounds." She looked at him as if saying, "Why bother?" If Masowe was willing to die in his place, they could at least make his pain bearable. "I think I have a bottle of water left. Pass it around. Make sure Doctor Tells drinks some. He looks dehydrated."

She glanced at Masowe's arm, the more serious of his injuries, if not the most painful. "I'll do what I can."

Alan took a last look at the swamp four kilometers beneath the earth. Whatever the outcome, it was better than dying in the belly of a volcano and joining the rest of the decaying vegetation to become oil for someone's chainsaw in a few million years.

22

July 6, 2016, 10:30 a.m.   *Ngomo* Mine, the Reservoir –
Verkhoen was pleased with himself. Dealing with Duchamps had
brought his mind back into focus. He was convinced that releasing
the water in the reservoir was the only solution. Duchamps had
unwittingly seconded his opinion. Flooding the mine would drown all
the creatures and wash them back to the lower levels, especially the
black devils that had killed his men. It would also take care of Eve
Means and Alan Hoffman. He shuddered at the look of hatred on
Hoffman's face when he had abandoned them in the lava tube.
Hoffman's burning glare frightened him almost as much as the black
creatures. Flooding the mine would solve all his problems. The
diamonds in his case would pay to pump the water from the mine and
restart operations, and more diamonds awaited him in the lava tube.
Plus that bastard Duchamps' stash.

The reservoir was simply a nine-hundred-meter-long horizontal
shaft. Dozens of airshafts connected the mine's many levels and
tunnels with a network of pumps and fans. There was no floodgate or
relief valve to empty it, but Verkhoen had conceived of a way to
achieve his goal. Ten levels above where he had left Duchamps, his
miners were blasting the gold-bearing rock face. They would not
have had time to secure the explosives before evacuating the mine. A
few bags of ammonium nitrate would shatter the roof of the tunnel
immediately below the reservoir. The weight and pressure of the
water would do the rest. 1.5 billion liters of water would race through
the mine like a flushed toilet.

Along the way, he passed two dismembered corpses wearing
camouflaged uniforms and carrying Heckler and Koch MP5 sub
machineguns. He recognized the single star on the bloody remains of

a beret and the sleeve patch, an inverted commando knife within a laurel wreath, as belonging to the SADF Special Forces. He cursed aloud. If the military had taken control of the mine, he couldn't escape through the elevators as he had planned. They had either overridden his lockout or rappelled down the shaft. If they caught him, especially with a suitcase full of diamonds, they would immediately detain and question him. His influence and status would be useless with the military authorities. He would have to find another way out of the mine.

He remembered his father's one folly, one both he and his father had worked fervently to bury in the past. Twenty years earlier, his father had drilled a vertical shaft five-hundred meters straight down on the far side of the mine and dug a horizontal adit to intersect one of the main shafts. It took three costly attempts to connect them. Within months, the vein in that direction played out, and he had ordered the shaft sealed. Few people other than the mine supervisor knew of its existence. He was certain no one would be watching it. To reach it, however, he would have to cross the entire width of the mine.

He discarded his R4 rifle, picked up one of the HK MP5s, and examined it. The six-pound weight felt familiar in his hands. He had trained with the .22 caliber version while in school and had become an expert marksman; however, this was the real thing, firing heavier caliber .9mm parabellum bullets at 800 rounds per minute. The Special Forces version he held came equipped with a noise suppressor, a laser sight, and a flashlight attached to the barrel. Pleased with his find, he gingerly removed a second clip from the dead soldier's uniform and slung the weapon it over his shoulder.

A spiral concourse connected 60 Level to 30 Level. This allowed him to avoid using the elevator and alerting the military to his presence. Reaching the shaft on 50 Level he sought, he located an abandoned explosives cart loaded with twenty bags of ANFO – Ammonium Nitrate Fuel Oil – a case of dynamite, a box of electric blasting caps, a full reel of wire, and a detonator. He whistled a few bars of Chopin, his favorite composer, as he rolled the deadly cart back to the ramp.

30 Level was as high as the concourse went. He had no choice but risk the elevator to reach 20 Level directly below the reservoir.

Punching in the code he had used to seal the elevators, he was delighted to find it still worked. If he were lucky, they wouldn't notice the elevator operating. If they did, they might attribute it to a SADF team. Either way, he would be gone before anyone came to investigate.

Carefully choosing a spot midway of the shaft, he piled the bags of ANFO against a wooden beam bearing the weight of a heavy crossbeam supporting the roof. He punched holes in several bags and inserted sticks of dynamite with fused blasting caps. He piled the remainder of the dynamite around the bags of ANFO. He ran the wire two-hundred meters along the mineshaft until he emptied the spool. Then, he connected the ends of the wire to the battery-powered detonator. He didn't need the entire spool of wire; the detonator had a built-in timer for delayed ignitions, but he preferred to be as far away as possible if something went wrong. He set the timer for three hours, the amount of time he estimated he would need to cross the mine and exit through the old shaft. He didn't want to risk becoming a victim of his own manmade flood. He smiled as he pushed the button starting the timer.

The passageway intersecting the old elevator shaft was on 22 Level, two levels below him. After setting the detonator, he trotted down the passageway to the airshaft. Just before he reached it, the lights went out.

Nothing to worry about, he thought. *The military is just playing games.*

Verkhoen switched on the flashlight attached to the barrel of the MP5 and used it to light his path. When he reached the airshaft, he played the light over the wire mesh grate. Two, red, glowing compound eyes stared back at him reflected by the light. Before he could fire, the screen crashed outward, followed by an enormous scorpion-like creature, its barbed tail lashing about like a bullwhip. Sharp pincers tipped the front pair of its eight legs, and its compound mouthparts clacked from side to side in anticipation of an easy meal. It leaped into the tunnel and bounded away into the darkness, avoiding his flashlight. In his haste to track it, he made the mistake of turning his back to the open vent. His ears detected the sound of another of the creatures crawling up the shaft.

"Sneaky bastards," he said. "Trying to set me up."

He spun on his right heel and fired a burst across the mouth of the opening, stitching a line of holes in the second creature's carapace. It hissed and fell back down the shaft, banging against the sides of the shaft as it fell. He turned his attention to the remaining scorpion.

He knew it was near. He could feel it, but he couldn't find it. Unless the beam of the flashlight reflected from its compound eyes, it was almost invisible in the darkness. He remembered an old survival tip a guide had related to him on a trip to the Kalahari in Namibia. When stranded in the desert without food or water, you could always count on nature's cleaning crew, vultures. They always showed up for death. If you remained motionless and played dead, they would approach to within arm's reach before attacking. Their meat was stringy and foul, but it beat starving, and their blood provided life-giving moisture.

He extinguished his flashlight, closed his eyes, and stood with his back against the wall to force the bug to attack from his front or sides. He fought down his fear of insects. He imagined the scorpion as a hyena, prowling the edge of camp while on safari. He listened. A soft scraping to his right repeated. He knew switching on the flashlight would spook it. He would have to rely on the laser sight. He would have time for only one shot. He would have to make it count.

He raised the MP5 and flicked on the laser sight in one fluid motion. The red dot painted an object just a few meters away. He knew it wasn't a wall. He fired on full automatic, allowing the recoil to push his weapon up and to the left. He sprayed the entire area with bullets. Satisfied he had hit the creature, he switched on his flashlight.

The scorpion lay on its side twitching, but a pool of yellow ichor ran from several tightly grouped holes in its head. One compound eye was smashed and dripping gore. He fired one last burst into it to finish it off. The creature stopped moving. He spat on it for good measure.

"Take that, you bloody bastard."

He picked up the case of diamonds and continued his journey across the mine. He met no more creatures, for which he was grateful. It meant they had not reached the abandoned tunnel. A fire-resistant brattice cloth hanging across the shaft marked the beginning of the older dig. When he pushed it aside, it was like opening the door to a blast furnace. A wave of scorching, dry air swept over him. The tunnel had no ventilation. The temperature hovered around 52^0 C, the temperature of a rare steak. The sweltering air quickly desiccated his lungs, making each breath a challenge. He wiped his parched lips on the back of his dehydrated hand and wished he had brought water.

There were no lights in the tunnel, and he had only the flashlight on the MP5. He was so exhausted from his long day of exertion that he barely had the strength to hold the weapon in his hands. In places, the shaft narrowed and the roof dipped to within one-and-a-half meters of the floor. He walked stooped over, dragging the case behind him, one hand brushing the blistering wall of the tunnel. He was dimly aware of the burning in his fingertips, but he ignored it.

When at last he reached the abandoned vertical shaft, he looked at the wire mesh covering the elevator cage and almost gave up. There had been no power to the elevator for over a decade. Even if it had electricity, he wouldn't trust it. The wooden floor was rotten and the cables were rusty. He didn't have the strength to remove the wire mesh, let alone make the long climb to the surface. He looked up the shaft, his eyes drawn to the miniscule square of daylight five-hundred meters above him. It was a long climb, but it ultimately led to safety.

He had no choice. It was either climb or die, and he was too stubborn to let death find him in such a deep, dark, and lonely place. He checked his watch, but the 6,000 US dollar Tag Heuer chronograph wasn't working. Somewhere along his journey, he had smashed it. He didn't know how much time he had left. He rested for as long as he could, but the thought of the ebony monsters somewhere behind him compelled him to action. He threaded the strap of his MP5 through the handle of the case of diamonds and slung both over his shoulder.

The climb was difficult and his progress was slow. He tested each rusty, two-decades-old rung before placing his full weight on it. His shoulders and his arms burned, but he reached one hand over the other and lifted each foot as high as he could, ignoring his aches and pains.

When he neared the halfway point, a shudder jarred the ladder. Dirt and rock sloughed from the walls and showered his head. He lifted his case to protect his bare head from falling debris. He clung to the rungs of the ladder as a blast of cool moist air swept up the shaft, bringing with it a myriad of smells. His explosives had detonated. He smiled, imaging the utter chaos he had created. He hoped Duchamps had managed to stay alive long enough to watch the flood racing toward him, washing him away like trash in the gutter.

His hands, already blistered from carrying the heavy case, burned from gripping the rough, rusty rungs. Slivers of metal dug into his fingers and the palms of his hands. He paused for a moment to wipe them on his shirt, but it only drove the splinters deeper into his raw, bleeding flesh. He spied a small niche in the wall of the shaft barely wide enough to curl up in, but he managed to squeeze himself and the diamonds into the shallow shelf to rest his muscles. He had taken far longer than he had anticipated. Daylight was fading quickly. He didn't want to roam the desert alone at night if any of the insects had found a way out of the mine.

He especially didn't want to meet one of the horrible black monstrosities that had devoured his men. He had seen a pride lions stalking a herd of wildebeest and had sensed that same determination and certainty of purpose in the creatures. Whatever hell had spawned them, they felt no more kinship with humans than the lion did the wildebeest.

He knew he couldn't it make out hampered by his heavy load, but he wouldn't give up the diamonds. They were now his Holy Grail, his *raison d'être*. He unhooked the MP5 and dropped it back down the shaft. It was nearly out of ammunition anyway. It only weighed three kilos, but every kilo counted. He hoped his decision didn't come back to bite him in the ass. Using the sling from the MP5, he draped the case over his neck and shoulder and continued climbing.

His motions became repetitive, requiring no conscious thought. Each rung conquered brought him closer to freedom. He reached for another rung, surprised there was none. He had reached the top. He dragged himself over the edge of the shaft and lay prostrate on the floor of the elevator, basking in the patch of sunlight filtering in through the gaps between the wooden planks sealing the shaft. He absorbed the sun's rays like a plant, allowing it to flush the darkness of the mine from his body. All that stood between him and freedom was a flimsy wooden barricade; and yet, he didn't have the strength to breach it.

He lay there until the path of the setting sun moved it from his face. His raging thirst forced him to his feet. He threw himself against the wall repeatedly until the boards snapped, feeling nothing with his numb shoulder. He pushed the boards aside and stepped out into daylight.

I'm free, he thought.

He walked along the perimeter of the fence surrounding Van Gotts' property until he came upon a water tank for cattle. A herd of multi-colored *Nguni* cattle lounged around the tank, resting in the late day sun. He pushed through them, heedless of their long, sharp horns and bellows of protest, and plunged his face into the water, submerging it until breathing necessitated lifting it out again. He set the case of diamonds by his feet, rolled over the rim of the metal tank, and fell into the water, splashing and laughing like a schoolboy. His body was a sponge, absorbing the water to replenish what he had lost. He stopped when he noticed a Bantu herder staring at him.

"I need food," he said in Afrikaans.

The herder said nothing.

He searched his memory for the Xhosa word for food. "*Ukutya*." To emphasize his need, he mimed eating.

Without a change in his deadpan expression, the herder pulled a bundle from his pocket and handed it to Verkhoen. Whatever it was, the aroma made his mouth water. He hurriedly tore off the wrapper and saw the bundle contained a ball of citrus-flavored rice and a piece of dried fish. He wolfed them down, barely bothering to chew, enjoying the sensation of food in his empty stomach. He stared at the reticent herder.

"I need to get to the mine."

The herder stared at Verkhoen for moment, and then, shifted his gaze into the distance, as if considering leaving the crazy *mzungu* in the water tank. Verkhoen, aware that his disheveled appearance and bizarre behavior presented a poor example of a white man to the Bantu native, fished a wad of wet rand notes from his pocket and handed them to the herder. The man's eyes grew wide and a smile creased his lips when he recognized the large denominations of the notes. The amount was more than the herder could earn in a year. He nodded his head, pointed toward the mine, and helped Verkhoen from the water.

Verkhoen smiled, not at the herder, but at the fact that he had made it. He had survived his encounter with the creatures from hell, a horde of giant man-eating insects, and his harrowing journey to safety. He had paid Duchamps back for his betrayal and silenced any possible accusations from Doctor Means and Alan Hoffman. Topping it all, he had brought out enough diamonds to bribe the necessary authorities to reopen the mine, allowing him to bring out the rest at his leisure.

In hindsight, things could not have worked out any better.

23

July 6, 2016, 2:30 p.m.   Magma chamber, *Ngomo* Volcano –
Eve cleaned and wrapped Masowe's arm, but the infection rendered it a swollen, useless appendage. A salve relieved some of the pain from his burns, but she could do little to treat them properly. They were much too serious for a simple first-aid kit. Throughout the entire painful procedure, the imperturbable Zulu security guard made no complaint.

Alan allowed them to rest for only an hour. He was eager to leave, but everyone had pushed themselves to their limits, even him. Doctor Tells especially needed rest. His irregular breathing and ashy-grey complexion worried Alan. He was afraid to push the old man harder for fear he might suffer a heart attack or stroke. The others managed a little sleep, but his anger at Duchamps prevented him from relaxing enough for slumber. The security chief had murdered his friend and co-worker and deliberately set loose the ravenous insects to cover his theft of the diamonds.

Verkhoen was high on his list of ruthless characters as well. While he hadn't personally killed Eve's husband, he had allowed Duchamps free hand to stop him. In Alan's eyes, the CEO's hands were just as bloody as Duchamps' were. His first task when they were out of the mine would be to report Verkhoen's actions to the proper authority.

Alan checked his watch – 2:30 in the afternoon. He wondered what the day was like on the surface. For some inexplicable reason he thought it was sunny out. Maybe it was just wishful thinking. He could wait no longer.

"Okay everybody. It's time to leave."

Doctor Tells was barely able to sit up. He leaned against the edge of the rocky platform that had served as his bed looking dazed and confused. Eve, knowing what was coming, moped around the edge of the camp with a long face. He had wanted to go to her while the others rested, but her body language had made it clear she wanted to be alone with her thoughts.

"Eve, it's time to go," he said.

She nodded her head.

"It has to be done."

"I know. It's just that … Well, I don't want anything to happen to you."

"Believe me; I'm not looking forward to this. Masowe's lifted the worst of the burden from me. He insists it's his right to die as a warrior. I'll admit I'm conflicted about that. It was my idea and my responsibility, but I don't want to die."

"Then don't," she said.

He noticed Masowe waiting impatiently at the foot at the path. "We have to go now."

At the crack in the wall, he bid Eve farewell. Their parting was fraught with unspoken hopes and dreams. Whatever budding romance had spawned between them during their ordeal, there had been no time to fan the flames of desire into passion. On his part, Alan regretted the side of him that automatically built a wall between him and any woman who threatened his defenses. It had cost him in the past and was doing so now. Both knew it might be the last time they saw one another.

"Eve," he said, fumbling for words, "I wish …" He shook his head. "Damn it, I think we would have been good for each other. In the past …"

She smiled and touched a finger to his lips to stop his rambling. "I know. I feel it too. You awakened something in me I thought long dead. It felt wonderful to live again."

"When this is over, when I do this, I want you to come to Nevada with me."

"Perhaps," she replied. "Maybe a dinner and wine first."

He nodded. "Oh, the hell with it." He took her in his arms and kissed her with all the passion he could muster, which to his surprise was a lot. Startled by his sudden bold move, she at first backed away; then, she returned his embrace and kiss with equal ardor. He clung to her as long as he could, but each minute's delay could foil their plan.

He broke away.

"Be careful." He shook Sandersohn and Tells' hands. "Let people know what's down here."

"I will," Tells answered. Sandersohn nodded.

He watched them crawl into the crack, Eve first, followed by Tells. Sandersohn brought up the rear to shepherd Tells along. When they had disappeared, he turned to Masowe. "No time like the present."

They reached the *Cerberus* without running into any of the insects or *Intulo*. Alan connected his laptop to the outboard USB port and brought up the control functions. To his great relief the machine was fully functional, except for the telephone. He typed a message for Trace, hoping he still manned the Shack. He wouldn't blame him for leaving. Things had to be as hellish up there as they were below.

Trace replied immediately, typing, "Verkhoen said you were dead. Glad you made it. What can I do?"

Verkhoen, Alan snarled. He had been hoping *Intulo* ate the bastard. "Give me complete control of the *Cerberus*," he replied. "I need to disconnect it and move it."

To his credit, Trace didn't question him. Alan watched the controls on his screen changed from the fiber optic cable connection to onboard control. They had tested the remote capabilities of the machine only a few times with as many failures as successes. He prayed this would be one of the successes. He switched the machine's functions to remote, disconnected his laptop, and tested the remote link by switching the lights on and off. Next, he detached the exhaust hose and the fiber optic cable and started the *Cerberus'* turbine. The noise of the turbine shook the walls of the lava tube, sending a shower of rocks and dust cascading from the roof.

"If there are any bugs around, they know where to find us," he told Masowe.

Masowe stood rigid, his eyes closed. His clenched fists and trembling jaw revealed an inner torment raging inside as he sought out *Intulo*.

Alan turned his attention back to the *Cerberus*. As long as he stayed within range of the *Cerberus'* Wi-Fi, he could operate it as he would a radio-controlled model car. The machine began rolling forward on its treads. Released from its tether, it could travel as fast as he could walk. Leading it like the Pied Piper, the machine followed him up the lava tube, crunching rocks to powder beneath its heavy treads. Guiding the lumbering behemoth with the keyboard was tricky. The navigation arrows controlled the port tread, and the numeric pad arrows controlled the starboard tread. Turning required stopping the appropriate tread in the direction he wished to turn by holding down the left or right shift key.

His hands were full. He had no time to explain his intention to Trace. He hoped the onboard camera would help him understand the situation.

There was no need to pick a careful winding path along the treacherous slope of the magma chamber. The heavy drilling rig plowed a path straight down the slope, climbing over rocks and pushing aside foliage. Small lizards and insects, flushed from hiding by the *Cerberus'* clattering treads, scurried away in fright. One of the ten-foot-long lizards Sandersohn had called an *ophiacodon* shot out of its underground den, brushing past Alan in its haste to get away.

Not even the muck and mire of the swamp could deter the cumbersome machine. Like the famous Abrams tank whose jet turbine engine he had chosen to power it, the *Cerberus* forced its way across the edge of the swamp to the granite pillar Alan had chosen.

He had shown Masowe the basics of the controls on the two-kilometer journey up the lava tube. The security guard claimed a superstitious upbringing, but his nimble mind, already familiar with the operation of most of the mine's heavy machinery, quickly picked up the basics of the laptop control panel. Alan had reduced the functions to a bare minimum – sliders to point the lights and camera, targeting the laser array, and engaging the treads if he needed to move it again. There was no need to shut it down. If his plan worked, the fifteen-million-dollar uninsured machine would be lost. If not, there would be no one left to recover it.

The roar of the jet turbine's echo in the cavernous magma chamber made speaking difficult.

"Press this and the lasers engage," he shouted into Masowe's ear. "It shouldn't take more than an hour to melt enough rock to make the pillar unstable. After that, gravity will take over."

Masowe nodded. His badly blistered face revealed none of the emotions that must have been churning inside him. He had set his mind to the task, and his stoicism refused to allow him to regret his decision. Perhaps he saw it as the only way out of the hell inside his mind. Alan had felt only the fringes of *Intulo's* mind, a dark, yawning abyss that swallowed everything it touched, and it had scarred him for life. The hive-creature had robbed him of an innocence he had not known he possessed, and its absence left a void he could never fill completely.

"I understand," Masowe said. "You must go now." He held out the dynamite and fuse Alan had given him. Alan worried he had cut the fuses too short for safety, but the Zulu had ignored his concern. "I will attack its offspring and allow *Intulo* to see in my mind what I am doing. It will come."

Alan felt guilty at leaving Masowe, but it was a one-person job. He shoved Masowe's revolver down the front of his pants. It had only two bullets left in the cylinder, but if he needed to use the pistol, more ammunition wouldn't make much difference. His salvation lay in the hope *Intulo* had already feasted on the insects in the mine and would make a beeline to the swamp to protect its young.

He laid his hand on the Zulu's shoulder. "You are truly a great warrior, Masowe. Your ancestors would be proud of you."

Masowe impatiently shrugged off Alan's hand. "Yes, yes, I am a hero. Perhaps they will build a statue of me and place it next to Mandela's." He laughed. "Two black heroes in South Africa. That would be something." He became more serious. "You must go quickly. I must call *Intulo*."

Alan took the time to write a brief message to Trace on his computer, but he didn't wait for a reply. He followed the *Cerberus'* wide path back to the edge of the magma chamber, hurrying from the cavern. As he clambered up the slope, Masowe engaged the machine's laser array. A shrill whine rose to a tooth rattling intensity, tapering off slightly when the spinning array reached maximum rpm's. The cavern lit up when he fired up the lasers. Alan took one last look back to see Masowe leaping up and down on the obsidian shelf, enticing the baby creatures from the water. He held sticks of dynamite in each hand.

He lit one of the fuses with the Zippo Alan had given him and lobbed it into the water. Scant seconds after leaving his hand, the dynamite exploded. Thick, oily water erupted in a geyser.

Simultaneously, the oxygen-enriched methane exploded. In a flash, a sheet of flaming methane gas spread across the surface of the lagoon, igniting the heavy proto-petroleum ooze slowly bubbling to the surface. The concussion reached the entrance to the cavern and knocked Alan off his feet. The firestorm engulfed the trees. The flames crawled up the tree trunks, creating blazing torches of them. Within minutes, the entire swamp was a raging inferno with ferns and the thick mossy groundcover feeding the conflagration. Dense black smoke billowed upward, obscuring the cavern's roof.

The *Cerberus*, unaffected by the flames, stood like Shadrach in Nebuchadnezzar's fiery furnace, spewing its own intense fire onto the pillar of stone, adding more smoke and heat to the mix.

The intense heat billowing from the mouth of the chamber forced Alan back. Coughing from the soot-laden smoke, he sought Masowe, but the Zulu security guard turned warrior remained obscured by the dense, black cloud. The smoke was so intense Alan worried Masowe would succumb to it before *Intulo* came. He could do nothing more. Turning his back on the inferno, he returned to the crack.

Away from the moist air of the swamp, he noticed the air in the lava tube was much warmer, but he didn't think it had anything to do with the Carboniferous bonfire behind him. He was sweating profusely. He wiped his forehead with the back of his hand, unzipped his jumpsuit, and unbuttoned the top three buttons of his shirt.

"They shut down the ventilators to keep any of the creatures from escaping," he surmised aloud. That meant the trapped smoke from the burning swamp would quickly fill the entire mine. He hoped any surviving miners had already escaped.

Crawling into the crack was like entering a silent tomb. He heard no sounds but his heavy breathing and his boots scuffing against the rock. The walls of the crack pressed in on him relentlessly, robbing him of his breath. He abandoned his hard hat but kept the flashlight clenched between his teeth as he crawled. The rock ate the light like a ravenous beast, leaving him in near total darkness, intensifying the pressure of the stone around him. Tendrils of smoke followed him through the crack. The hot air felt too heavy for his lungs to move and tasted bitter. He concentrated on the tiny patch of light in front of him, ignoring the dread feeling something other than the fire was behind him, pursuing him. That it might be *Intulo* behind him drove him onward even faster.

The alarming thought occurred to him that separate parts of the hive-mind creature might be able to act independently of one another. If so, some of the ebony meta-millipedes could follow him, while the remainder confronted Masowe, a flaw in his plan he had not accounted for. He could only pray there was a limit to the *Intulo's* capabilities.

He finally emerged into the mineshaft coughing and half-blind from the smoke. His lungs sucked in the clean air in great gulps. He forced himself to calm down. Fear could kill him as quickly as one of the insects. His left arm ached from crawling through the winding crack. The pain had grown from a constant annoying presence, to a throbbing agony, pulsating with every heartbeat. It had swollen until the bandage bit into his irritated flesh. He loosened the bandage and peeked at the wound. Angry red lines radiated from the gashes. The wound suppurated a Dijon mustard-yellow pus. He hoped it wasn't gangrenous. He re-wrapped it to avoid looking at it, almost biting his tongue to quell the pain.

When he reached the crack in the roof of the tunnel he had widened with dynamite, it dawned on him that he might have difficulty climbing out with only one good arm. Sandersohn was strong enough to help Eve and Tells, and Eve could help him up, but he was alone. The only solution he could come up with was to carry rocks to the spot below the crack and pile them high enough to stand on to reach the floor of the tunnel above. It was backbreaking work. Forced to carry larger rocks with both hands, the effort of using his injured left arm brought tears to his eyes.

When he thought his mound of rocks was high enough, he climbed up and leaped for the floor above. It took three tries, but finally he wedged the edge of the opening under his left arm and pulled himself up with his right hand. He lay there for a few minutes gasping for breath, but his urgent fear drove him to move. He emerged at the now demolished wooden door outside the emergency shelter on 136 Level, hoping he could remember the circuitous route back to the #2 elevator.

The power in the mine was off. Without the ventilator fans pumping cooler fresh air into the mine, the mine had become a stagnant hothouse. He estimated the temperature at 125 degrees

Fahrenheit. It was hotter and drier than the deserts of Nevada, but in the desert, even the coyotes sought shade when temperatures reached the lethal range. He didn't have that luxury.

Racing down the maze of mineshafts with only his flashlight and his memory to guide him, his imagination conjured *Intulo* in every murky shadow. The walls of the tunnel seemed to produce darkness, oozing it from tenebrific pores and spilling it in his path. He was more than a little surprised when he reached the elevator unscathed. Without power, the cage was useless. He stared up into the daunting dark void of the elevator shaft with mounting apprehension. He located the metal ladder mounted to the side of the shaft and began climbing using only one hand. The climb was tiring, made even more difficult by the intense heat and his handicap. He wanted to stop and rest, but he had no choice. It was either climb or die.

He found Eve and the others by accident. When he reached the top of the elevator shaft, he lay there panting while he caught his breath. The air was stifling, an oven set on broil. He allowed himself only a few minutes before setting out for the main elevator that would take him to 70 Level and the ore conveyor belt out of the mine. He stopped when a sharp noise around the corner of a junction startled him. Thinking it was one of the deadly insects, he took out his pistol and waited. He relaxed when he heard Eve's voice.

"Here it is," she said.

"Thank goodness," Sandersohn said. "I don't think we could walk another meter."

Alan stepped around the corner and said, "You'll have to."

Eve was ecstatic, "Alan!" She ran to him and threw her arms around him. "Thank God you made it."

"We're not safe yet," he said, wincing from the pain her tight embrace caused. "The entire swamp is burning. Without the fans, the tunnels will quickly fill up with smoke. We have to hurry."

"This might help," Sandersohn said. He pointed to one of the electric mine carts used to move about the mine. A pool of blood beside the cart and more splattering the seat left little doubt as to the fate of the one who had last driven it. Luckily, it was fully charged. Tells, pale and barely conscious, lay on the back seat. "He's almost had it. The heat and the running are too much for him. That's why we sought out a cart." He handed Alan a short, stubby machinegun. "It's one of the army's MP5s. I found it in one of the shafts. I still have the rifle you gave me."

Alan took the weapon and turned to Eve. "Eve, you drive. Sandersohn, you ride shotgun with me. If you see any creatures, fire only if they attack." Alan climbed into the front seat beside Eve with Sandersohn on the opposite side in the back seat so they could cover more territory. "Where are we going?"

"Doctor Tells can't climb, and I won't leave him," Eve explained. "There is a spiral ramp at the end of the corridor that will take us up ten levels. That only leaves five levels to climb."

"Sounds like a plan."

They passed a junction where cobwebs covered an entire side tunnel. They ignored the human-shaped bundles hanging from the web like ornaments on a macabre Christmas tree. They encountered no live insects, but Alan considered the remains of insect carapaces, legs, and patches of dark viscous fluid more frightening than a horde of the creatures. *Intulo* had been there.

He rubbed his left hand. The itching from the scratches had become unbearable. He had broken open the scabs while climbing the ladder. The pus stained the bandage ocher.

Eve noticed as well. "My God, Alan! That looks awful."

"Feels like shit, too," he replied, "but there's nothing we can do until we're out of here."

"It's badly infected. There must be a first-aid kit somewhere around here."

"We don't have time."

"You could die."

He had considered that possibility. "If we don't get out of here soon, we'll all die."

She drove with one eye on his hand, refusing to give up. "It won't take long …."

As the cart careened around a curve in the ramp, he saw a man in a white jumpsuit standing on the ramp. "Look out!" he yelled.

The cart skidded and careened sideways, almost hitting the man. He closed his eyes and cringed in fear as the cart slid by him, missing him by a hair's breadth. He opened his eyes and moved toward them, limping from a bloody cut on one leg.

"Go back," he warned. "The insects are all over the next level."

"We have no choice," Alan told him. "We're going to 70 Level." He looked at the man's leg. "How is your leg?"

"I'll live," he answered. "I had a run in with a big beetle."

"Are you alone?"

He grimaced. Alan thought it was from pain, but when he replied, "I am now," he realized it was an expression of the man's anguish. "One of the creatures killed my companion. The army sealed the elevator shafts and trapped us down here. I'm a mining supervisor. My name's Cody Bray."

"Listen," Eve interrupted the introductions. "What is that sound?"

Alan listened, hearing a faint rumble, growing louder. "Insects?"

"No," Bray answered, his face turning pale. "I recognize the sound. It is water."

The ground began to shake as the rumble deepened. A strong wind blew past them. Then, a meter-high wall of water surged around the curve and crashed into the wall in front of them. It curled back on itself and rushed toward them. A dozen insects preceded it. They had set aside their differences in their mutual haste to flee. Sandersohn began firing to keep the creatures off the cart. Alan joined in, laying the rifle across his lap and firing one-handed. Luckily, the insects were more concerned with escaping the water than in attacking them. They parted around the electric cart like incoming surf around a rock.

"Someone released the reservoir!" Bray cried. "It will flood the lower levels."

Alan knew immediately who was flooding the mine –Verkhoen.

The surge of water grew deeper and the current stronger. The cart began to slide sideways back down the slope.

"How much water does the reservoir hold?" Alan asked Bray.

"Enough to wash us away," he replied.

"Eve, turn us around."

She looked at Alan as if he had lost his mind. "We'll never outrun it. We have to go up."

"No, down," he insisted.

She turned the cart around, heading back down the ramp. The water pushed against the back of the cart trying to lift the rear wheels from the ground. Soon they would become just another piece of flotsam washing downstream. Eve pressed the accelerator to the floor and pulled slightly ahead of the water. They exited the ramp at full speed, just ahead of the flood, but it was catching up quickly. He had to find another way up.

Ahead of them, the lights of the cart reflected from an emergency exit placard above a dark opening in the wall of the tunnel, an airshaft. "Where does that go?" he asked Bray.

"70 Level."

"Then that's our ticket out of here. Eve, park it there."

The cart's wheels struck the twin loco rails running down the middle of the tunnel and bounced into the air. Out of control, it rammed the wall beside the opening and shuddered to a stop. Alan used the forward momentum to leap from the cart and kick in the metal grate. The impact felt as if it would rip his injured hand from his wrist. The roar of the water rushing at them drowned out the sound of the grate falling down the shaft. The water was knee deep and swifter than a mountain stream. They held hands to form a human chain to reach the open vent. The strong current threatened to send them rolling down the tunnel to their deaths. Sandersohn led the way. He practically pushed Eve into the opening.

"What about Doctor Tells?"

"I'll bring him along. You climb."

She crawled into the shaft, but she stared back down at him as she climbed.

"Your turn," he said to the mine supervisor.

Bray hesitated. "With this bad leg, I might not make it," he said.

"Use your hands and your good leg. Dogs can manage on three legs. You're better than a dog, aren't you?"

Bray grinned and followed Eve. That left Doctor Tells. Like Eve, he wouldn't leave the old man behind. He would keep his promise to Eve. With his injured arm, Alan didn't want to slow any of the others down. The water and the noise had roused Tells, but he was still groggy. Alan picked him up and dragged him through the water into the shaft, clinging to the rungs by bracing his legs around the ladder to support both their weights. The water washed the cart down the tunnel out of sight and began spilling over the edge of the opening, creating a waterfall down the shaft. More water dripped on his head from openings above making the rungs slippery. He hoped they managed to reach the conveyor before the shaft flooded entirely, trapping them, which, he realized, must have been Verkhoen's plan all along. He wanted no witnesses.

"Bray, Sandersohn," he yelled up the shaft. "When you reach the top, find a rope, and lower it to me."

"Saving yourself, eh?" Tells moaned. "Well, I don't blame you."

"You're awake. Welcome back to the land of the living, Doctor."

"I take it that we are in grave danger is the reason you are carrying me like a piece of luggage."

"A considerable amount of danger, yes."

"It would be best to abandon me. I am an old man, and I have slowed you down enough already. I feel my usefulness as a traveling companion is at an end."

"Don't be silly, Doctor. You're as light as a feather."

"Hrumph! I weigh 13 stone. That's 86 kilos, or 190 pounds to you Americans. Leave me here; besides, I do not wish to be manhandled in this manner."

"We have to hurry, Doctor," Alan said in way of apology, as he placed Tells' feet on the rung beside his. "Just wrap your arms around my shoulders and hang on. I'll do all the heavy lifting."

His left hand was swollen and practically useless. His fingers were numb but gripping the rungs sent a throbbing pain from his wrist to his elbow. He climbed by laying his wrist over the rungs and pulling up, using his injured wrist for leverage. His wrist was soon raw and bleeding, but he couldn't stop. The water had hit the bottom of the airshaft and was rising rapidly. Something had washed into the lower vent blocking it.

Bray reached the top while he and Tells were less than three-quarters of the way up. Alan heard Bray cursing as he beat on metal. "The metal grate is in place and barred!" he yelled.

"Force it," Alan replied. They had to exit the airshaft soon. The water was less than twenty meters below him, and he was making poor time hauling Tells piggyback.

Bray continued pounding on the grate, but it wouldn't budge. Sandersohn, waiting below him, said, "Wait. There's a catch on the side. If I can reach my fingers through, maybe I can move it aside."

All went silent for several minutes, except for Tells' heavy breathing and the gurgling of the rising water level. Alan silently urged Sandersohn to hurry.

"Got it!" Sandersohn yelled triumphantly, and Bray kicked the grate aside. Alan watched his three companions disappear through the vent.

There was no time to search for a rope. The water was lapping at Alan's feet. He struggled to assist Tells up the ladder. The old man made a valiant effort, but he was too weak to help. Groping for the rungs with only one good hand, while attempting to maintain a grip on both the ladder and Tells, made a slow go of it. He was glad to see Sandersohn crawling back down the ladder.

"I couldn't find a rope." He reached his hand down for Tells. "Put your arms around me, sir. I will help carry you up."

Alan pushed Tells' feet while Sandersohn pulled. The two of them managed to get Tells up the shaft. He crawled through the vent after Tells.

"Thank you," he said to Sandersohn. To Bray, he said, "Where to?" Water began pouring from the airshaft they had just vacated. "We can't stay here."

"There's the abandoned shaft."

Alan looked at Bray in surprise. "An abandoned shaft?"

"Yes. The company sealed it years ago. Few people know of it."

"You can bet Verkhoen does. Where is it?"

"About 700 meter above us on 22 Level and across the mine for a couple of kilometers."

Alan shook his head. "We'll never make it. It's too far to climb and we don't have time."

"The water is moving down the mine. It will below us."

"Yes, but smoke rises. Soon, we'll be breathing burning swamp fumes."

"There's the skip elevator on 65 Level, but the military has sealed the shaft on the surface."

Alan looked at the bedraggled company. Bray had an injured leg, he had a bum hand, and Tells was too fatigued to be fully aware of where he was. Alan shook his head. "No, we stick to the original plan and try for the ore conveyor on 70 Level. It's closer, and the military probably haven't sealed it."

"We have six levels to climb yet."

"It's better than sixty."

"We've only seen the leading edge of the flood. Most of it is winding down the ramp and the elevator shafts, but the mine is a gigantic maze with hundreds of interconnecting shafts and tunnels. It will soon work its way back to us."

"I'm more worried about what's below us."

"The insects?"

"No, *Intulo*."

Bray laughed. "That old legend. You've been listening to too many superstitious miners."

"Whatever the creatures we saw are, they're no legend. The insects are afraid of it. I'm afraid of it," he admitted.

The mine supervisor stared at him a moment in disbelief, but Alan's admission of fear and the nods from the others convinced him. "I think I know a short cut."

Once again, they began marching through the dark mine.

24

July 6, 2016, 3:30 p.m.   *Ngomo* Mine, 30 Level –

Duchamps was dying and he knew it. His hand was numb from pressing it to the wound in his side. Blood leaked from between his fingers. The air was chilly in spite of the heat. He was shivering as his extremities shut down in a futile attempt to conserve blood for his brain and heart. He would die happy if he could have killed Verkhoen. Instead, Verkhoen had the diamonds and was free to blame him for the carnage. Verkhoen would come out of the entire disaster without a blemish.

He had given up hope of rescue. The army hadn't reached his level. That meant they were being cautious, retaking the mine one level at a time, sealing each level behind them to prevent any insects from escaping. They had shut down the fans to prevent the creatures from using the ventilator shafts to move about, which explained the rise in temperature. He didn't know which would kill him first, the bugs, the heat, or Verkhoen's bullet.

The floor shuddered beneath him. He had forgotten about the reservoir and Verkhoen's threat to destroy it. Now, he had a fourth option – drowning. The rushing water would sweep him down the tunnels like a pebble in a river, grinding him to an unrecognizable pulp. Verkhoen would enjoy that.

He groaned as another spasm of pain wracked his body. The millipede venom was still playing havoc with his system. His mind had wandered in and out of lucidity for hours. He thought he had heard insects scampering around in the dark, but for some reason they had not approached him. He presented an easy target. His rifle lay across his lap, but his finger was too numb to pull the trigger. He no longer knew which sounds were real and which ones his delusional mind had conjured. Perhaps insanity would overwhelm him before death. If so, dying would be simple. He probably wouldn't even realize he was dead.

When he felt a presence in his mind, he thought he was hallucinating. "Maybe it's just ghosts," he said to the empty tunnel. His words echoed. He repeated himself louder to enjoy the sound of his voice. "Maybe it's just ghosts," he yelled. The echo proved he was still alive. The tingling in his mind didn't go away. As it grew stronger, fear dredged up from somewhere deep within his psyche rose like a fountain of black despair to taunt him. There were no words, no language, and even the images exploding in his mind were incomprehensible. They did have one common theme. They all evoked a sense of hunger and a craving for more than food. He felt like a piece of meat in a butcher's display case with a patron licking his chops. Was this the devil that Verkhoen had ranted about? Had they dug too far and reached hell?

"Come and get me, Devil," he called out and laughed.

Pain exploded in his head and spread throughout his body. He went into convulsions. He felt ribs crack. The rifle slid from his lap, and a fresh stream of blood gushed from his wound.

So much for taunting the devil, he thought.

The convulsion and the pain subsided, but the presence in his mind didn't. He felt as if someone had wrung every thought, every emotion from his body, leaving only a husk. He feared if the presence left, there would be nothing left of him. The devil came closer. He could hear him in the tunnel, slithering like a serpent across the rock. The floor of the tunnel shuddered again, *the thunder of the devil's footsteps*, he thought. Using what little strength and willpower remained, he flicked on the flashlight.

The devil was a black carpet gliding across the floor toward him. "What are you?" he asked.

The devil paused. He felt it was staring at him, licking its chops. *Trying to decide how many licks to my chewy center.* His lack of apprehension surprised him. When drowning in fear, fear didn't seem important. The floor of the tunnel began quaking. Shards of rock fell from the roof. A strong wind bearing the heavy ozone smell of the air just before a summer shower rushed down the tunnel. He tore his gaze from the devil and pointed the flashlight in the other direction.

A wall of water reaching almost to the roof swept down the tunnel toward him. *Drowning wins*, he thought. *Too bad devil.*

The black mass broke into a dozen ebony creatures that looked something like the giant millipede that had bitten him, but he knew these were infinitely more deadly. They were supercharged millipedes. Suddenly, the group retreated, slithering down the tunnel away from the water and quickly disappearing among the shadows. At first, he thought it was fleeing from the water, but through the tenuous threads of consciousness linking him to the devil, he knew the devil wasn't fleeing, but rushing toward something else at the bottom of the mine with a sense of anger so strong it dispelled all other thoughts. When the devil, if devil it was, fled, a sense of calmness he had not felt in many years enveloped him. With serenity came acceptance.

The wall of water was a speeding locomotive, smashing into Duchamps, snapping his spine, and pulverizing his head into the rock floor; then picked up his broken body and flushed it like sewage from the mine.

25

July 6, 2016, 4:00 p.m.   *Ngomo* Volcano –

The searing heat blistered Masowe's skin, but he was oblivious to the damage the hot obsidian inflicted on his bare feet. He had discarded his boots and his clothing and danced the Hunter's Dance naked before the largest campfire in the world – *Ulungu*. The great swamp beneath the earth was burning. The trees and plants had become a blazing inferno, fueled by pockets of methane gas and proto-petrochemicals oozing from the ground and the water. Flames soared halfway to the roof, spilling heat like rain over the entire chamber.

The roar of the flames overshadowed the high-pitched whine of the *Cerberus* eating away at the base of the pillar of stone holding up the roof of the magma chamber. Where the lasers cut into the hard granite, globs of red-hot molten rock ran down the side of the pillar like candle wax. Not for millions of years had the stone felt such intense heat, not since the lava drained from the chamber, flowing back to its origin near the Earth's molten outer core.

Masowe had no one to play a *pedi* flute or *ugubhu* mouth bow to accompany his dance. No goatskin *isigubhu* drum pounded out the beat to which he danced. He wore no *umfece* ankle bracelet made of moth cocoons filled with small pebbles to jingle with his steps. He danced the Hunter's Dance alone, in anticipation of facing his enemy, without stabbing *assagi* spear or cowhide *isihlangu* shield. He did not have an *impi* band of warriors to protect him in battle. His weapon was his mental connection to *Intulo*, and his shield was his faith in his *sangoma* father's teachings.

The air was thick with suffocating smoke. It parched the inside of this throat and baked his lungs. He could see for only a few meters around him, but he had no need for vision. He was not hunting his prey. It hunted him and he was not running from it. He had opened his mind to *Intulo*, treading carefully in the dark nether regions of the creature's mind lest it wholly consume him. Through his eyes, he showed the creature the destruction of its lair and the slaying of its offspring. *Intulo*'s rage rose until it became a dark, roiling storm cloud pierced by flashes of ebony lightning. Its unrestrained fury seared through the mental link between man and creature.

A normal man would have shut down his mind or fled in abject terror from the blasts of elemental hatred assaulting him, but he was a warrior, a member of the Zulu tribe. He was no longer a security guard working for the Van Gotts Corporation. He was Shaka Zulu reborn.

He knew now the creature was not truly *Intulo* and the magma chamber was not *Ulungu*, home of the gods. It was just a creature from the forgotten past, a misanthropic evolutionary dead end. Without its giant insects for food, it would turn to men to satisfy its craving. He must stop it.

The link between them ran both directions. Through *Intulo*'s alien mind, he saw images of the flood sweeping through the mine. Soon, the wall of water would reach the inferno where the intense heat would flash it into steam. The magma chamber was a sealed pressure cooker, allowing the expanding steam nowhere to go. Pressure would build, further weakening the surrounding rock. Between the machine's belching heat melting the support pillar and the force of pressurized steam, the roof would collapse. He would kill his prey.

Intulo was coming. Masowe could feel its presence. The individual creatures that comprised the hive-mind monster outpaced the torrent of the flood in its haste to stop the destruction of its young. It fired bolts of dark agony at Masowe. The mental shield his father had taught him to create deflected most of the power, but enough got through to wrack his body with pain. He collapsed on the ground, his chest heaving for breath in the cloying, black smoke. Above the din of flame and manmade laser energy, he heard the deep rumble of falling rocks and the sharp, brittle cracking of the roof above him. A shower of rock pelted the glassine obsidian shelf with the sound of rain on a window. The laser drill was weakening the pillar and the roof was beginning to collapse.

Masowe did not regret dying. His only regret was having no trophy of his kill to display on the wall of his mining camp room. He crawled across the shelf to where he had discarded his clothing. The agony of his naked body pressed against the heated rock made each movement torture. His hands sought his pants pocket. He withdrew a small, beaded gourd, his *ishungu* to ward off evil, and clasped it to his chest.

Intulo flowed down the rocky slope of the chamber, an avalanche of evil careening toward him. The creatures did not pause to observe the destruction of its domain. They slithered up the slope to the shelf intent on punishing Masowe. Cracks raced up the flanks of the granite pillar as it swayed in an invisible zephyr. At last, its enormous weight grew too heavy for the weakened base to support, and the colossal spire of stone slowly toppled. The roof cracked, at first where the pillar pulled fee, but then fissures radiated outward, reaching for the walls of the cavern. With a sound of the rending of a world, the chamber began to tear itself apart.

Intulo waited before devouring him, savoring his terror as an appetizer. Masowe stared up at the horde of ebony creatures rearing on their rear legs, encircling him, staring at him with an intensity that would have crippled its normal insect prey, but his agony weakened their hold on him. As the fringes of the deluge reached the inferno, flashing instantly to steam, an earsplitting hiss erupted, shaking the ground. *Intulo*, intent on its prey, ignored the devastation around it. Masowe forced a smile to his blistered lips just before the creature ripped into his mind with a sledgehammer blow, and then enfolded his body in a dozen tight, deadly embraces. He did not feel the burst of scalding steam spilling from the cauldron. Nor did he hear the thunderous roar, as the entire magma chamber collapsed in on itself, pulling the surface above down into the void created by its demise. Hunter and prey both lay entombed beneath kilometers of solid rock.

Masowe hoped his ancestors would be proud of him.

26

July 6, 2016, 5:30 p.m. *Ngomo* Mine, 70 Level ore conveyor –
Bray stopped at small alcove in the tunnel they had been
following. A 55-gallon drum of hydraulic fluid and a smaller drum of
lubricating oil took up most of the space. A rack on the wall held two
grease guns, an oil-stained gallon bucket, and a flashlight dangling
by a string. A locked toolbox sat below it.

"This is it," he announced.

Alan stared at the alcove searching for the promised way out.
"Where?" he asked.

Bray rapped his knuckles on an unpainted wooden door set into
the wall. To Alan it looked like a cupboard. Bray opened the door,
revealing a metal cage barely large enough to accommodate one
person, suspended from a steel cable the diameter of his thumb.
Wisps of smoke drifted up from below.

"What is it?" Alan asked.

"A dumbwaiter. The maintenance crew uses it to reach the main
motor housing for the belt conveyor and the rollers. It keeps us from
shutting it down when they need to grease the bearings. There's just
enough room to squeeze from beneath the conveyor and reach the
walkway. We'll have to go up one at a time," he added.

"I don't think I'll fit," Tells said.

Alan sat the doctor on the toolbox. His face and skin were a sickly
gray. Alan worried he was near having a heart attack. The smoke
drifting up the shaft set off a spasm of coughing. His hands shook as
he braced himself on the toolbox to keep from keeling over.

"You're positively svelte," he said. "This heat has melted the
pounds off like a sauna."

"You are an excellent liar, young man, but I appreciate your attempt to humor me."

"We'll get you out, Doctor," Alan said. "We're not leaving you behind."

On the journey to the maintenance shaft, thick smoke filled the tunnels making breathing difficult for all of them, especially Tells. Alan and Sandersohn had supported the doctor by resting his weight on their shoulders while he struggled to put one foot in front of the other. Seeing where they were going had been a challenge. They had followed Bray's unerring lead. Without his intimate knowledge of the mine, they would never have made it through the labyrinth of tunnels.

"Sandersohn, you go up first. Take the machinegun just in case any creepy crawlies are up there. I'll bring up the rear."

Sandersohn laid the MP5 in the bottom of the cage and crawled inside. "Cozy," he said.

"Pull that cable down," Bray said. "It's weighted on the other end and won't take much effort to lift you to the top. When you get out, send it back down using the crank up there."

"Right," Sandersohn replied and began pulling the cable. "Don't dawdle," he said as the cage disappeared up the shaft.

"This time I'll go last," Bray said.

"We'll flip a coin later," Alan replied.

As the dumbwaiter bearing Sandersohn climbed the shaft, Alan pulled Eve aside. He hadn't had much time to speak with her, to explain how he felt about her. He didn't want to die without having said it. Her beauty enraptured him. She wasn't magazine model beautiful –high, thin cheekbones, pencil-thin eyebrows, and eyes so dark with mascara they looked racoonish. His ex-wife, Sharon, possessed that kind of beauty, but she was cold and aloof. Eve had what he called a cute-girl-next-door beauty, magnified by her lack of makeup and her inner determination to survive. Soot from the smoke streaked her cheeks, and her hair lay plastered to her scalp beneath the hardhat, but even in the harsh glow of the flashlights, her face looked angelic in spite of her fear.

"I want to thank you, Eve."

"For what?"

"For making me realize my work has been a crutch. I substituted the *Cerberus* for a chance at any relationship and thought I was coming out on the winning end. I was wrong. I like what I see in you and what I feel about you. It's like you kick started my heart."

"You made me live again, Alan. I was dead inside, bitter and angry at what life had done to me. Now, I think I could love again. Maybe I already do."

He drew held her to him, relishing the feel of her body against his. For a long, tender moment, he forgot where they were and what they faced. The sound of the cage descending brought it all back in a painful rush.

"Ladies first," he said, ushering her into the waiting dumbwaiter.

She peered through the open metal-grate bottom of the dumbwaiter down the shaft and took a step back, shaking her head. "It's not safe."

"Of course it's safe," Bray insisted. He reached in, grabbed the side of the cage, and shook it, rattling it against the side of the shaft. "See?"

Eve glanced at Alan. He nodded his head. She smiled, crawled inside, and smiled back at him. Then she began pulling the cable.

Alan checked his watch. Two hours had passed since leaving Masowe in the swamp. He didn't know how much longer they had. He looked at Bray. "I'll go last."

Bray cocked his head to one side and stared back at him with a wry grin. "Look, you said an inferno was raging below us in a volcanic magma chamber. After what I've witnessed today, I believe you. This smoke backs you up. Your plan is to collapse the roof of the chamber, right?"

"If everything goes according to plan."

"The mine has hollowed out this old chunk of rock like a wheel of Swiss cheese. It's almost a half-century old. Some of the wooden supports are as old as the mine. The flood washed out God knows how many of those supports. Small tremors can shut us down for days. A major shake can collapse tunnels. What do you suppose will happen when a chunk of rock several kilometers in diameter crashes to the ground?"

Alan was embarrassed that he hadn't considered the possibility. As an engineer, albeit not a mining engineer, he should have made the calculations. His original plan to close the *Cerberus* tunnel had morphed into a more ambitious project to seal the entire magma chamber and lava tube system. Its conception had been spontaneous and had changed with the circumstances. Beyond his goal to stop the creature, he had given no thought to the wider aspects of his scheme.

"I see."

"Get the others out of the mine. Don't worry. I don't intend to remain behind, but this leg will slow me down. You'll have your hands full with the old man. I can take care of myself. It's my mine, my decision," Bray replied. He turned to Doctor Tells. "You're next."

Tells was too weak to pull himself up. It took nearly fifteen minutes for Sandersohn to get the dumbwaiter up the shaft using the hand crank. Alan waited impatiently for cage to come back down, expecting the floor to give way beneath him at any moment. Finally, it was his turn. As he crawled into the cage, the floor shuddered. The toolbox bounced across the floor. A grease gun fell from the rack.

"It's starting," he said. "There's room for both of us in here if we suck in our guts and hold our breath."

Bray shook his head. "We might fit, but only one of us can reach the cable. One person can't lift two, especially a man with one arm. Sandersohn can't lift us either. Hurry. Don't waste time arguing."

Alan grabbed the cable with both hands, but let his right arm do most of the work. Another tremor struck, stronger than the first. The dumbwaiter swung like a pendulum, banging against the sides of the shaft. He pulled faster. When he reached the top, Sandersohn reached in and dragged him out of the dumbwaiter. He crawled into the narrow gap between the conveyor rollers and the floor. He didn't envy anyone whose job entailed working in such a confining space while the conveyor was moving just inches from their faces.

"Did you feel the tremors?" Sandersohn asked, as he released the brake and began frantically cranking the handle to lower the dumbwaiter to Bray.

"Yeah, we don't have much time."

"Get Eve and Doctor Tells out of here."

Alan hesitated. He was getting tired of leaving people behind.

"Don't be a fool, Alan," Sandersohn snapped. "You can't help here. Now, get out of my way."

He crawled from beneath the conveyor. Eve and Tells sat on the tough, steel-fiber infused fabric of the two-meter-wide belt. Rollers along the edge folded the belt upward to form a trough to keep the ore from spilling out.

"Help me with Doctor Tells," he said to Eve.

Together, they got him to his feet and began walking down the conveyor. Another tremor hit. It was the strongest one yet. If not for the curved edges of the conveyor, Alan would have toppled over the side, taking the others with him.

"The cable snapped!" Sandersohn yelled from beneath the conveyor. "It fell down the shaft. I can't bring Bray up." He was frantic. When he poked his head out from beneath the conveyor, his stricken face highlighted his panic.

Alan cursed himself for not planning their escape better. *How many others are going to pay for my mistakes?* "There's nothing we can do for him," he said. "We have to get out of here."

"We have to do ..."

The walls of the tunnel groaned a low, mournful note. For a moment, Alan thought it was calling his name. Alan's uncanny ability to know when a collapse was imminent went into high gear. The magma chamber was collapsing and taking the mine with it.

"Get out from under there," Alan yelled to Sandersohn.

The low groan rose in tenor to become an agonized scream as rock shattered under the enormous pressure from above. The conveyor heaved, tossing all three to the belt. Alan landed on his injured arm with Tells sprawled across him. A knife blade of agony plunged into his brain. He fought the darkness dragging him down into unconsciousness. The tremors came on top of each other like waves crashing on the beach. This time the shaking did not subside, but grew worse. The mine was collapsing around them.

His warning to Sandersohn came too late. Overstressed metal ripped like paper. The bolts of the conveyor frame sheared away, dropping the entire conveyor to the floor of the tunnel, crushing Sandersohn beneath tons of steel. The crash drowned out Eve's scream. The roof cracked, a fissure ten-meters long sending a shower of rocks cascading down on them. The floor of the tunnel rose and bucked beneath them as the manmade wound in the earth tried to seal itself.

"Get up," he told Eve.

She shook her head. "I can't."

"Then crawl, damn it!" he shouted. "I won't leave you here."

She rose to her knees, and then used his leg to climb to her feet. Together they half-dragged Tells down the conveyor. Blasts of hot air, filled with smoke and dust, created a wind tunnel, propelling them forward. Ripples raced along the conveyor fabric, trying to trip them. His flashlight was useless in the engulfing cloud of dust. He could see nothing. The wind at their back guided them.

The clamor of the mine plummeting into the magma chamber became a crescendo building to a climax. He could hear the tunnel collapsing behind them, chasing them as if determined that no one should escape its wrath. Ahead, through a break in the smoke and dust, he saw a faint patch of lighter shadows. *Just a few more yards.*

They emerged into twilight. After countless hours in the murky mine, it seemed like high noon. He urged Eve and Tells on. The conveyor ended abruptly with a five-meter drop to a waiting ore truck. He located a ladder on the side of the conveyor support platform. Eve climbed down first to help him with Tells, but lowering him was too much for his injured arm. When the ladder began bouncing, he dropped Tells the last few feet to the ground, and then lost his grip on the ladder and tumbled after him. The impact knocked the breath out of him.

He regained awareness with Eve tugging on his arm, yelling at him to get up. He got to his feet unsteadily and lumbered after her. He fell again when the ground heaved. Behind him, the conveyor platform groaned and collapsed on top of the ore hauler. If Eve hadn't roused him, he would be lying beneath the pile of mangled steel rubble.

Tells. He looked around for the elderly scientist. A rush of relief flooded over him when he saw Tells sitting on the ground with his back against an oil drum. Eve had dragged him to safety. The old man was awake but in no condition to continue. Alan wasn't sure about himself either.

They were near the bottom of the old mining pit. The only exit was the switchback road circling the sides of the pit to the top. Boulders shaken loose by the tremors bounced down the terraced sides of the pit. He watched as one massive rock broadsided one of the ore haulers abandoned on the sloping roadway. It tipped the truck onto its side and shoved it off the roadway. The thirty-six ton vehicle tumbled to the bottom, strewing pieces of metal along the way.

"There!" Eve cried.

She pointed to an open jeep. Alan prayed the keys were in the ignition. He helped Tells to his feet, leaned his shoulder into Tells' belly, and laid him across his shoulder. Staggering under Tells' weight and his own unsteady legs, he carried Tells to the jeep and dumped him unceremoniously into the back. Eve pushed Alan out of the way when he began to climb behind the wheel.

"You can't drive with one arm," she said.

He didn't argue. He could barely pull himself in beside her.

The keys weren't in the ignition, but Eve found them between the seats. She cranked the jeep, shoved it in gear, and spun sideways in her haste to leave. Alan cringed as she raced up the sloping gravel roadway at breakneck speed, the left tires coming perilously close to the crumbling edge. She darted around rocks crashing across her path, slewing the jeep from side to side in a daring game of dodge ball. He gripped the door handle with his good hand. Poor Doctor Tells, half-unconscious, rolled around the back of the jeep, careening off the sides in a personal game of pinball.

The jeep skidded sideways as Eve powered it around a switchback. A truck door appeared in front of them through the dust, wrenched from the crashed ore hauler and imbedded in the roadway. Eve jerked the wheel to the left to avoid it, scraping the left side of the jeep along the side of the cliff. A stream of gravel and dirt gouged out by the shattered mirror pelted Alan's face. The truck door smashed the driver's side mirror. Eve ducked as it sailed over her head.

As they rounded the last curve, she punched the accelerator, urging every remaining horsepower from the engine. Alan glanced across the pit. The entire slope above the conveyor tunnel was collapsing, slowly sliding down into the pit. If they had delayed another minute, they would have been surfing the avalanche of dirt and rock to their deaths. The jeep cleared the ground as it reached the flat surface surrounding the rim of the open pit. Tells groaned as the jeep slammed back to earth. The jarring impact sent a shooting pain ripping through Alan's infected arm. He gritted his teeth and cluing to the door handle with his good hand.

A plume of dust rose from the pit behind them, which grew wider as the edge adjacent to the underground mine inched slowly toward the elevator shaft and mine buildings. In its last act of revenge, the dying magma chamber was eating the entire mine and surrounding countryside. *Intulo* and its brood would either die or be trapped forever beneath kilometers of rock. The mine could not produce enough gold to make reopening it worthwhile. Verkhoen had lost.

Alan had lost as well. He thought of Vince and Bill, victims of Verkhoen and Duchamps' greed. He had lost his beloved *Cerberus,* buried in a tomb he had helped create. His father had lost the most. Now, Verkhoen would have no need of three boring machines. Hoffman Industries would go bankrupt. He and Verkhoen shared equal responsibility for that.

Headlights blinded him. Eve threw the jeep into low and jammed on the brakes. The vehicle slid sideways to a grinding halt. The jeep shuddered and the engine sputtered and died when she released the clutch. A five-ton army truck blocked the road. A soldier stepped out of the truck. A second soldier stood beside the truck with his weapon pointed in their direction.

"Who are you?" the first soldier yelled.

Alan saw the captain insignia on the man's sleeve in the truck's lights. "Alan Hoffman, Doctor Eve Means, and Doctor Tells, Captain. We were in the mine."

The captain motioned for the soldier to lower his weapon. He checked the clipboard he carried and read off their names. "Alan Hoffman, Doctor Evelyn Means, and Doctor Simon Tells." He looked up in awe. "We presumed you were dead. Glad you made it." He pointed to the pit. "We saw the dust and smoke rising and came to investigate. Did anyone else make it out?"

Alan shook his head. "Just us three."

"What about Mister Verkhoen? We heard he was in the mine."

Verkhoen's absence startled him. "You haven't seen him?"

"He hasn't reported in. We assumed he was dead as well."

Alan had his doubts. The true bastards were hard to kill. "Have any of the creatures escaped?"

"A few did, but we killed them all. They attempted to break out several times, but we beat them back. Your engineer said there is another creature down there, some kind of monster." His face clouded with doubt. "None of our people saw it."

Alan nodded. "Yes, there was, but I don't think it survived. Verkhoen dynamited the reservoir. The lower levels are flooded and the magma chamber cavern is collapsing, pulling the entire mine down on top of it."

The soldier stared at him. "I don't know anything about that, but when the tremors started they evacuated everyone from the mine and the surface buildings surrounding it."

"Did that include my engineer, Trace Morgan?"

"Yes, sir. Mister Morgan refused the evacuation order. When we sent troops to remove him, he became quite insistent and combative, decking one of the soldiers. I believe we have him in custody. He insists we allow him to have his iPhone. He is not happy."

Alan grinned. "No, I don't suppose he would be. I'll go to him shortly before he tries to break out."

"Would you please come with us?" the captain asked. His tone left little room for refusal. As they walked to the truck, he noticed Alan's arm. "You look like you could use a medic, sir."

"Doctor Tells is in the back of the jeep. He needs help more."

The captain yelled at the truck. "Private Diggs, you and Dawson bring a stretcher." The two named men jumped out of the rear of the truck. One of them carried a collapsible stretcher.

"We'll see to him, sir," the captain told Alan.

The ground groaned and shook as more of the surrounding landscape sank into the expanding sinkhole.

"Perhaps we'd better vacate the premises," Alan said. "It looks like the Ngomo Volcano hasn't uttered it last gasp yet."

The captain studied Alan's face for a moment. "Volcano? If you say so, sir. Please follow me."

Alan looked on as the two soldiers carried Doctor Tells to the rear of the truck. He helped Eve into the truck. Tells looked up at them from his litter. In spite of his pain, he smiled. "That was some ride. If I can survive that, I can survive anything."

Eve offered an apology. "We were in a rush."

More quietly, Tells said, "They will never believe us, you know."

"Believe what?" Alan asked.

"The story about the swamp and *Intulo*. They will have to accept the giant insects. We have video and doubtless, there are a few dead specimens lying about, but the concept of an eons-old, hive-mind creature will be too much to accept. I advise caution when speaking of it lest you are considered too dangerous for the public welfare."

"But we saw it … them," Eve said, dumfounded by Doctor Tells caution. "They exist."

Tells nodded. "Yes, and we must be vigilant for any others of its kind, but we have no proof, and proof is the difference between an amazing discovery and just another tall tale from a UFO nut."

Alan realized Tells was right. Who would believe them? He hardly believed it himself. It already seemed like a nightmare from which he was slowly awakening. By dawn and the revealing light of a new day, he might not believe it at all.

"Maybe you're right. I'm just a mechanical engineer trying to improve mining conditions. Maybe I should stick to that. If I don't lose everything. I'm out one fifteen-million-dollar machine and the prospects of selling two more."

"I wouldn't worry about that. The video Eve posted acknowledges the marvels of your *Cerberus*. Eve insisted on that. I'm quite sure offers will soon pour in. With Van Gotts' loss, other mines will prosper. So is the way of big business. Perhaps there is little difference from one prehistoric creature eating another."

The truck started up. Alan put his good arm around Eve as it jerked into motion. "After a shower and a shave, perhaps we could have dinner and a bottle of wine."

She smiled. "We could skip the dinner and the wine," she said, "but I insist on the shower."

As the truck rumbled past the chain-link fence surrounding the mine, the main elevator shaft tower collapsed. Moments later, the buildings around it disappeared into the yawning chasm with the shriek of shredded metal, crushed masonry, and splintered wood. Alan hoped his efforts had been enough to kill *Intulo* and its brood. Even so, he would continue to build his machines, but he would remain on the surface. The lure of deep, underground mines had worn off.

27

July 6, 2016, 6:30 p.m.   *Ngomo* Mine, Perimeter fence –
Klaus Verkhoen followed his herder guide along the chain-link perimeter fence of the mine. He was pleased with his handiwork. He would stash his diamonds until things calmed down at the mine, and then convert them to bearer bonds, which were much easier to sell than raw diamonds. He would pump the water from the mine and retrieve all the remaining diamonds. Duchamps, Hoffman, and Means' deaths had erased his past sins. No one would ever learn of his unsafe mining attempts, his murderous efforts to conceal them, or his somewhat overzealous method of eliminating the insects.

He approached the mine from the pit side to avoid the military presence near the main gate. With a shower, a shave, and a change of clothing, he would resume control of his mine. The Board of Directors would be irate with him for recent events, but they would not remove him, at least until he had cleaned things up. He would be their public scapegoat. *Let them stew*, he thought. By the time they voted to remove him as CEO, he would have retrieved the remaining diamonds. With such tremendous wealth at his disposal, he would be beyond their reach.

He no longer needed Van Gotts Corporation. It might have been enough for his father, but his ambitions ran higher. Wealth was power and he would wield it like a scalpel, delicately slicing into the flesh of high society and slipping in through the open wound. "Control the controllers," his father had always told him. Verkhoen would heed his father's advice. Wealth bought influence both political and social. He would not place himself in the limelight. Instead, he would quietly pull the strings from behind the curtain, safe from retaliation and investigation.

He turned to his silent herder companion. "How would like a job as my new aide? You could learn to wear real clothes and abandon those filthy, smelly cattle. The pay is very good, and your taciturn manner makes you highly qualified for the job." The herder glanced up at him and quickened his pace. Verkhoen laughed. "Perhaps you're right. You have found your niche in life. Everyone should know their place."

As he neared the pit, the ground shuddered beneath him. His guide turned to him, his face a mask of sheer terror. Before Verkhoen could stop him, he raced away into the darkness back toward his herd of cattle. *It's just the water knocking out a few old supports,* he said to himself. *A few tremors are to be expected as the earth settles.* When the ground heaved and groaned a second time, louder than ever, he suspected the situation might be more problematic than he had anticipated.

A cloud of dust rose from the pit, silhouetted against the twilight gloom. A third tremor struck; this one strong enough to slam him to the ground. He scrambled for his case of diamonds, clutching it to his chest like a security blanket. A knee-high tsunami of dirt rushed toward him, ripples caused by the quake. When it struck him, the ground bucked beneath him, tossing him into the air. He landed heavily on his back, knocking the breath from his lungs. The chain-link fence vibrated like a plucked violin string, keening a low, one-note dirge. The ripple of soil raced past him, wrenching steel fence posts from their concrete foundations, and flinging them into the air. As he watched, the main elevator shaft collapsed.

After a handful of seconds, the earth tremors subsided. He picked himself up from the ground and brushed off his clothing. The billowing cloud of dust and smoke erupting from the pit drew him like a beacon. He needed to see what was happening. It could affect his plans. As he stood at the brink of the pit, he was at first mystified by the glowing pool of liquid spilling from the conveyor shaft, but as the intense heat and the sulfurous stench of molten rock reached him, he knew his mine was finished. He laughed. *Even the bloody planet is conspiring against me, coughing up its molten guts to entomb my diamonds.*

The silence didn't last long. He watched in horror as the side of the pit broke free and slid to the bottom, plunging buildings and equipment into the growing pool of magma. The edge continued to crumble, devouring everything in its path. The expanding chasm came for him like a vengeful spirit, the ghosts of the mine's dead seeking retribution for their lost lives. Running would make no difference. The mine was swallowing the entire compound, taking everything to its grave. He knew instinctively Alan Hoffman had a hand in its demise.

Verkhoen set his case of diamonds beside him, took his cigarette case from his shirt pocket, and placed a cigarette between his lips. He removed his cigarette lighter, but had no time to light it. The ground disintegrated beneath his feet, and he plummeted into the dark, yawning abyss.

28

July 8, 2016, 10:45 a.m. Protea Hotel, Klerksdorp, South Africa
–

Alan and Eve sat on the second-floor balcony of his hotel room. The day was bright and beautiful, made even more so by the pitcher of Black Velvet cocktails sitting on the table between them. The mixture of Hennessey Black Cognac, sweet vermouth, Maraschino liquor, and orange bitters was a little too sweet for his taste, but it was cold and alcoholic and Eve seemed to enjoy them. Her opinion and comfort now meant more to him than his. If he intended to pursue a relationship with the beautiful biologist, he would not make the same mistakes of his failed marriage and his less-than-stellar subsequent relationships.

It had been two days since they had escaped the mine. The military continued to cordon off the area around the mine, but he had managed a helicopter ride to view the destruction by using his credentials as a geologist. The open pit mine was now a five-kilometer-wide, fifty-meter-deep depression, reminding Alan of photos of sites of underground nuclear explosions. A jumble of razed buildings and wrecked equipment that had been the Van Gotts Ngomo Mine littered the bottom of the chasm. Wisps of smoke and rivulets of lava rose through cracks in the rock. The molten magma, released from its pool fifty kilometers beneath the earth by the destruction of the upper magma chamber, would continue to rise until it filled the depression, erasing all signs of the mine and the horrors buried beneath it. It seemed a fitting end. Nature was healing the wounds created by man. *Ngomo Volcano* would take its place on the geological survey maps.

The military had no accurate count of the dead, but most estimates placed it at one-hundred fifty-two. Publically, they were attributing the disaster to the sudden eruption of a previously unknown underground volcano. No word of giant prehistoric insects had yet leaked to the public, but soon the video Eve had uploaded to the internet would find its way to legitimate news outlets, and the shit would hit the fan. He thought of the memory stick in his pocket containing the video of the magma chamber Trace had recorded. He had watched it one time through. Even though the quality was poor because of the obscuring pall of smoke, *Intulo* was plainly visible, as was the raging inferno. It looked like the lake of fire in hell. The images captured before Masowe had ignited the swamp showed the Carboniferous flora and fauna in all its glory.

It also showed Masowe sacrificing his life to defeat the creature. He wanted that information distributed as widely as possible. The Zulu security guard was a hero and the world should know.

Doctor Tells was recovering in hospital. He was a tough old bird and would soon be driving the nurses crazy. Alan flexed his arm. It was still sore and somewhat swollen, but draining the wound of pus and the series of antibiotic shots the attending physician had administered seemed to be working. At least it hadn't hampered his and Eve's nighttime escapades.

"When must you leave?" Eve asked.

He looked over at her and grinned. The past two days with her had been the best in his life. Nothing could erase the deaths of Vince McGill and Bill Bakkerman or the horrors he had experienced, but the side of his life that had suffered the most, his love life, had reached a new level. What he and Eve felt might not yet be love, but it was the first step toward what he hoped would be a lasting relationship.

"Since I don't have much to pack or ship back home, Trace and I are scheduled to fly out tomorrow morning. The military authorities have hinted that they would appreciate my leaving the country as soon as possible. They're afraid of what I might say."

"They can't shut me up," Eve insisted. "Someone has to know what really happened."

He handed her the memory stick. "This might help," he said.

She looked at his mischievous grin and asked, "What's on it?"

"Proof. I would prefer you wait until I am safely out of the country before releasing it."

She leaned over the table and kissed him. "I knew I loved you for some reason."

"Whoa," he said. "Let's not rush this. Sex first, love later."

She became suddenly serious, nodding her head. "Whatever you say."

"Here's another gift for you. I was hoping to get it made into a ring, but ..." He handed her the diamond Vince had stashed inside his computer bag. He had found it while checking the computer before packing it for shipment to Vince's parents. By rights, the diamond was Vince's, but given the circumstances, he thought Vince wouldn't mind sharing.

She stared at the diamond with her mouth open. "My God, it's gigantic."

"Yeah, there's a lot of that going around lately.

"What am I supposed to do with it? Allen Hoffman, is this a proposal?"

"No, I usually get down on one knee when I do that. I could never sneak it by customs. I thought you might find someone to cut and polish it. I don't think Vince would mind if you had a jeweler slice off a few carats, just enough for a ring for you. We can call it a friendship ring for now. If you can sell the rest of the diamond, I'll send the money to Vince's parents."

"Alan, that's so sweet of you."

He blushed. "Yeah, I'm like that sometimes."

She frowned as she stared at the stone in her hand. "All those diamonds down there ... Do you think someone will ever dig them out?"

"Through all that magma? Let's hope not. Let whatever is buried down there remained buried."

"Do you think there are other places like the magma chamber, places deep in the earth with living creatures like the Intulo?"

He smiled. "Vince would think so." He shook his head. He had given a few hours restless thought to that very subject without deciding. "I don't know. If we keep boring deeper and deeper, we're bound to find something inimical to mankind's welfare. It's in our nature."

"I suppose so," she agreed. "When I finish this lecture in

Johannesburg, would you mind very much if I visited you in Nevada?"

"I'm counting on it. The desert can be a lonely place."

She held out the raw diamond. Though it looked more like a shiny stone than a jewel, the sun glinted from its crystal surface. "Can you afford to give this to me? Are you going to be broke? I don't know if I can love a pauper."

"Doctor Tells was right. My father informed me the company has already received six orders for our mining machines, and NASA is taking a closer look at our smaller *Charon* version for a future lunar mission. I think we can hold off the creditors for a while. I might be busy, but I won't be a pauper."

"Alan?"

He looked across the table at her and saw the playful look in her eyes. "What?"

"Since you're leaving tomorrow and I might not see you for a few weeks, I thought ..." Her voice trailed off, as she winked and rose from her chair. On her sensual stroll back into the room, she removed her blouse and bra and dropped them on the floor, freeing her luscious breasts. He skirt quickly followed. He was surprised that she wore no underwear.

As he got up to join her, he thought, *I wonder if Van Gotts is still paying for this room. I hope they don't bill me for a new set of box springs.*

The End

SEVEREDPRESS

 facebook.com/severedp

 twitter.com/severedpre

CHECK OUT OTHER GREAT DINOSAUR THRILLERS

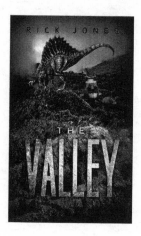

THE VALLEY
by Rick Jones

In a dystopian future, a self-contained valley in Argentin serves as the 'far arena' for those convicted of a crime Inside the Valley: carnivorous dinosaurs generated from preserved DNA. The goal: cross the Valley to get to the Gates of Freedom. The chance of survival: no one has eve completed the journey. Convicted of crimes with little o no merit, Ben Peyton and others must battle their wa across fields filled with the world's deadliest apex predator in order to reach salvation. All the while the journey i caught on cameras and broadcast to the world as a realit show, the deaths and killings real, the macabre appetite o the audience needing to be satiated as Ben Peyton lead his team to escape not only from a legal system that's more interested in entertainment than in justice, but also from the predators of the Valley.

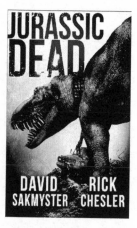

JURASSIC DEAD
by Rick Chesler & David Sakmyster

An Antarctic research team hoping to study microbial organisms in an underground lake discovers something far more amazing: perfectly preserved dinosaur corpses. After one thaws and wakes ravenously hungry, it becomes apparent that death, like life, will find a way.
Environmental activist Alex Ramirez, son of the expedition's paleontologist, came to Antarctica to defend the organisms from extinction, but soon learns that it is the human race that needs protecting.

CHECK OUT OTHER GREAT DINOSAUR THRILLERS

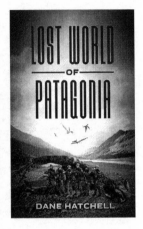

LOST WORLD OF PATAGONIA
by Dane Hatchell

An earthquake opens a path to a land hidden for millions of years. Under the guise of finding cryptid animals, Ace Corporation sends Alex Klasse, a Cryptozoologist and university professor, his associates, and a band of mercenaries to explore the Lost World of Patagonia. The crew boards a nuclear powered All-Terrain Tracked Carrier and takes a harrowing ride into the unknown.

The expedition soon discovers prehistoric creatures still exist. But the dangers won't prevent a sub-team from leaving the group in search of rare jewels. Tensions run high as personalities clash, and man proves to be just as deadly as the dinosaurs that roam the countryside.

Lost World of Patagonia is a prehistoric thriller filled with murder, mayhem, and savage dinosaur action.

SAVAGE ISLAND
by Alan Spencer

Somewhere in the Atlantic Ocean, an uncharted island has been used for the illegal dumping of chemicals and pollutants for years by Globo Corp's. Private investigator Pierce Range will learn plenty about the evil conglomerate when Susan Branch, an environmentalist from The Green Project, hires him to join the expedition to save her kidnapped father from Globo Corp's evil hands.

Things go to hell in a hurry once the team reaches the island. The bloodthirsty dinosaurs and voracious cannibals are only the beginning of the fight for survival. Pierce must unlock the mysteries surrounding the toxic operation and somehow remain in one piece to complete the rescue mission.

Ratchet up the body count, because this mission will leave the killing floor soaked in blood and chewed up corpses. When the insane battle ends, will there by anybody left alive to survive Savage Island?

32798387R00149

Made in the USA
Middletown, DE
18 June 2016